cage

vance phillips

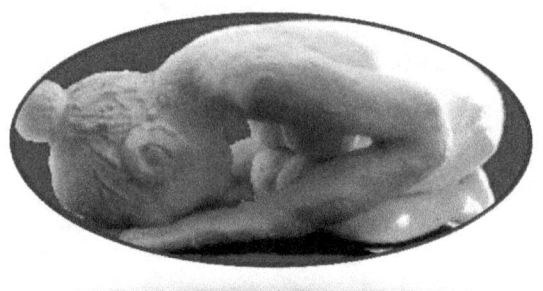

Butterscoth Publishing Incorporated

ISBN: 10-0990482707
ISBN: 978-0-9904827-0-3

The publisher acknowledges the copyright holder of this work as follows:

CHAPTER 1

It was a Wednesday afternoon at the ass end of June. Hard to believe it was so hot with dense, rain-heavy clouds looming in the grey sky. It was so humid that I could lick a drink right out of the air.

The words: *floating on a couch in the Gulf Stream* entered my mind.

In his dirty southern drawl, Critter interrupted my concentration to ask me, "You thank what they said was true, Danny?"

The two of us sat on overturned paint buckets behind Broutal Correctional Institution's central warehouse, where I worked. We leaned with our backs against brick walls on opposing sides of the loading dock's wide garage doorway. The door hung coiled above us, and through its opening I felt the breeze of an industrial fan as cool air swept across sweat dribbling down the nape of my neck.

I fanned a fly that buzzed around my nose. "True about what?"

"What they's talkin'bout in that newspaper. 'Bout how them prisoners kilt them guards way up there in Iowa."

"Not Iowa," I said. "Idaho. It happened in Idaho."

"I wouldn't know 'bout that. You know I cain't read myself—on account of my Pa was better at givin' whoopin's than lessons, but I listen good. That's what whoopin's do—teach you to let your Pa do the talkin', while you listen. So when Ms. Jenkins—you know her don'cha, Danny? She's the high-yella black guard with the big ol' ass that er'body calls Big Booty Trudy."

Yawning, I nodded along. "I know who she is."

"Well, she stopped to talk to me while I was doin' my gard'nin' down to the medical buildin'—that's what I do for work around here,

Danny. I'mma gard'ner. That means I plant flowers. I plant pansies and violets and rooster combs. I'm almost as good at gard'nin as I am cookin' shine. That's what I grow'd up doin', moonshinin'. That's how we make our money back home in Franklin County, Virginia. I was raised on Sugar Creek Road, where..."

"What about the newspaper article, Critter?"

He stopped talking and stared at me—stared through me. His eyes went still and vacant. I imagined his thought as an elusive butterfly that his slow mind tried in vain to grasp.

Snapping back to attention, he said, "Officer Jenkins...she told me 'bout how them boys up and kilt a hun'ert guards because they tried to take the TV's out of their prisons. She said they th'owed down on 'em with shotguns, and then chopped off their heads with meat cleavers."

"Meat cleavers?" I raised an eyebrow. "Where did they get meat cleavers and shotguns inside of a prison?"

He shrugged. "Hell, I'ont know. That's why I ast you, Danny. You're the smartest black man I know, all the time readin' them smart books and magazines. My Grandpa Earl used to say a black man ain't worth two teaspoons of duck butter, but hell Danny, you're so 'telligent...I bet you got every mystery of the whole wide world sorted out in that brain of yours. I'd tell that to my Grandpa Earl if he was here too. Mm-hm. I'd tell him that you're worth more'n two buckets of duck butter!"

I snorted a laugh while recounting all the stories I'd heard of Grandpa Earl and how he felt about a black man. I thought about that and how I wanted to wring his scrawny neck too.

Aside from that, Critter's question reminded me of the newspaper article I'd read about a group of inmates in Idaho who had staged one of the most violent prison riots in American history. It had taken place a month ago, and although the incident had been reported on the news and in the papers, no clear explanation for the cause of the riot had been given. All anyone knew for certain was that it had lasted twenty-seven days, and the death toll tallied at six guards and thirty inmates.

The mere mention of prisoners sticking together had some inmates at Broutal in an uproar and ready to start their own riot, here in North Carolina. Rumors circulated amongst us about the noble causes the Idaho inmates may have rioted over. Maybe the Idaho prison administration had been planning to remove televisions and free weights from their institutions; or maybe they were going to force the inmates to work without pay or the promise of an early release. To be honest, it didn't matter *what* the Idaho prison officials had been planning to do, the inmates there didn't like it. The fact that thirty of them had been slain didn't seem to be an issue to North Carolina's inmates. Comparisons between the two prison systems were made, and inmates at Broutal agreed that we had reasons to fight as well.

But so far, no plans had been made to follow through with it.

In a way, I too admired those men for standing against authority, but I also remembered reading that their demands had not been met. After the riot, Idaho's prison officials implemented the new policies they had been planning all along. The riot had only prolonged the inevitable.

Their violence was in vain.

Those men died for nothing.

For me, that was a good enough reason not to riot.

I couldn't explain that to Critter. He wasn't equipped with the mental abilities needed to comprehend much more than simple commands. His feeble mind was attracted to the glory of the fight because he could not understand its futility.

Not wanting to explain it to him over and over again, I said, "Maybe it happened, maybe it didn't. Idaho might as well be a million miles away."

"Yeah," he replied, nodding along. "I reckon so."

Staring into the grey sky above, I spotted a distant break in the clouds where a brilliant blue shone through. I hoped it wouldn't rain. I hoped that it would be a beautiful day.

After a time had passed, I asked Critter, "When are you going to work? Sarge has told me over and over that you can't be here when trucks come to deliver supplies. I don't want anyone accusing you of stealing if the inventory is off, especially since you aren't supposed to be here in the first place."

He didn't reply.

I looked over and saw his head tilted back against the brick wall. His wild, auburn hair hung in clumps over half-closed, blue eyes. His tanned face was heavily freckled. His sunken chin was overshadowed by thin, pink lips that he struggled to keep closed over chunky, protruding teeth. His flat nose had been broken a few times, and its smashed flesh carved deep wrinkles around its base making his face resemble a ferret, a chipmunk, a rat, a rodent—some species of a squinting *critter.*

The sleeves of his white tee shirt were rolled up high upon stout shoulders, broadcasting muscular arms decorated with a collage of blurred prison tattoos. His brown uniform pants were cuffed and bunched around his knees, showing off milk-white legs stemming from dirty, black prison boots.

I wasn't sure if he was asleep or in a drug-induced trance. That was Critter. One minute he was riding in the passenger seat beside you, and the next he was off on a long journey all by himself. Where his aimless mind led him, only Critter knew, but he never told a soul.

He'd been that way for the fifteen years we'd been pulling time together.

Deciding not to bother him, I dug into my back pocket for the pen and notepad that I always carried with me. Carefully, I flipped past pages that were filled with my sloppy handwriting.

Settling on a page with just one line scribbled in at the top, I read the words aloud, *"floating on a couch in the gulf stream."*

I read them over and over again, trying to remember the intention behind every word—trying to retouch the same feelings and emotions I'd felt when I had written the phrase the day before.

My eyes closed as I leaned deeper into the brick façade behind me. In my mind, the prison housing me began to fade away. The industrial fan, whirring inside the building, became turbulent winds whipping waves all around. The scent of freshly-cut grass, wafting in the air, became a fragrance of saltwater and seaweed. Murmuring pigeons, perched in rain gutters above my head, became bleached sea gulls soaring high into a sky as endless as the ocean beneath it.

"floating on a couch in the gulf stream..."

I could not recite the words silently. They were born to be said aloud, brought forth with rolling syllables and soft vowels. Only by spoken word could their secrets endow the essence of what was in my heart.

Repeating the words again, I imagined her face and superimposed it over all else I experienced at that moment.

"riding her love like...like..."

Words rushed in and out of my head so fast that I almost fell over while jolting from my stupor to write them down. Her face, framed within the four corners of my notepad page, drove me like a madman fueled by relentless obsessions. It felt as if I was whispering those living words into her ear instead of scribbling them on paper destined to brittle and wither away like dead leaves fallen from their tree.

Yes, her face guided me. Her image was as much a part of my hand as the ink my pen smeared across parchment to chronicle the feelings I felt.

I smelled. I heard. I saw. But most of all, I wrote.

At the age of thirty, I have already served fifteen years on a sentence of life, without parole. I've been working in the warehouse for three of the six years that I've been housed at Broutal.

The warehouse supplies everything from ink pens for inmates to uniforms for officers. I unload delivery trucks, keep a log of the inventory, and I deliver the orders processed. To some inmates it sounds like a lot of work to do for seven-dollars-a-week, but I don't work most days. Usually, all I do is hang out and read for eight hours.

The loading dock, where I sit year-round, lies at the back of the prison overlooking a wide expanse of blacktop that ends at a sally port of fences. Flanked by two guard towers, the sally port is where delivery trucks enter to drop off products to the prison. Beyond that is a main highway running past the institution. It is the only gateway to the real world that I have known in a long time.

When I was first assigned the job, I would go out to sit on my bucket and stare at the sally port, dreaming of the free world on the other side. Sometimes I read a book. Sometimes I slept. Sometimes I thought about the bad man I used to be and how sad it was that so many of us were wasting away in prison. And sometimes I just sat.

That was before she came along.

That was before she made me a poet.

Finally, I finished writing and wiped the sweat from my brow. I sat back, drumming my pen against the notepad, combing my brain for any stray words I may have left behind.

Satisfied that all of my thoughts were on paper, I lowered my eyes and read aloud what I had written: *"floating on a couch in the gulf stream. running my fingers through the froth of her sea. stroking her thighs and the treasure between. riding her love like the waves beneath. deeper and deeper and deeper we go. till depths so deep only eternity knows. in a black so dark living plankton won't glow. lost at sea where only true love grows..."*

Gasping behind me, she declared, "Danny! That was beautiful! Did you write that?"

Startled, I twisted on the bucket and it threw me off like an ornery bull. I landed flat on my back, staring up at her angelic silhouette haloed by the burning sun behind. The sight of her oval-shaped porcelain face mesmerized me as she returned my awkward stare with one of her own through big, brown eyes over glazed by her obvious amusement. She offered an apologetic smile with full lips as roseate as her blushing cheeks.

I noticed that the sky was now as clear and blue for as far as my eyes could see.

To mask my embarrassment, I said, "I'm okay."

Her smile widened. "You dropped your notepad, Danny."

"No..." I watched in horror as she stooped to pick it up. "Please, don't."

She stood and leafed through the dog-eared pages anyway. "What are these? Poems?"

I didn't answer.

Crinkling her chestnut eyebrows, she paused on a random page and read what it said aloud:

"wood of the willow.
there is a passage that will lead you straight to my heart.
you may lose your way if you can't navigate the dark.
but if you can find this twisted path leading to me,
i'll be surrounded by tears, beneath the willow tree.
what wisdom i offer cannot be promised.
but when you leave me, you will leave with vast knowledge.
i've seen hell on earth and heaven in a cage.
i've seen the world's goddess with her body on display.
i've seen vagabonds battle over a slice of bread,
 and I've seen a gladiator humble himself to be fed.
i've seen smiles from a child who knew no love,
and i've seen tears on the faces of so-called thugs.
this is what you'll hear, beneath the willow tree...
if you can ever find the twisted path leading to me.
 wood of the willow."

She gasped yet again. In the consuming silence I could still hear her sweet voice pouring over my words. From her tongue had I heard them as they were meant to be spoken: with passion and tenderness.

I remained frozen on the concrete, watching as she shifted her weight from one leg to the other. She smiled while flipping pages and skimming their contents here and there.

Finally, she stopped on one page. Her smile faded down into a frown as she began to read:

"why?
why would she want me?
i have nothing—i offer even less.

i possess not the confidence most men profess.
why would she want me?
i have no aspiration, no dreams to fulfill...
no fast talking words to make her feet stand still.
my emotions are fragile; self-esteem has been killed.
why would she want me?
brutal truths are too truthful, their honesty i know.
yet I find myself basking in her radiant glow.
golden lamp lighting darkness, she spotlights my show.
her pleasure—center stage—but i script sorrow.
why would she want me?
my heart...so dark as a raven on a wire.
so craven as a coward cowering beneath sire.
when fanning the flames of my sensual fire,
i'm hidden as the sheep, cloaked in wolf's attire...
hiding the desires my soul secretly admires.
so why would she want me?
why?"

Placing a hand over her heart, she glanced down at me, then looked back to my words on the page. "My god," she whispered. "It's like you were speaking right to me." She took a deep breath and let it out. "Is that how you feel, Danny?"

I didn't say anything.

Looking over the poem again, she told me, "I had no idea that you were so talented. I mean, I always thought of you as smart but...I had no idea that you could do..."

I still didn't reply. I climbed to my feet, facing her. She peered up into my eyes. She didn't offer my notepad, and I didn't try to take it. Her chest heaved with every breath.

"Who did you write that about, Danny? Somebody you care for?"

You, Officer Anderson. I wrote it to you. It's what I've been doing since I met you. I put pointless words to paper thinking that eons would pass without you ever knowing they existed. Most every word that I have written was for, about, or to *you.*

You are the heaven that I found in a cage.

Ignoring my thoughts, I mumbled, "I just like to write, Ms. Anderson. That's all."

Neither one of us spoke for a dangling moment. Rebel strands of her chestnut hair danced between us, broke free from the loose tangle banded at the back of her head. Air from the fan blew cool on one side of my face, while the sun's heat roasted the other. I didn't feel much of anything except searing desire burning holes through my heart.

We didn't notice Critter until he was nearly standing between us. "What's goin' on, Danny?"

Without taking my eyes from Officer Anderson's, I said, "Nothing is going on. Why would you ask that?"

His gaze bounced between her and me. "'Cause y'all standing there starin' like you ain't ever never gonna see each other again. Sho' looks like somethin' is goin' on to me!"

Ms. Anderson let out a tired sigh and looked at Critter with the same annoyed expression that she would give a four-year-old child. "The gun tower called, Critter. We have a delivery truck coming in."

Critter's lower lip sagged as he contemplated her words. His eyes glazed over with the effort until he realized that it was time for him to go. "I gotsta leave anyhow," he said. "Cap'n Turner say he got some rose bushes to plant for the secretary down front of the operations buildin'.

"Cap'n Turner can't stand roses, but the secretary likes 'em, and I thank he sweet on her. They been lookin' at each other the same way y'all two was just a minute ago.

"One time, I was down to the operations buildin' trimmin' the shrubs, and I had to pee real bad. They ain't got no john for inmates down there, but hell, I had to pee. I snuck inside real quiet—so's not to 'sturb nobody. When I opened the bathroom door, there was Cap'n Turner, kneelin' 'tween the secretary's legs with the hem of her dress draped over his head. Now I'ont know what he was doin' down below, but she sho' gave a holler when she spotted ol' Critter standin' in the doorway.

"Cap'n Turner chased me from one end of the operations buildin' to the other. He was so mad—I thought he was gon' kill me! But when he got tired and settled down, he took me alone and said that he would give me anything *I mean anything*—that I wanted in the whole wide world if I never told a soul about what I saw him and her..."

"Critter!" Ms. Anderson barked. "Don't you have some flowers to plant?"

Cocking his head at an angle, he softly told her, "Well that's what I do for work, Ms. Anderson. I'mma gard'ner. That means I plant lilies and pansies and rooster combs and..."

"I know what you do!" She punched a fist to her hip. "Now get out of here before the truck shows up!"

He nodded his agreement. Anderson and I watched all five-foot-one of him strut through the warehouse toward the exit.

Shaking her head, she said, "I swear that boy is on something."

I wanted to tell her that he probably was, but I kept my mouth shut.

Anderson leaned against the brick wall with her arms crossed over her chest. My little notepad of poems was tucked between two of her fingers. She stared at me in a way that I had never been stared at by a woman.

"You take care of him, don't you?" she asked.

"Why would you say that?"

"This is a tough place. We as officers don't know about everything that goes on in here, but we know enough. It's not hard for me to imagine you protecting him."

Most people assumed the same thing because Critter is small and white, while I'm tall and black.

I thought about explaining how it was between Critter and I, but talking to c/o's about what goes on in prison beyond their eyesight is a taboo. It's something that convicts aren't supposed to do.

But so she wouldn't ask again, I told her, "Critter can hold his own." And I was telling the truth.

I had met Critter three days after my fifteenth birthday—on the very same day that I began serving my life sentence at the Morganton High Rise for boys.

Critter was seventeen at the time, and he slept in the neighboring cell. As a two-year veteran of the prison system, his only advice upon meeting me had been, "Git yourself a knife and stick the first sum-bitch to look at you wrong. Don't thank they won't try you 'cause you're black like them. They try er'body."

Back then, Critter wore the same compact build. Slim waist and legs. Thick chest and arms from years of pumping iron and doing push-ups. While staring into his wild, blue eyes I had sensed that he wasn't right in the head from the very start.

Because of that, I didn't take heed to his advice.

I regretted my doubt when two bigger, black kids cornered me near the shower. One asked where I was from. He smiled as if were friends. I told him Roanoke Rapids. The other asked if I was a gang member. He didn't smile. I said no. They both wanted to know if I had money in my prison account. I tried to answer, but the words went cold in my throat.

Looking out into the cellblock around me, I saw a hundred other kids glued to the scene as it played out. No one wore a look of surprise. I sensed that the same thing had happened to each of them. If those two hadn't approached me, two others would have. Those silent eyes staring told me that if I bowed down this time, I would be bowing for the rest of my life.

I felt like the gladiator in the center of a coliseum—maybe not as brave a gladiator, but on spectacle like one—knowing that I had to fight and I didn't want to.

The gooey feeling in my knees made me hit one of them before they hit me. Red hot pain shot through my knuckles as they connected with his chin. He stumbled back. The crowd of boys whooped and cheered, "Beat his ass!" So I charged on, swinging wildly while trying to aim through squinted eyes.

His friend dipped low and tackled me at the waist. My head smashed into the concrete wall, and a kaleidoscope of colors clouded my vision. Somehow I held my ground, slamming my elbows into the kid's spine as he tried to wrestle me down.

The other kid rejoined the fight, picking his poison, punching me in the face at will. His fists moved in slow motion as if we were fighting under water. My head jolted back with each concussion and only lowered again to be pummeled once more. I was slowly slipping into a peaceful darkness.

Out of the blue, I saw a flash of metal, and a mist of blood sprayed my face.

The guy who'd been punching me now laid motionless on the concrete floor with his eyes wide open and vacant. A dark trickle of blood seeped from a gash on the side of his head. I had no idea what had happened.

My other attacker pressed his back against a wall with his hands thrust out in surrender, begging for his life.

Through fear-filled eyes I spotted Critter inching toward the guy while twirling a looped belt with a steel padlock fastened to the end like Sir Lancelot himself twirling a spiked mace on a bloody battlefield.

Critter gave the guy some running room, and he bolted, leaving his busted-up friend bleeding on the floor.

When all was safe, Critter looked up at me and said, "I told yo' dumb ass to get a knife! You cain't fight worth shit."

We'd been friends ever since.

"Officer Anderson!" Came booming from deep within the warehouse.

She and I froze, recognizing the heavy voice of Sergeant Thompson. Quickly, I held out my hand for her to give me the notepad. She shook her head no and slid it into the back pocket of her navy blue uniform trousers.

Sarge stepped onto the loading dock with a scowl across his face. He said, "Y'all have some explaining to do."

At six-foot-four, Sergeant Thompson stood a few inches taller than me. He was twenty-something years older, seventy-five pounds heavier, and white. The round belly that he carried on chicken legs had him waddling when he walked. His uniform always smelled clean but looked sloppy. He wore ancient, wire-rimmed glasses beneath balding, blond hair. His double chin was clean-shaven, and what hair he lacked on top of his head sprouted in a bushy mustache that hid his upper lip.

Sarge had been the *Officer In Charge* of the warehouse for as long as I could remember. Always a good-natured kind of guy, Sarge had never spoken down to me or treated me as a lesser man. Although I knew a little about his private life, we rarely spoke of personal things. He'd brought me turkey after Thanksgiving and candy canes at Christmas, but a barrier remained between us—the wall of inequality that segregated officers and inmates.

To Anderson and I, Sarge said, "I told y'all that I don't mind that boy Critter being in here *sometimes,* but not on truck days."

"That's on me," I admitted. "Critter walked in here on his own, but I didn't have the heart to tell him to leave. I won't let it happen again."

After studying my face, Sarge's frown spread into a sly grin. "Yes you will. His little ass'll be in here first thing in the morning—just as sure as shit. He'll probably be waiting at the front door with a story about how he caught the lieutenant pissin' in the warden's coffee pot—the lyin' little bastard!" We all laughed, and he said it again, "Just don't have him up here when the trucks arrive. He ain't too bright, and he'll only get in the way."

I nodded. "Alright."

To Ms. Anderson, he said, "I've got some bad news for you. State inspectors are at the front gate, and Warden Shelly has assigned me to lead their tour group around the prison."

"Damn it!" She spat. "How long will you be gone?"

He shrugged. "Couple hours. All day most likely."

"But Sarge...I was supposed to take a half-day off. I need to run some errands and do some other things too..."

He held up his hand to stop her. "Do you want me to tell Warden Shelly that I can't show the safety inspectors around because you want to go home early?"

She didn't say anything. She hung her head low.

"I didn't think so," he said. "You can take your half-day tomorrow. That's the best that I can do. I tried to get a substitute officer from one of the housing dorms to help us out, but they're spread thin too. The whole damn prison is short staffed; has been since the governor put that hiring freeze on us. But I guess it doesn't matter, because we'll have to make due with what we've got. All I need you to do is supervise Danny until he finishes unloading the truck."

Ms. Anderson turned her gaze toward me.

I saw something in her eyes that made my knees go weak. I thought of my notepad idling in her back pocket and the passionate way she had read the words buried within.

After looking back to Sarge, she smiled and said, "I'm sure we'll be fine. Make sure to call ahead and let me know when you're coming back."

CHAPTER 2

The delivery truck dropped off ten pallets of assorted supplies.

By using a manual jack, I lined-up the pallets down the warehouse's central corridor in a long row. Ms. Anderson signed the truck driver's invoice and waved as he pulled away. After watching the eighteen-wheeler disappear through the sally port, I yanked down the garage door and locked it.

Broutal's central warehouse is divided into a maze of thirty chain-link cages that secure the products stored with heavy locks on all the cage doors. Each cage is further divided into aisles of sheet metal shelves, the items categorized by alphabet or nature of usage.

Fluorescent lighting in the warehouse is sparse. Walking lanes between the cages are illuminated by huge skylights imbedded in the tall ceiling, causing shimmering squares of golden sunlight to bathe her in a glowing glory as she walked ahead of me to unlock the sixteen-cage so that I could begin stocking its shelves.

I couldn't steal my eyes away.

The sight of her was divine—beauty defined by her own standards. Nothing like the stick-figure models in most magazines, Anderson wore a natural shape with round hips that tapered into a healthy waist. Short and slightly heavier than most women, the navy blue uniform she donned did nothing to hide her ample curves. She was pleasantly plump. Beautifully ordinary. Perfectly plain. Simple—a simply sensuous woman who set my heart afire.

After she had unlocked the gate, my eyes lingered over the swell of her breasts for a moment too long. She leaned against the open cage, watching me stare, waiting for me to start.

I began stripping the pallets box by box.

Eventually she left and brought back a stepping stool. She placed it near the mouth of the sixteen-cage and sat to supervise me working.

Ms. Anderson had only been assigned to the warehouse for seven months. She got the job after Officer Brown, an older black man, retired.

Although I'd seen her on post in other areas of the prison, prior to her starting in the warehouse, we'd never spoken. Even after we began working together, I kept conversation to a minimum.

That was the safe thing to do.

Women employed at Broutal outnumber male employees at a ratio nearing two-to-one. They hold positions in every department. They are officers, captains, mail clerks, food service supervisors, self-defense instructors...and they work under a constant cloud of suspicion.

In the prison environment it is acceptable for a woman to belittle or command an inmate forcibly, but for her to be seen talking to a convict for too long or too often displayed a sign of weakness.

Weakness leads to wrongdoing.

For that reason, friendly women are often scrutinized by their co-workers. At times, scrutiny leads to an investigation by the prison's Internal Affairs unit; even if the only evidence is hearsay.

Investigations lead to termination.

Consequently, women who value their jobs don't talk to inmates.

I tried to lose myself in the work by finding a comfortable rhythm, but it was hard to concentrate with her brown eyes tiptoeing over my every movement. Strange sensations that I drew from her both exhilarated and frightened the hell out of me. I got the feeling that she knew what her eyes were doing and she only persisted to draw a reaction, but I didn't give her one. I kept on working, pretending that she wasn't there.

For a while she sat on her stool, watching me with wondrous eyes.

I noticed her reading from my notepad as I began stripping the third pallet. Once engrossed in my work, she gave no physical hints as to how my poems affected her. She read a page and then flipped to the next. Her actions were nonchalant. Innocent.

It became a chore to focus on my job. I tripped over my own two feet. I put boxes on shelves where they didn't belong. Snippets of my expressed emotions echoed in my mind as I glanced at her more often than I should have...

my feelings are burdens.
Painful.
one so lovely as you doesn't deserve them.
Angel.
Or...*how can my admiration remain secret, when longing looks expose my regrets? i should gladly pluck out my betraying eyes, for gaping and gawking each time she walks by.* It crossed my mind that she could turn me in if what I had written offended her. I didn't like thinking that way, so I reminded myself that I hadn't planned for her to see my poems—that's just how it had turned out. Besides, every poem wasn't directly about her. Some I had written wishing for her to see life through my eyes. Maybe those would throw her off the scent.

> *children of the chain*
> *during saturday cartoons in a polk youth center dayroom.*
> *billy got his wig split with a broken-off broom.*
> *other inmates laughed and ran off to spread the news.*
> *while billy lay dead, on the floor, until noon.*
> *too old to be tamed, yet too young to be ashamed.*
> *too stubborn for change, we were just children in chains.*
> *rappers on the radio sung us the wisdom of life.*
> *we learned of sex from pictures; masturbation at night.*
> *films gave us role models with a gangster's insight.*
> *scarface was our hero when toting pride to a fight.*
> *too old to be reclaimed, yet too young to be insane.*
> *too naïve to be blamed, we were just children in chains.*
> *my celly was my brother, his pride: justification.*
> *through his eyes i decide: my actions were his contemplation.*
> *from his failure i gained a bastardized education.*
> *of aging in prison where survival is graduation.*
> *too old to be saved, yet too young to be enslaved.*
> *too unknown to be named, we were just children in chains.*
> *children of the chain*

Halfway through the eighth pallet, I stopped for a break. Hot, sweaty, and with my tee shirt plastered to my chest, I leaned against the cool chain-linked cage. After catching my breath, I looked up and caught her staring again. Her head was cocked at an angle. Her big, brown eyes never faltered from mine.

> *if my fingers could circle her waist, they would be like mouths devouring her taste. if they could knead the texture of her strawberry flesh, i would feed and feed never stopping to rest.*

We paused like that for a minute or so, staring at each other, me wondering if she had it figured out. When suddenly, she hopped up and stalked off toward the small office she shared with Sergeant Thompson. I followed her with my eyes until she disappeared around the corner.

My notepad was nowhere near the stepping stool she'd sat on.

Damn. Why did I write those poems? Why didn't I leave them in my cell? How could I have been so stupid? *Damn.*

She returned twenty-minutes later as I was scribbling in figures on the inventory sheet. She paused within a glowing ray of sun, shaped by the square skylight above. Her long chestnut hair was now free of its tie, brushed and water falling in waves down past her shoulders and farther still. Her face was freshly made-up. She smiled at me with glossed lips as slick as honeydew.

Stepping too close for my comfort, Officer Anderson offered me a cold bottle of water.

I shook my head. "I can't take that."

She kept on smiling up at me. "Danny, I have been watching you work for two hours straight. The very least that I can do is give you a drink of water. I know you're thirsty."

She was right. I could have built a sand-castle on my tongue, but she'd taken me by surprise. She had never offered me anything before.

"I don't know, Ms. Anderson..."

She took a bold step closer. "Don't offend me, Danny."

The sweet scent of her filled my nose. We no longer stood on stiff concrete in a cold penitentiary...

we faced each other in the center of an open field amidst tall grasses and white wild flowers waving with a warm summer's wind. the sky was purplish-red with wispy clouds weaving throughout in silvery threads...

"Danny. Don't offend me," she said again.

"No ma'am." I shook my head. "I wouldn't do that."

She shoved the bottle against my palm and wouldn't let go until I got a grip on it. I unscrewed the cap and took a long swig. She smiled up at me wearing a grin of victory like she'd just conquered Rome.

The water was fresh and clean and cool, and I was grateful for what she had done.

She moved closer still as I lowered the bottle from my lips. With less than a foot between us, she said, "Now don't you tell anybody that I gave it to you, and I might just give you something else."

Her sugary voice sounded smooth and soothing. Her accent was southern and soulful.

Panting from the long drink, I couldn't find words to reply. I reached up and put the bottle on a shelf.

She asked, "How come you don't talk to me?"

An uncomfortable silence grew between us. I hurried to fill it. "I do talk to you."

"No, you say '*Hi* and *Bye, Ms. Anderson. Can you open the six-cage for me, Ms. Anderson?*' You never talk about where you're from, what you like or don't like. You never ask about me either."

I thought of the convicts I knew who had fallen in love behind bars. Some had fallen for guards, some for an old flame, some for mail order pen pals, but one fact remained the same. They had all fallen for love like it was some divine entity destined to drop out of the sky and turn water into wine.

I understood the logic.

Affectionately, being in prison was a lot like wandering through the Sahara alone and miserable. Maybe love was an oasis that tricked the heart into making one moment in life seem far better than all moments preceding it. Or maybe it was an illusionist that kept a person poised in awe until the lights went up as the curtain tumbled down and the magic faded away.

I had never known love, but I had seen just as much pain in those men's eyes as I had seen joy. Being in love and in prison created obvious complications, no matter the circumstances. Somewhere down the line, I realized that I couldn't handle the frustration.

So I kept what I felt to myself.

"Sometimes its better that way, Ms. Anderson—better not to talk and ask questions." The sour look she gave said that she wasn't satisfied with my answer. Wanting to end the conversation, I said, "I've been in prison so long that I don't have much to say anyway."

"Mmmm," she purred. "Your sure have a lot to write about." She licked her lips. "No one has ever written about me before."

A pang of fear shot through me. "What makes you think the poems are about you?"

Her smile faded. For a moment, she looked unsure of herself—second guessing her instinct. Finally, she smiled again. "Some of them are about me...aren't they?"

I yearned to tell her about the *things* I felt when writing for her. The *thing* that built in the pit of my belly and struggled to claw its way out. The *thing*—some indescribable *thing* that fought tooth and nail for escape, like a beast in a cage or an explosion of rage. An expanding *thing* that swelled my insides, filling me with overflowing imaginations of her absolute pleasure. Some*thing* alluring and hideous too. An animalistic *thing* of savage lust that prowled around my reasoning to make what I wanted dangerously sweeter.

But I could not tell her so. To admit what I felt would only undo me in the end. We could never be more than what we were. My greatest fear was that I would give in and find myself expecting an affection that she wasn't willing to offer.

The safest thing to do was to stop before it went too far. "I don't think about anyone when I write. I feel a certain way and jot down the first thing that comes to mind."

Her eyes said that she didn't believe me—that she knew I was lying.

"You're different, Danny."

My sweaty tee shirt began to dry, and I became aware of its musk. I worried if my breath was stale, or if my bald head was too greasy. I wondered if she saw the same faults in me that I saw in myself.

"Different how?"

"Don't you know?" she teased. When I remained silent, she said, "You speak differently, for one."

"I do?"

She nodded. "You don't talk...*black*. You don't use slang or sound like any of the other inmates—you don't talk like you're from the ghetto."

"I'm not," I blurted. "I'm not from *the ghetto*..."

It was her turn to look nervous. "I didn't mean it like that."

"I know you didn't. My dad was strict on the way that I spoke. I didn't know that it was a bad thing."

"It isn't," she rushed to say. "There isn't anything bad about you at all. *Different* is good, Danny. *Different* is refreshing. Most people I know do everything they can to *not* be different."

I didn't understand. "Why is that?"

"I don't know," she said. "Maybe they're unhappy with who they are. We spend our lives trying to be someone else. Individuals are a dying breed. The radio tells us what songs to like. Television teaches us how to dress. The web has us comparing our tastes to the rest of the worlds. Even if we take one idea and blend it with another to call our own, we're still just a mixed-up mirror image of something that we thought was better than what we were before. We're no more than clones. We're all living the same, exact life. We say all the same things, except we think that we stand out because we shout the same words in our own distinct voices. *But not you.* You say the things no one else is saying."

A thin smile graced her lips. "You're perfect. Your poems are perfect. They've touched me in a way that nothing else has, and so have you. That's why you're *different*."

Her smile died as her eyes traveled the cage, landing on the barred skylight above, and then the padlock hanging from the gate. "I just wish you weren't in here."

My mood spun downward in a somber spiral. Her confession was the sweetest thing anyone had ever said to me. I couldn't understand why it made me so sad to hear it.

I whispered, "All I have are poems."

"You don't need anything else, Danny. What you write is a reflection of what's in your heart. That's really all a girl wants—to know how a man truly feels about her."

Her compliments lowered my guard, but shed light on my insecurities. "You talk like there isn't a good man waiting on every street corner for a woman like you to come along."

"What makes them *good* and you *bad*, Danny?"

"I'm locked up. They can take you places…buy you things. Don't you think that you deserve that?"

"It's not the same," she said, shaking her head. "Dinner is okay, and flowers and candy are nice things. But you've given me something better. I've never felt the way I feel right now. You make me feel alive. You make me feel wanted."

I do want you, but I can't have you.

Truth boiled inside me, but denial fought to cool its steaming passion. Denial was safe. Denial would keep our relationship strictly business. Denial would return things to the sterile way we were meant to be.

But *denial* was not truth.

"You're beautiful," came sputtering from my mouth. "Beautiful…" My beating heart banged against my ribcage. "You're funny and smart and considerate…you're everything that a woman should be."

Her mouth went wide with a gasp.

"Ms. Anderson, I can't remember a time when I didn't have a crush on you; when the sound of your laughter didn't make me smile too; or when I thought of anything other than you."

Tears pooled in the wells of her eyes like hot rain swelling in the hollow hands of summer leaves...but she didn't cry. The droplets hung suspended as her fingers rose to cover her gaping mouth. "Danny..." she exhaled with a grimace that spread into a slow smile. "Thank you, Danny."

Burdens that had once weighed me down were now like balloons floating up and away. It felt great to let it all go, but, "I hate feeling this..."

"Why?" She begged, desperate to know.

I didn't have a good explanation to give her. I had only thought of the feelings I felt—that's what I wrote about, the feelings—never the motivations behind them.

"Because I see how you are with other men—male officers, I mean. You poke them in the ribs. You whisper in their ear. You hug them. With them, you're natural.

"You change when you're around me. If you're on the phone when I walk by, you cover your mouth as if what you're saying is too important for me to hear. You never *ask* me to do something, you *tell* me to do it."

"Danny..." she reached out to touch me, but her hand paused in the space between us. She stared at her own fingers as they curled into a fist that she dropped at her side. "I didn't know I was doing that. I'm sorry if I..."

"It's not just you. It's all of you. I never thought that you did it on purpose. You're doing your job—being an officer. That's how it is. We see each other every day, but we may as well be strangers for the roles life forces us to play."

Her hands clasped together and her fingers fidgeted with each other. She sighed, then bit her bottom lip, then sighed again. She had the look of a woman thinking too many things at once—a woman who couldn't decide on what was most important to say.

Finally, she muttered, "And to think...you've been toting those feelings around for months, but I was blind to it."

"You weren't supposed to know."

Anderson inched closer until her chest met mine and the pounding of her heart was thunder in my own veins. "But I do know...now. So things are different between us, right? Better."

I moved to step away, but a vicious flow of electricity was an electromagnet between us, holding me there.

Our lips brushed as she whispered, "Don't you believe in destiny, Danny? Maybe we're supposed to be right here, right now." Her hands rose to the face of my shoulders. "Have you been locked up so long that you can't see?"

I felt her breath against my chin. "See *what?*"

"That they built walls to keep you in prison, but there are no walls to keep you from me."

Her arms crawled around the base of my neck, and she hugged me. She sniffled while pressing her cheek to my chest.

For her, there was nothing abnormal about it.

Fearing this alien closeness and the strange way that it felt to have a woman in my arms, I said, "Ms. Anderson, somebody could come back here. I'm not supposed to touch you this way."

She pulled back. "How else are you supposed to touch me?" Her smile was easy and confident. "You're as human as I am. If you care about someone, you have to show them. That's what makes life worth living. Without other people to make us feel good, it would all be meaningless."

I opened my mouth, but no words came out...just a defeated croak that betrayed the loving things I wanted to say.

She was wrong though. There were walls between us—walls that I never knew existed until she tried to tear them down.

I knew all about that *meaningless* life.

I'd spent my adolescence in prison. My role models had been child molesters and serial killers. When most kids had been learning to drive, I had been fighting to survive. No Friday night lights for me. No junior or senior prom. No first date. No first kiss. No first love.

I came of age in a cage.

Ms. Anderson's expectant eyes stared up at me, and I didn't know what to do. Primordial instinct guided my quivering lips closer to hers until the flesh of our flesh was almost one and I breathed in from the breath of her lungs.

I'd never been so close to anyone in my life.

Never.

Any sane man would have kissed her.

A sane man.

But I didn't.

CHAPTER 3

Running full speed toward the warehouse's exit, I burst through the heavy steel door and spilled out into the Four-tunnel with my heart racing. Streams of sweat poured from my face as I doubled over, heaving for air.

It was cooler in the Four-tunnel. I felt no pressure. No fear.

I couldn't believe I had been so close to her.

I couldn't believe the things we'd spoken of.

I couldn't believe that I'd forgotten to get my poems!

The warehouse door slammed shut behind me, drawing my attention. I knew that I would never look at that door the same. It was no longer the entrance to my place of work. Now it was a portal leading to an altered dimension of confusion—a gateway that led back to my cowardice.

The thought of mingling with the prison's killers and rapists was comforting compared with meeting her brown eyes once again. I could face the penitentiary. It was the only life I knew.

I couldn't go back in there to face her.

"Danny?" A female voice called to me. "Are you okay?"

Glancing up, I spotted three female officers waiting at the slider-door leading into Housing Dorm Four. The women were all young and black. They wore fresh faces and styled hair. Their dark uniforms were ironed and neat. The three of them were escorting a middle-aged, black con named Booby-Doo with his hands cuffed behind his back.

"Ms. Darcy," I said, greeting the only c/o whose name I knew.

"What happened, Danny?" She crinkled her nose above a playful smile. She nodded toward the warehouse's entrance. "Did something scare you in there?"

I envisioned Anderson's plump, pink lips. I imagined her succulent tongue sliding between them to take a slow tour from one corner of her mouth to the other.

I shook my head no. "It's really hot up there. The air is on the fritz." The four of them continued to stare as if they knew I hadn't told the whole story. To change the subject, I asked Booby-Doo, "Why are you in handcuffs? Are they taking you to the hole?"

Smacking his lips, he threw hateful eyes toward Ms. Darcy. "This drunk-ass bitch talkin' about she seen me jackin' off on her in the shower when she was makin' her rounds in C-block. I told the Sergeant that I was just washin' my ass, but she…"

Ms. Darcy wheeled on him. "You were masturbating while looking at me!"

"Why you keep tellin' everybody that?" He asked her. "You lyin'!"

"You were all lathered up and slippery," she said. "You had your hand on your privates."

Booby-Doo turned to me. "I was in the shower. Ain't I supposed to be lathered up with my hands on my privates?"

"Don't act stupid," she told him. "You know what you were doing!"

Booby-Doo said something else, and their argument grew louder and more intense. In my eyes, Ms. Darcy was wasting her time. Everybody knew about Booby-Doo. He was a *gunslinger*: a habitual masturbator.

North Carolina's prisons are bursting with perverts like him: created by a statewide ban on all nude images in correctional institutions. The ban left straight inmates with no form of sexual release other than fantasizing about the fully-clothed women who work in prisons, destroying a convicted felon's notion of sexual normalcy. I imagined opponents of pornography in prisons arguing that a sexual predator would change if he wasn't exposed to nude pictures of women, but the ban had the opposite effect. The ban on pornography in prisons trained incarcerated men to become sexually aroused when in the presence of a dressed woman—in an everyday setting—rather than with a magazine in the privacy of his cell.

"Don't worry about it!" Ms. Darcy shouted. "Jack off on the forty-five days you're going to do in the hole! Masturbate on that! *And* I'm going to write you up for calling me a drunk-ass bitch!"

Booby-Doo smiled her way. "Please, girl—that lil' time ain't nothin'. I done rode this rodeo befo'. Besides, I'm servin' life anyway, so fuck you and your write-up!" Ms. Darcy's eyes went wide. Booby-Doo continued, "I don't understand why you took a job in a man's prison if you afraid to see some wood anyway. That shit right there don't make no damned sense."

The door leading into Dorm Four slid open to the hissing tenor of its air compressor. The women prodded Booby-Doo into motion with their extended steel batons.

After watching the door close behind them, I walked in the opposite direction toward *The Center*.

I knew very little history about other prisons where I had served time. Most of North Carolina's sixty-three prisons had sprung up during modern years. Only a handful of the state's prisons were old enough to have a history worth telling. The fact that I'd heard Broutal's story many times from elderly convicts and near-retiring officers said a lot about its relevancy. Its birth encompassed more than just the building of a prison. Broutal had been the foundation for North Carolina's modern penal system.

In 1950, the first Broutal *prison farm* was erected on three-thousand acres of farmland just two miles outside of Bonnieville, North Carolina.

In theory, Broutal was meant to be a self-supportive penal facility where the inmates who worked on a state-owned farm grew all of the vegetables they ate and learned to take pride in their newfound skills. The Broutal Project was designed to be the model for a new era of prison reform; a smart alternative to the costly, age-old practice of archaic confinement. This idea was based on the belief that a convicted criminal would renounce his life of crime because he had grown accustomed to hard work.

This line of thinking served two purposes. On one hand, reformation of criminals was possible through forced working habits. On the other...bureaucrats had found a way to make prisons pay for themselves.

Politicians quickly realized the benefits of such an endeavor.

Not only did the Broutal Prison Farm produce enough food to satisfy its own needs, but the farm's production also fed sixteen other prisons that were scattered throughout North Carolina, as well as non-correctional institutions like public schools and hospitals. The governor of that time reasoned that if such good progress continued, funding for more work farms would be allocated, and their crops could be sold on the open market.

Although the *governmental organization* of forced labor was new to the North Carolina penal system, such practices were not new to southern states. Prior to 1950, prison work camps had been in existence since the abolishment of slavery: used to supplement the workforce stolen from the south by Abe Lincoln.

By abusing a legal process known as *Peonage*, tens of thousands of black men were unjustly arrested by southern officials and charged with frivolous citations for vagrancy or whistling at white women. Following the conviction of a trumped-up charge, the convict's *bond* was then purchased, from the convicting county, by a private business owner in need of cheap labor. From there, the purchased inmate went to work on a farm, in a mine, or at a factory until the expiration of his prison sentence.

This practice of under-the-table slavery lasted for more than fifty years.

Reformation of the criminal justice system, just before World War II, outlawed forced peonage in the United States. That change proved beneficial to state prison systems who—now freed from the bondage of private business—took up the reins and developed *Correctional Enterprise:* the new plantations of the south, where even white men were branded slave if they had been convicted of a crime.

The Broutal project was North Carolina's test run of this new venture.

Viewed as an archetype instead of a bona-fide facility, the prison had been thrown together in a matter of weeks—in the event that the project failed and the buildings had to be torn down quickly in order to resell the property.

The main compound consisted of eighteen ramshackle buildings peppered across the southwest corner of the farm. The inmates lived in three-fourths of these, and their bunk houses were without running water or electricity.

The inmates weren't allowed recreation. They worked without pay, and they slept. Fed scraps of the vegetables they grew, the inmates loaded bushels of the choice morsels onto trucks and watched hungrily as they were shipped off to be sold elsewhere.

Harvest season was the hottest time of year. Ripe with mosquitoes, bees, and biting wheat bugs long hours in the fields were as unmerciful as the tyrants who supervised them.

Armed correctional officers oversaw work in the fields. Two rode on horseback and two walked on foot to supervise a progression train of sixty inmates. Workers moved freely without restraints, and few attempted to escape because Broutal's land holding was huge—too huge for a man to get away on foot. Also, it was a known fact that an overseer would be rewarded with a paid vacation for killing an inmate attempting to escape. At that time, rumors circulated amongst law enforcement officials that most of the inmates killed while working in the fields were killed for insubordination, not escape; although *attempted escape* was the most justifiable excuse usually given in written reports.

Those rumors were never investigated.

Though lawful, murders at Broutal weren't a common occurrence. Most violent incidents were reported as whippings for lagging behind in work or complaining about the harsh conditions the men were forced to work in.

Regardless, the first Broutal *Prison Camp* thrived during its eleven years of operation. New federal guidelines concerning fair treatment of prisoners forced its closure in 1961.

The second Broutal went up in 1965 after the remnants of the first had been levelled. Out went the ramshackle bunk houses for a new five-hundred-inmate facility complete with running water and electricity.

This improved Broutal *Correctional Facility* had a cannery to process and distribute the crops grown on the farm.

The state bought more land surrounding the newer Broutal to cap off its total holding at twelve-thousand acres. Two smaller prisons, West Oak and Ashenden, were built along the farm's perimeter to help haul in the crop.

Broutal *Correctional Facility* operated for thirty-five years before being condemned in 2000.

The following year it was replaced with an interior metropolis that was sure to pave the way for the next wave of North Carolina's prisons in both structure and technology.

Broutal *Correctional Institution* resembles a flat octopus with eight tunnels as its tentacles sprouting in all directions from a central hub called *The Center:* an underground crossroads where all the tunnels intersect in a doughnut-shaped ring.

The core of *The Center* is a command post called *Master Control:* a two-story tall structure circled with tinted windows all the way around. *Master Control* is the heart and brains of the institution. All directives originate from within its bowels. Very few doors can be opened by key in Broutal. Most of the electronic doors are operated by an officer stationed in *Master Control.*

Serving as streets or byways, each tunnel leads to either one of four housing dorms, or one of four *Correctional Enterprises* now operating at Broutal: a new cannery to process the food grown on the farm, a state-of-the-art printing plant that handles all of the state's literature and stationary, a denture plant, and an optical plant that produces eyeglasses worn by inmates as well as civilian Medicaid recipients.

I left the Four-tunnel and stared up at the black beast, *Master Control*, as I rounded *The Center:* It was impossible to see through its tinted windows, but I knew that someone could see me. Little surveillance cameras are mounted above every slider-door, and in areas of the prison where inmate traffic is the heaviest. An officer stationed in *Master Control* monitors what the cameras capture at all times.

Because I was the only inmate assigned to work in the warehouse, a camera had never been installed there. But whenever I was in the tunnels or in my cellblock I was mindful that eyes were on me.

Over the intercom an officer from *Master Control* shouted: *"The dining hall is now serving dinner for institutional janitors!"*

Three officers were on post in *The Center*—three young, black males laughing amongst themselves. They ignored me as I walked past them. They were talking about the riot in Idaho and how they wished they'd been there to kill inmates.

I fell in with a group of cons heading toward the Two-tunnel for chow.

"Danny! Yo! Danny!"

I spotted New York waddling my way. He was a dark, black con who stood at five' eight and was just as big around the middle. I had known him for a little over a decade, and we'd always been friendly if not friends.

I wasn't in the mood for company, but I found myself waiting for him all the same. I needed a distraction to get Ms. Anderson out of my mind.

"What's good?" New York bellowed once he'd caught up. We bumped fists as his eyes roamed my sweaty forehead. "Them white folks workin' the shit outta you in that warehouse!" He laughed in my face. "What they got you doin' up there, son? You 'pickin cotton and pullin' the plow at the same time? I ain't seen a nigga sweat like that since the last time OJ went on trial!"

I gritted my teeth in reply. I began to think that waiting for him had been a bad idea.

New York had a friend with him, a mulatto kid who couldn't have been a day over twenty-one. He was shaved clean with shoulder-length black hair. Thin and frail, he stood with his hands buried in his pockets, wide eyes darting everywhere. The kid tried his best to hide behind New York. "You need to come work first shift in the kitchen with me," New York said while rubbing his belly with a smile.

The chow line was so long that it snaked out of the Two-tunnel and into *The Center*. I didn't realize that we had made any progress until we stood beside a huge number 2 painted on the wall, signifying what tunnel we were in.

I said, "I'm not going to wake up at 3 a.m. every morning. I've done that before, and it's not something I look forward to doing again."

"Eh, you get used to it," he went on. "You eat what you want, and you wouldn't have to unload trucks or pull delivery carts all over the prison."

"I like my job," I confessed.

New York shook his head sympathetically. "They got you brainwashed, son. *Institutionalized*. You sound like a slave and shit. Don't nobody in their right mind like workin' for the sweat-shop salaries the state is payin' us. We might as well be workin' for free. It's the twenty-first century and they only pay us forty cents-a-day, seventy cents...a dollar. That's why they talkin' about a strike."

It was news to me. "A strike?"

"Yeah. The muslims are puttin' together a sit-down. Some guys don't want a sit-down. Some of them want to set it off like they did in Iowa."

"Idaho. It happened in Idaho."

"That's the place—*Iowa*. Them guys laid down the blueprint, so now it's on us to follow it."

I told him, "A riot won't get us anywhere. A sit-down could. They've got a lot of money tied-up in the plants. We could get something done if we quit working and stopped a few checks coming in, but a riot is pointless. All those people died for nothing." New York shrugged. I said, "Those inmates never got what they were fighting for. Didn't you read the article?"

"I ain't got time to read no article." He pointed to the scrawny kid with him. "Kelly read it and told me what it was about."

I looked to the young man. "Kelly?" I asked him. "Did your parents give you that name?"

He nodded with pride. "My dad is black, mom's Irish. Her maiden name was O'Kelly, so to pay respect to her heritage, she..."

"Kelly is comin' to work with me in the kitchen." New York draped his arm across Kelly's shoulders, all but kissing his ear. "Ain't that right?"

Ignoring what I'd seen, I asked, "What about the strike?"

New York dropped his arm from Kelly's shoulders. "Like I said, son—they *talkin'* about a strike. Ain't nobody *really* goin' on strike around here. These dudes is soft, son. Look at 'em."

As we entered the chow hall, I took a gander at the men serving time with me. Though most were African-American, seated at the many tables was a mixture of inmates representing every race known to mankind. The majority were serving lengthy sentences—over half for some form of sexual deviancy. There were those that committed armed robbery, bank fraud, midnight burglary, drug dealers, addicts, and con men. The felonies binding them were as diverse as the spectrum of their skin tones.

The only characteristic they shared was a lack of malice in their eyes.

Inmates strike in order to gain power over an oppressing administration. Quite naturally the governing body that holds such power is reluctant to give it up. It doesn't matter what the inmates want, the administration will do all it can not to give in to them. There will be a lockdown, and officers at Broutal will retaliate. Life behind bars will become much worse than it had ever been before.

And so begins a battle of wills in which the administration has the upper hand.

Because strikes are self-inflicted wounds, it takes hard men to see one through properly. It takes disciplined men who are willing to sacrifice the pacifiers of modern prison life for a long period of time. During a strike, there is no television, no yard-call, no telephone, and no junk food from the canteen. There will be no comfort. Only endless weeks of solitude behind a cell door.

Most inmates don't want that. Most are set in their ways. They're afraid to miss an NBA game or a re-run of a popular sitcom. They've become addicted to the microwavable sandwiches and sodas that are sold in the canteen. They are satisfied with their mundane lives of working, watching TV, and sleeping. That life is consistent. Creatures of habit don't like turbulence in their smooth sailing. They have found comfort within the discomfort of confinement. To riot would ruin their lives of ease. To strike would do the same thing.

Even if a majority went through with it and refused to go to work, the few who went against the grain would destroy the *all or none* principle of unity needed to force a change.

New York strained his neck to get a glimpse of other inmates' food trays as they sat to eat. "Turkey pot pie again!" He complained. "They feed us that shit four times a week! I eat so much turkey—I'mma turn into a fuckin' turkey, I swear!" Disappointed and shaking his head in disgust, he asked me, "Did you hear about that chick who worked in Dorm one? Ms. Parker?"

I'd heard him. I'd been staring right at him, but I hadn't seen New York. Instead...I remembered Anderson and the interested look in her eye after she'd read my poems.

"Danny!" New York snapped his fingers in my face. "Danny? You okay? You startin' to act like that crazy-ass Critter you hang around with."

I pushed her out of my mind. "What did you say before?"

"Ms. Parker," he barked.

"Oh. The brown-skinned woman who wears the tight pants and the little braids."

"That's her. Shorty got *walked-out* this morning. They patted her down as she was coming into work. She got caught with three cartons of cigarettes taped to her stomach and back."

In the fifteen years that I have been doing time, I had only seen one female *walked-out* of a prison. Of course it is now a regular occurrence with the number of females working in male prisons, but it is something usually heard of instead of seen.

The woman had been the prison's dentist; except she'd been the one getting drilled in the examination chair, by an inmate, and not the other way around. I had seen her physically *walked-out* of Pamilco Correctional with her hands cuffed behind her back. During the walk of shame, she'd kept her blond head down while paraded past gawking inmates and whispering officers.

"Three cartons of cigarettes?" I mumbled, thinking it over.

New York told me, "They say she was bringin' it to Sweet Pete. You remember him?"

I nodded. "He was in the single-cell unit with us at Polk Youth Center. He slept in the end cell on the third tier. He used to sell weed."

"That's him." New York stepped forward with the chow line. "I heard Ms. Parker was dumpin' three cartons a week. Do you know how much a carton goes for in here? Three hundred! They were makin' almost four-thousand dollars a month, son! Hard to believe a man can make so much money while sittin' in a tin can all day, huh?"

Rising medical care costs of the inmate population had been the driving motivation behind North Carolina's decision to pass a bill banning tobacco products from all state properties in 2009. As a direct result, cigarettes became the prison system's biggest illegal enterprise.

Unbeknownst to frugal senators and congressmen, they'd opened the door for a twenty-first century version of Al Capone's prohibition era gangsters where smart-suited wise guys of yesterday's past were superseded by underpaid c/o's wearing ironed-on badges. Luckily, the prison's crooked cops were able to stop smuggling in illegal narcotics that could land them in prison as well. The ban made it safer for an officer to smuggle in a five-dollar pack of smokes to sell to an inmate for fifteen or twenty.

I asked New York, "Did they catch Sweet Pete with anything?"

"A cell phone," he said. "He had one of them big ones—the kind you can watch movies on. I got him to e-mail my cousin one time. He offered to let me use it, but I ain't trying to get caught with no phone."

Getting caught with a cell phone meant a six-month stint on long-term segregation: lock-up: the hole. Twenty-four hours in a cell except to recreate in a man-sized dog cage for an hour twice a week.

Officer Parker's only punishment was to lose her job.

"Yo! I want my broccoli with the heads on it, mutha-fucka!" New York yelled at the inmates serving food on the kitchen side of the Plexiglas window. "Don't give me that dry-ass rice on top!" He banged on the plastic shield. "Dig down to the bottom and scoop up that soft shit!"

Other inmates shook their heads at New York with contemptuous eyes. His little friend Kelly looked embarrassed to be seen next to him; if he'd had a shell, he would have climbed inside of it. For a moment, I wondered about the nature of their *friendship*, but I let it go because it was none of my business.

My wandering mind traveled back to Anderson. I thought of her squeaky, rubber-soled shoes that always perked my ears, her sweet smelling shampoo that kept my nose rising behind her scent, and other everyday expenses she may have. How much did all of it cost? What about her rent or car insurance? Was she the type to budget money wisely, or did money burn a hole in her pocket anxiously urging her to spend, spend, spend as soon as a paycheck hit her hand?

I thought about Ms. Parker and the fact that she didn't have a job anymore.

What if that happened to Anderson? How bad off would she be if she lost her job? How bad would I feel if she lost her job because of me?

We took our trays to an empty table where New York complained because they had served apples for dessert, instead of cake, while stuffing his mouth with turkey pot pie.

Kelly sat silent, staring in awe of New York in action.

I glanced down at my own tray. Broccoli stalks, no heads. Crispy rice smothered in wet cornstarch idled next to stale bread and a heavily bruised apple.

New York pointed to my broccoli stalks. "You gonna eat that?" He asked with rice sputtering from his mouth.

I licked my lips. Tasting slick remnants of Anderson's gloss made my eyes close in ecstasy, remembering how our lips had barely touched. I could still feel her breath beating against my chin as she'd whispered, "But I do know...now. So things are different between us, right? Better."

Or were they better? Even as a thirty-year-old man, I'd never experienced a relationship with a woman other than them as officers and me as an inmate. I didn't have a clue about what a woman wanted or how I was supposed to act. The feelings that I felt were an overwhelming mystery.

The burdens I bore created an awkward imbalance that I didn't know how to carry. I cared for her and I wanted us to explore what we felt, but I didn't want to get caught. If we took it any further I would have to find a way to protect us both. I couldn't let her meet the same fate befallen to Ms. Parker and others before her, but the only way to ensure that Anderson never got walked-out was for me to leave her alone in first place. That was the harshest truth to admit.

"I'm not hungry." I slid my food to New York. "You can have it all."

He had my tray hovering above his own, shoveling my food on top of his before I had even stood up from the table.

As I left the chow hall, I heard other inmates talking about a strike and how they would love to see every convict in Broutal standing up for a change. Listening to them, I realized that I wanted to see it too.

The Two-tunnel was empty. I felt suffocated while waiting alone at the slider-door heading into *The Center*. She consumed my every thought. I felt lightheaded and faint...weak. I wanted to find some hole and crawl inside of it to be alone.

"Danny! Wait up!" Kelly called out as he approached me.

His eyes were light brown and girlish with long lashes.

"Where is New York?" I asked him.

"Where else?" He gave an uneasy smile. "He's still eating."

Right off, I could tell that Kelly wasn't from some impoverished slum like most young men of color in prison. His speech was crisp and proper.

I asked, "Why didn't you wait for him?"

He averted his eyes from mine. "He's okay, I guess. I just met him yesterday."

I didn't say anything more. The slider-door opened, and I stepped aside to allow a group of guys heading to chow to walk through first.

Kelly followed me into *The Center*. His new, prison issued sneakers squeaked against the concrete floor. He asked, "Will you show me where the gym is?"

As we neared the Four-tunnel, my eyes stared toward the warehouse's entrance. Anderson was still inside, probably wondering why I had ran from her. I hoped she didn't think that it was her fault. I felt a compelling need to go back there and explain that I was messed-up in the head, but that would only make the situation worse.

I told Kelly, "The gym is down the Six-tunnel."

"Where's that?"

I pointed at the huge numbers painted beside the slider-doors all around the perimeter of *The Center*. "It's not hard to find."

"I don't know anybody," he whined.

"You don't know me either."

"I – I don't want to go there alone," he confessed.

I stopped in my tracks and faced him. The sudden movement made him back off. "I'm not New York, Kelly. I don't need a sidekick."

He threw up his hands. "I just want to know how to find the gym."

But I sensed something more. Naivety exuded from his every pore. He sought guidance in this strange land that he didn't understand. He reeked of fear and uncertainty. Weak men like him aligned themselves with alpha-males in order to survive in prison. They can't stand on their own two feet, so they join gangs hoping strength in numbers will prop them up. Guys like Kelly stumble into the pitfalls of prison life because they don't know how to avoid them.

"I'm not like New York," I said again." He does the boys."

The kid scrunched his eyebrows. "What do you mean?"

"Think about it, Kelly. He *does* the *boys*. It's not hard to figure out."

Examining his young features, I was able to pinpoint the exact moment when what I'd said sunk in.

There was rage in his eyes as he glanced back toward the Two-tunnel where New York was no doubt still stuffing his face. "I'm not a *boy!*"

"You don't need to convince me," I said.

A Mexican, male officer on post in *The Center* stepped to us and said, "You guys have been standing here too long. Do either one of you have a Hall Pass?"

"No sir," I said. "We were heading to the gym from chow."

The officer nodded. "Move your ass then."

I started walking again, bypassing the Four-tunnel, and running from Anderson.

Kelly fell in step. "Why does he think I'm a...that I'm a *boy?*"

"How long have you been down?"

He shrugged beside me. "What does that mean? *Down?*"

I let out a long sigh. "Cons don't ask: 'When did you come to prison?' We ask: 'How long have you been *down*,' or 'When did you *fall?*' Because coming to prison is like *falling down* on hard times, or like *falling down* on your luck." I asked him again, "How long have you been down?"

Nodding with understanding, he answered, "I *fell* two months ago. Before that, I was on the street. I was out on bond awaiting my trial."

I took another look at his young features. It saddened me to see his face in a prison. A convict doesn't get shipped to Broutal with less than a twenty-year sentence, so I knew that he was in for a long haul. Seemed like such a shame to know that he was set to face the same hardships I had. A damned shame.

Passing the Five-tunnel slider, I asked him, "If you knew that you were coming to prison, why didn't you cut your hair?"

He combed fingers through his black locks. "My girlfriend likes long hair."

"Is she here now? Is she sleeping in the cell with you?"

He shook his head.

"Then it doesn't matter what she likes." We held up at the entrance to the Six-tunnel, waiting for the slider to open. "Can you grow a beard?"

"Yeah," he said, "But it's sparse. That's why I shave." I told him to get a haircut. "Get it cut low."

He eyed my slick, black pate with a gulp. "Bald? Like yours?"

"No. Get a buzz cut or something. A guy named Ward is the barber in Dorm One. Tell him you want a *Caesar*. And let your beard grow. It doesn't matter how much hair you have, the point is to have some."

"Will that keep people from thinking I'm gay?"

"It's a start."

A group of inmates piled up on the opposite side of the Six-tunnel slider. There were quite a few young men in the crowd. I saw Kelly examine them through the Plexiglas. I hoped he noticed that they all wore beards or goatees, exhibiting some physical semblance of masculinity.

The door opened and we stood aside to let the men pass before making our way down the Six-tunnel.

"You need to change your name too," I said.

"But I like my name."

"Why don't you tell everyone to call you Susan? Melissa? What about *Amber*? They'll think the same thing if you tell them your name is Kelly." He winced at my advice. I tried to soften the blow. "Nobody goes by their real name in prison anyway, so get over it."

"You can say that. Your name's Danny."

"People *call* me Danny. It's not my real name."

Kelly's jaw muscle tensed as he gritted his teeth. Fresh tears glistened his inexperience eyes. "I don't understand why I can't be myself in here."

"Because you aren't man enough. Not yet."

It took a few seconds of silence for him to suck up his tears. I made sure to walk the Six-tunnel slowly so he'd have time to pull himself together before entering a gym full of savages.

Kelly explained, "My lawyer told me that I'd have it hard in here. He said guys who come in with charges like mine get *taken care* of first. It's like with New York—I explained to him about what happened. He seemed to understand. How was I supposed to know that she was fifteen..."

I held up my hand to stop him. "I don't want to know what you're in here for."

"But it wasn't my fault..."

"It doesn't matter." We stopped just outside of the gym's open doorway. I pointed to an elderly black man who was playing a game of chess by himself. "That's Roscoe. He's been in prison longer than you and I have been alive, and you know what? There isn't a soul on this compound who knows what he did to end up in prison. That's how it's supposed to be. With us you're a clean-slate. You're another guy doing hard time. Don't expect anyone here to feel sympathy for you because you're innocent. *Everybody* is innocent."

He was on the verge of tears again. "It's not right, Danny. I don't..."

"No, it's not right. But the point you're missing in this is that it isn't about you or what you want. It's about *them*."

A group of guys headed toward the door to exit the gym, so I pulled him aside. I spoke low but in a frank tone. "To make it in here you have to be something like a psychologist, Kelly. You have to study these men and the things that motivate them. You have to know them better than they know themselves. Sometimes you'll have to be a psychic, able to predict the stupid things they'll do before they do them. And you'd better be able to handle yourself if something involves you, or be able to get the hell out of the way if it doesn't."

Kelly's tears were gone. His eyes were wide, peering up into mine.

I said, "The key to prison life is *perception*. If you project weakness, they will treat you like a weak man. You need to know how people view you at all times. You must know that, and how to *control* their perception of you. I don't know what you thought about convicts before you came here, but this is a thinking man's world. Some of the most intelligent men are behind these walls, and they are heartless. They will throw on the charm just to deceive you.

"I'm not saying that you need to put on a mask or pretend to be something that you aren't. These men only need to know what you stand for, and it's better to show them that at a first glance. Most of the time that's enough to keep them off of your back."

He nodded slowly with his eyes lowered to the floor.

"But you don't have to listen to me." I raised my hands out to my sides. "What do I care? It's your asshole. Not mine."

He asked me, "What was that barber's name again?"

"Ward. His shop is next to the library in Dorm One, why?"

Kelly turned and began walking toward *The Center*, the direction from where we had come. "I'm going to get a haircut."

"Now?"

He nodded. "Why wait?"

"I thought you wanted to see the gym?"

"I'll see it tomorrow," he said. "But thanks for the help."

I almost laughed. "I didn't help you. I told you how you could help yourself." He kept on walking. I called out, "Kelly!"

He turned, pausing in the middle of the Six-tunnel. "Call me, K! It's just, K, from now on!"

I laughed then, watching him walk away. I wondered if I'd been so naïve when I first started doing time.

A gangster rap song was blasting over the stereo when I entered the gym. I spotted a handful of shirtless cons lifting weights. The recreation officer, Mr. Tingles, was shooting pool with an inmate at one of the seven tables.

The gym was a cacophony of clanking weights, music, slapping jump ropes, and popping ping pong balls.

But not one of those sounds competed with the pounding of my heart when I glanced inside of the all-purpose room and spotted the Mexican smash Critter's head into the concrete wall.

My feet were running before my brain knew what was happening

CHAPTER 4

At one time the all-purpose room was home to a small boxing ring and the pugilistic equipment needed to train incarcerated fighters. But as prisons grew overcrowded, and physically-fit prisoners too violent to control, the system banned the boxing program sometime in the early nineties. Broutal's *progressive* recreation staff had installed a universal weight machine to replace the ring. After years of heavy usage the weight machine grew too old to repair, but no money was ever provided to buy a new one. With the ancient weight machine on its last leg, the rec staff removed it in hopes that they would soon be able to purchase some other useful pacifier to occupy the inmates' time.

It never happened.

So now the all-purpose room is an empty, concrete cube where inmates go to beat each other senseless whenever they have a gentlemen's misunderstanding.

If opposing gangbangers want to go at it without sparking a war, they go into the all-purpose room. If Little Jim owes the Lowball poker table more that he can pay, all debts can be settled in the all-purposed room.

Convicts challenge each other to fight for any and all reasons: an argument over who's the better ball player—Kobe or Lebron? Who's the best rapper—Jay, Kanye, Nas, or Kendrick? One guy snitched on another's homeboy. Somebody is always using the last drop of hot water from the coffee pot, and he never wants to fill it back up.

We fight over television, sports, cards, dominoes, words, money, work, hard looks in the chow line. We fight like children in a school yard—

childish adults too immature to recognize that the true basis behind violent confrontation doesn't stem from an obvious superficial issue.

The root of all violence is our own foolish pride.

I pushed through two Mexicans who blocked the doorway to get inside the all-purpose room. My eyes locked on Critter kneeling next to the concrete wall with his palm pressed against the blood-soaked side of his head.

The bald Mexican that he was fighting danced on the balls of his feet with his bloody knuckles raised. "What's up now? You called me in here to fight!" He taunted Critter. "Here I am!"

Adrenaline charged my body. Fists clenched. My shoulders swelled with blood and fury. It was hard to stand there and do nothing, but it was a one-on-one fight. When two cons *shot-the-one*, no one broke it up. As men we watched them go at it until they couldn't go anymore or the police intervened. Those were the rules.

Critter staggered to his feet. Drunkenly, he raised his fists. He was way too uncoordinated, too dizzy, too *something!* My temper raged hotter knowing that he was in no shape to finish the fight.

His opponent took a good look at Critter. "Yo...you look like you've had enough. Just give me my money and I'll let you live." The bald Mexican dropped his fists and stood all the way up. "Look, you're bleeding all over the place."

Though blood poured from the side of Critter's face he gritted his teeth and charged the guy, punching him in the nose before he had a chance to protect himself. Blood spewed forth as the Mexican slunk away.

"Now you bleedin' too," Critter spat.

The sucker punch hadn't taken his opponent out of the game. He recovered quickly and attacked with more murderous motive than before.

As the taller of the two, the Mexican was able to lean back as he punched so that Critter's stubby arms could not reach him. Critter swung and missed—the Mexican popped him twice. Critter swung and missed again—the Mexican popped him thrice and then swung a hard right that caught Critter in the same spot that was already a bloody mess.

Critter sloppily tried to defend himself against the onslaught, but it was no use. One short burst of blows laid Critter out.

"That's enough!" I ran over and pushed the guy away as he tried to mount my friend. Kneeling next to Critter, I surveyed a deep gash to the side of his left eye. The bloody pulp was wide open with clumps of Critter's auburn hair matted inside.

The Mexicans behind me shouted, "You ain't got nothin' to do with this, dog! We're leaving here with our stamps or both of you are gonna get it!"

I kept an eye cocked in their direction though I focused on my friend.

Critter squinted up at me. "That you, Danny? When'd you git twins? I'll be, y'all look 'xactly alike too. Mm-hm. All seven of you."

I asked him, "Are you alright to walk?"

"*Hell naw*, I ain't alright! Them sum'bitches try'na kill me, Danny! Fuckin' Mexicans! My granpa Earl bought me one them piñatas for my tenth birthday. I hit that thang 'til my arms like to fell off, and I couldn't bust it. Whole day passed and Grandpa Earl say I cain't have no candy or cake 'til I bust it open. So I beat that thang and beat that thang all day long and ain't git no candy or cake for my birthday. I ain't liked nothin' Mexican since! Hell naw, I ain't! Not tacos or burritos or beans or El Caminos or egg rolls or shrimp fried rice neither—I ain't liked nothin' Mexican, at all, since my tenth birthday when I ain't git no candy or cake!

"And that's what they's try'na do to me, Danny—beat me like a Mexican piñata, but I keep tellin'em I ain't got no candy!"

The Mexican men laughed. One said to his buddies, "He's fucking *loco!*"

Though bleeding and battered, somehow Critter wore a euphoric grin, smiling at a secret that only he knew, feeling no pain at all. His pupils were tiny as pinpricks.

I asked him, "What are you on?"

His head lolled loosely on the concrete floor. "A half-dose of methadone, eighteen—hun'ert milligrams of neurotons...a thirty of morphine..."

"What are you trying to do, *kill yourself?*"

"Naw, Danny!" He declared through a crooked smile. "I was try'na git high. It's just that the methadone makes me itch worser'n the time I 'tracted the crabs from my aunt Tammy Faye. I knowed she was nasty, but I couldn't stay away. My Pa made me shave my peter to rid me of the crabs, but she gave 'em to me again and again and again. What's funny 'bout the whole thang is that I caught my Pa shavin' his peter too, but I never knowed why.

"Shavin' you peter won't rid you of the drug itch—trust me, I done tried it a few times—it makes you itch worse. That's why I came to the gym to buy some *Bennies* from ol' Julio over there—*Bennies* is really Benadryl. They take away the itch and git you high too, so it's a double whammy. Mm-hm. But Julio robbed me. He took my fifteen stamps and ain't give me my dope. He said I still owed him from last time."

"Did you?" I asked.

Critter blinked fifteen slow times. "Did I what?"

"Still owe Julio from the last time?"

He said, " Hell, I'ont know. I owe a whole lotta people. I wants to git high, Danny. I don't wants to pay. Only time I thank 'bout payin' what I owe is when I wants to git high again."

"That's why I beat your ass!" The bald Mexican said. "You're bad business! I'm gonna tell everybody not to sell you shit!"

"Fuck you Julio!" Critter shouted, trying to sit up. "If you're stupid enough to give me dope for free, then I'mma be smart enough not to pay!"

The Mexicans whispered to each other in Spanish. The menacing glances they cast our way told me that they wouldn't let it go easily.

The tension was too thick for my comfort. "Time to go, Critter." I tried to help him stand, but he was a wet fish in my hands—as useless as a bag of bones. I propped him against the concrete wall with his legs straight out in front of him. Through clenched teeth, I hissed, "You need to stop doing this! It's not worth the drama!"

Critter's head hung so low that his chin touched his chest. He seemed to chuckle silently. "Ain't nothin'else to do around here, Danny. All I do is work and sleep. I git high to help the time pass by, and I ain't gon' stop 'cause you don't like it."

I glanced toward the Mexicans, then back to Critter. "What if it kills you someday? Did you ever think about that? What if it kills you?"

With some effort he lifted his glassy eyes to mine. "Then I just be dead."

The three Mexican men approached me. I stood to face them. It was obvious that they were gang-related. One of them had TS-16 tattooed in block letters across his forehead, advertising a dangerous Mexican street gang. The look in his eyes told me that if I had a problem getting Critter out of there, he would be the root of it.

I stood between them and my friend.

I was taller than them all. Broader in the chest. My body carried no fat. I felt the corded muscles tense as my veins pumped adrenaline mixed with hot blood.

Tattoo pointed to Critter. "This ain't over! He still owes us thirty stamps, and he ain't leavin' until we get paid!"

It occurred to me that I didn't owe those men anything. It wasn't my beef to settle. I had every right to walk away.

Looking down at Critter I realized that he was a dumb, racist, junkie, red-neck who would never amount to anything; but he was my friend. Of all the fights Critter had fought, I only knew of one that his mouth or drug addictions hadn't aggravated. That was the day he'd saved my life so long ago. For that I would always be in his debt.

I swung hard, nailing Tattoo on the lump between his eyebrows. Before I could follow it up, one of his friends launched an arching right hook. I leaned back an inch and felt the wind from his knuckles as they whizzed past my nose. I popped the guy with a lunging jab. He stumbled back. I charged in, throwing my hands with all I had until he crumpled to the concrete floor.

Tattoo regained his composure, I turned on him quickly, and we stood face to face. I spied the bald one Critter had fought from the corner of my eye. He stood to my left with his forearms crossed over his chest like he had plans to enjoy the show. I was grateful that he gave Tattoo and I the honor of *shooting-the-one*.

Crouching into a fighting stance, I took two steps toward Tattoo.

There was no fear or gratification in what I had to do. I didn't think about the fact that I could kill or be killed within that moment. I saw a man who had plans to hurt me, and I was going to do everything in my power to stop him.

Tattoo parried and sidestepped like he'd been trained as a boxer. His body moved as one, compact unit—a machine. He kept his chin tucked behind raised, knobby knuckles.

I jabbed with the left as an opener. He back-pedaled easily. I threw another and another and another, reaching for him. He bobbed his head at a safe distance, avoiding my attack fluidly, watching my efforts fall short or their mark.

Usually, I was a calm fighter. At six' one and two-hundred-fifteen pounds, my mass of lean muscle was enough to make most of my opponents cower beneath me. My hands were fast. My power unmatched. I was a wide-horned bull stomping any and every challenger.

But not Tattoo.

I couldn't hit the guy.

I shot a jab/right-hook combo. Tattoo slipped the jab, ducked under the hook, and slid inside. His fists jack hammered my ribs. When I dropped my elbows for protection, he snuck in a swift uppercut to the underside of my chin. I thought I'd been kicked by a mule.

Staggering, I barely had time to raise my hands before he attacked again. Tattoo stayed with me, moving where I moved, pistoning his punches in a mechanized flurry. His knuckles landed solidly on every inch of my face, but determination would not let me fall.

Dipping low, I dove at his waist. I wrapped him up tight and lifted him off his feet. His fingers clawed at my face in the seconds before I slammed him down to the concrete. His head bounced off the floor, and I thought I heard a bone snap. Tattoo let out a howl of pain that made me wince with regret for what I'd done to him, but what other choice did I have?

After straddling his chest, I latched on to his throat with my left hand and raised the right in poise to strike. "Is this over?" I shouted, needing a strong assurance that Critter and I could still stroll the tunnels of Broutal without worrying about a shank in the back. "Is it over now?"

Tattoo didn't speak. He spat blood in my face.

I hit him so hard that it knocked him out. I hit him again to wake him up. The third hammer that I smashed him with split the flesh over his eye and ran a river of red down the side of his head.

I stood up, leaving him leaking on the floor. Looking to his only standing friend, I said, "Critter doesn't owe you anything anymore. That debt is settled. If you want something from him, come to me to get it."

The guy didn't speak or nod or acknowledge that he'd heard me. He just stood there staring with his arms folded over his chest.

Worn out, my eyes washed over the all-purpose room. It looked like a bomb had went off with the blood sprayed across the white walls and pools of it on the floor.

A handful of inmates stood inside the doorway. They watched me with something like awe in their eyes. No one spoke, blanketing the room in an eerie silence.

Four officers pushed their way in. Two were overweight black women, already heaving for air and drenched in sweat upon arrival. One was Harrison, a friendly black man.

The last to enter was that asshole Maloney.

Immediately the two women rushed to the downed inmates. One called in a medical emergency with her hand-held radio as she knelt next to my friend Critter.

The two men stepped to me.

Harrison asked, "What happened here? Did you do all of this?"

I didn't reply. I didn't have to. They were going to take me to the hole just for being there. Admitting my guilt would only make things harder for me.

Maloney stepped closer, crowding my space. Standing in the neighborhood of six' seven, he was a Clydesdale and I was a mule. His broad shoulders, twice the size of mine, were rounded like boulders straining his uniform shirt. His neck was a railroad tie. His chin, a steel wedge. His head, a helmet.

Maloney's hair was cut so high and tight that I couldn't distinguish its color. His emerald eyes were the only humanistic feature on him, but even they lacked the warmth of morality. His pasty, white skin was a road map of bulging blue veins crisscrossing his flesh. I could hear his muscles rippling—I could smell the testosterone and steroids and fat burners and whey protein seeping from his pores.

"Are you deaf?" He asked, his dialect devoid of a southern accent.

"Officer Harrison asked you a question." Maloney's green eyes looked over my blood spotted tee shirt. "What happen in here?"

Still feeling Tattoo's face against my knuckles, I said, "Nothing."

His teeth clenched. "Why are you sweating then?"

"We were having a push-up contest."

He pointed to the men sprawled out on the floor. "What happened to them?"

After a casual glance to the victims, I told Maloney, "They lost."

Before I could brace myself he twisted a hand in my tee shirt and slammed his free forearm into my throat, shoving me against the wall.

His leverage jacked me up and up until I was a ballerina balancing on my tip toes.

There he held me, snarling.

Officer Harrison was in his ear, "Maloney! You can't do that! Let him go! You're going to get us both walked-out of here!"

Maloney ignored him. With a voice like crunching gravel, he rumbled, "Don't play with me. I own your ass in here."

I tried to wedge a hand between his arm and my throat, but he was too strong. My eyes bulged from their sockets as I gasped for air.

Very calmly, Maloney asked me, "Are you going to tell us what happened here? Or do I have to beat it out of you?"

I hated to fight, even though I had never backed down from one. I fought in prison so the mangy wolves would see a battle-scarred panther, instead of a timid rabbit, when they looked my way. Sometimes

I won. Sometimes I lost. But to predators, my point was always proven: I will fight.

You can't win by fighting the cops. You might get the best of one, but there will be many more. A hogtied inmate can't defend himself against pepper-spray and steel batons. First they'll beat you half-to-death, and if you survive that, they'll keep you locked-up on long-term segregation for a few years to make sure the lesson sinks in.

It's a loose, loose situation.

"This place is full of guys like you," Maloney said, keeping one arm against my throat. "You think you're tougher than us." With his free hand, he removed the retractable baton from his utility belt. "I want to see how tough you really are."

He jerked the weapon to its full length.

I didn't move. I didn't even try to.

He raised the baton and whacked me across the knee.

A bright burst of pain shot through my body. I wanted to fall down, but I was held in place by his forearm in my throat.

"You ready to talk yet?" He asked me.

Tears flooded my eyes, but I wouldn't cry—not from pain, and not for his joy. He raised the baton and hit me once, twice, three times…

My boss, Sergeant Thompson, ran over and pushed Maloney off of me. Sarge backed him into a corner with a finger pointing in his face. "What the hell are you doin'? You crazy fool! What's the matter with you, hitting these guys like that?"

My legs buckled beneath me. I slid to the floor and stayed there. I had no idea where Sergeant Thompson had come from, but I was happy to see him.

Just inside the doorway stood the six *Department of Public Safety* inspectors that Sarge had been leading on a tour of the prison. I counted four white men and two grey-haired white ladies, all toting clipboards and ink pens. They stared at me with their mouths gaping open.

One of the white ladies clutched her throat, asking, "What kind of prison are they running here?"

Warden Shelly stepped to the forefront wearing his signature turd-brown business suit. His balding, sun burnt scalp gleamed a ferocious pink above beady eyes.

The warden rushed to Maloney. "What are you doing, Officer?"

Maloney thrust his hands behind his back in an attempt to hide the baton. He explained, "Mr. Tingles, the gym coordinator, called in a code for inmates fighting. We ran in here to break it up."

Warden Shelly's eyes locked onto Maloney's. "You know damned well that's not what I'm talking about."

While on the floor behind him, I saw a steady stream of sweat soaking the back of Maloney's neck. He had a tattoo there that read: USMC.

He told the warden, "It's not what it looks like, sir. I was trying to find out what happened in here, but the inmate wouldn't tell me, so I..."

"Decided to beat it out of him..." He finished for his subordinate.

Maloney dropped his head.

Warden Shelly turned toward the inspectors, smiling at them, showing his control. *Bloody murder* screamed his eyes once they rolled back to Maloney.

"Why don't you take the rest of the day off," the warden told him. "An unpaid vacation might help you reflect on your inappropriate actions. Maybe then you'll realize why we don't do things *that way* at Broutal." He put his hands on his hips and thought about it a bit more. "As a matter of fact, don't report back to work unless we call you."

To my boss, Warden Shelly said, "Lock them all up, Sarge—" waving a hand over us convicts. "I'll lead the tour from here. Come along ladies and gentlemen. You have yet to see Broutal's own Cannery. I hear tell they've got some fresh ears of barbecued corn on the grill out back. If you're polite, I'll see if I can't convince one of the inmates to serve us up. They do take pride in their work."

Maloney pushed through their crowd, bumping Warden Shelly so hard that he almost knocked him down.

In shock of his audacity, one of the ladies asked the warden, "What was that officer's name? I missed his name tag."

Warden Shelly smiled down on her. "Now Mrs. McGovern, I can't see why you would be interested in a thing like that. All of this was an isolated incident, and I assure you that we have the situation under control. This is a correctional institution, very stressful indeed. The men and women who risk their lives working here are not perfect, and these things will happen." He clamped a hand around her elbow to pull her away. "So if you'll come on with..."

She shook free with an ump. "Warden Shelly! That officer assaulted an inmate right in front of us. Do I need to remind you that this is a *Safety* Inspection—not at all limited to usage of wet floor signs and the proper storage of chemicals? It is my job to make sure that you are providing a safe living environment for the inmates, and I take my job seriously. What I saw today was not an example of a *safe* environment. I

46

intend to inform my supervisor about this. And did you forget that my husband is North Carolina's Secretary of Agriculture? He speaks to the governor daily. I will also tell him about what I saw. And if you insist on withholding that officer's name—well I don't mind at all. I'll just assume that you condone his actions when I make my report to..."

"Maloney," he blurted. "His name is Officer Michael Maloney."
"Spell it," she said, scribbling on her clipboard.

CHAPTER 5

*I'm going to the hole for a long, long time...*I thought, while seated on a steel bench inside a holding cell in Housing Dorm Four.

The holding cell is a layover spot for inmates transitioning from the general population to A-Block: the segregation cellblock—one located in each of the four housing dorms.

Fronted by a clear, floor-to-ceiling Plexiglas wall, the holding cell gave anyone walking past a view of a lone fish in his dirty bowl.

Missing a toilet, there was a wet spot in one corner that stank of stale urine. I silently thanked the last occupant for leaving such a treat behind. On one white wall, *FUCK THA WERLD* was misspelled with smeared feces so old that I couldn't smell it.

I'd been sitting in there for hours trying to make sense of the punishments that lay ahead of me. Not only had I fought two inmates, but I'd been in a scuffle with an officer. I knew that I would be sentenced to thirty days for the fights with the Mexicans. I could handle that with no problem.

The situation with Maloney wasn't so cut and dry.

How far would Warden Shelly go to protect his own? Sure he had put on a noble show for the inspectors, but he hadn't fooled me.

Correctional officers like Maloney instill a notion of fear within the inmate population. Their presence alone helps to keep order amidst the chaotic *disorder* of the prison environment. They are the lurking threat in the back of a troublesome inmate's mind; a detached conscious; a second thought; a living, breathing repercussion that holds an inmate in line by sheer reputation alone.

Whispered word of his arrival passes from ear to ear upon shift change. No inmates get high or smoke cigarettes during a Maloneys twelve-hour reign. Drug runners refuse to deliver. Loan sharks close their books. Poker tables shut down. Boys and their daddy's keep their hands to themselves.

Maloney types go by the book when it suits their needs. They perform random shakedowns and strip-searches, daily. They'll write you up for possessing an extra pair of socks or on ink pen that isn't clear. They go above and beyond what must be done during a twelve-hour shift.

Most officers loathe working with a Maloney because they create unnecessary problems. They're unpredictable. Uncontrollable. Bull-headed and arrogant. They take everyone out of their comfort zone. They want the inmates to fear them—never giving thought to the principle that fear breeds violence.

But no matter how hated they may be, Maloneys are essential to natural order. They belong in prisons as black bears belong in mountains, or lions roaming the dusty plains. Without predators like Maloney, the monkeys would have the run of the jungle.

There would be no balance of power.

The only sound in the holding cell was the steady hiss of an air-conditioning vent overhead. I sat listening to it and the hollow noise of my own depressing thoughts in the long hours before two female c/o's came to pick me up. One was short, round, and black. The other was short, round, and white. Well into their fifties, both of them looked to be in the wrong line of work. They were a reflection of the cold-hearted economy of the outside world where people took a job wherever they could find it.

The white lady handcuffed my wrists behind my back. Neither of them spoke.

The hole was calling my name.

There is an instance in a convict's life when he knows that harsh punishment for a wrongdoing is imminent. Most likely he's been there before, so he knows what to expect and accepts his fate whether he is destined to be beaten by correctional officers or locked away in segregation. It is an instance of clarity when he realizes that he cannot take back what he has done.

There is no *hope* for a better outcome in that moment; only what the moment itself creates. Hate. Rage. Anger. Fear.

I felt regret.

Regret...because I had squandered my time with Officer Anderson.

I expected the ladies to escort me to A-Block where I would be locked in a segregation cell to begin serving my whole time. Instead, we left Dorm Four and entered the Four-tunnel.

They led me into the warehouse, where I worked.

The office light was on, but we didn't go inside. As we walked past the open door, Anderson poked out her head to look at me. The blank expression on her face hid whatever true emotions she felt, but I was happy to see her, and I sensed that she felt the same.

An analog clock, on the wall above her head, read eleven-nineteen.

Out on the loading dock, Sergeant Thompson sat on Critter's bucket. Through the open bay door, a crescent moon hung like a fishhook beneath the surface of a black sea speckled with twinkling coins—stars upon whose wishes had been heard and long since forgotten.

The air was clean and crisp and fresh as we drew near.

It was the first time that I had seen a night sky unimpeded by dusty, Plexiglas windows in eight or more years. Staring up into the black sea above, I was saddened by the fact that this may be the last time I ever stepped past the loading dock door.

Sarge told the escorting officers, "I've got 'im from here."

The white lady removed the handcuffs. When she was done, she told me, "You have a nice night now, Sugah."

As the women left, Sarge said, "Sit down, Danny."

I did as told, but I didn't relax. He and Ms. Anderson should have headed home five, six hours ago. They were still at work because of the trouble I caused.

Without looking my way, Sarge asked me, "Them women gone yet?"

Glancing down the central hallway, I didn't see anyone. A country song blasted on the radio in the office. All else was still. "Yes, sir. They're gone."

"Good." Sarge pulled out a pack of cigarettes and a lighter from his breast pocket. He shook a cigarette halfway out of the pack and held it toward me. "Want one?"

I shook my head, knowing how valuable a cigarette could be down in the dorms. "I don't smoke," I said. "Besides, we're not supposed to have those in here."

He laughed and slid the cigarette between his own lips. "We ain't supposed to do a lot of things." Sarge left it at that. He lit the cigarette and took a long drag. After blowing out a stream of smoke, he asked me, "Why didn't you defend yourself against Maloney? Why did you stand there and let him hit you?"

Of all the things I thought I would hear, I had not expected that. I gave the first reply that came to mind. "Because he's an officer, and I'm an inmate."

Sarge blew smoke into the night air on the wings of a tired sigh. "He's a man just like you." He let me think about that while he smoked. Finally, he met my eyes again. "Do you *really* think he's got a right to beat on you any ol' kinda way 'cause you're in prison?" This revelation seemed to mystify him.

I shrugged. "Doesn't he?" The old man stared at me. His expression was a question mark awaiting an answer. "It happens every day in here, Sarge—you know it just as well as I do. I don't think it's right, but what can I do about it? I'm in prison. That's just the way that it is. I guess it's different for people who live on the outside, but…"

"Ain't no difference, Danny. Wrong is wrong. It don't care what color stripes run across your hide, what side of the fence you're on, whether you're short, fat, tall, yella, blue, or cockeyed. *Wrong* is *wrong*."

It was an easy thing to say as a free man. He drove home every single day. The worldly ideals that applied for him didn't apply for me. There was no way to make him understand that, and I wouldn't try. He had his own thoughts about how the world was and how it should be. But the distinction did not lie between right or wrong. It settled with a willingness to accept my place in the world and the hardships that went along with it.

A long-limbed silence stretched between us before he said, "I don't know how you see yourself, Danny, but I think you're great. You work hard. You don't steal. You never complain about nothin'. I'll bet that if I left you in charge while I took off for six whole months, things would be running just as smooth when I came back." He took a last drag from his cigarette and squeezed the hot cherry onto the ground. Sarge stuffed the burnt butt in his pocket. "I trust you more than I trust some fools in my own family."

"I'm the same as the other inmates."

Sarge held up a finger, then pointed to me. "That—you are not," He said. "You weren't a threat to Maloney. You didn't deserve what he did to you. Any other inmate would have jumped on 'im, and I would've had to pull a state boot out of his lily-white ass. You're a thinking man, Danny. That's why you aren't the same as everybody else. There's no doubt in my mind that you could have whooped Maloney from one end of the prison to the other, but you didn't. And I respect you for that."

I turned to look out into the night sky, wondering if Sarge knew that he and I were having the father, son talk that I once needed to have with some faceless mentor long ago—long before the nigrescent soil of penitentiary life had spoiled the roots of my manhood.

I hated the fact that he had to convince me of my abuse, because my institutionalized state of mind wouldn't let me see it for myself.

"You know what, Danny?" He said. "I'd never looked up your file until tonight. I'd never had reason to. You do what I ask. You're the best worker I've ever had..." he trailed off, searching for words. "My God, Danny. You've been in prison since you were fifteen-years-old?"

"That was a long time ago, Sarge."

"I understand if you don't want to talk about it. I won't beat a dead horse, you know. All I'm sayin' is—realizing what kind of life you've been forced to live has opened my eyes." He took a moment to think about it. Soon after, he chuckled to himself. "Reading your record was like reading a war report. How many fights have you been in? Hundreds?"

I sat there.

He asked, "Did you know how to fight before you came in?"

I shook my head. "I was a fast learner."

He laughed heartily; he slapped his knee and laughed again.

I didn't laugh along, but I smiled with him, amazed that he seemed to like me much more than I had ever known.

"Before reading it, I thought I had an understanding of who you were," he went on. "Not to say that you're a troublemaker outside of work. I just couldn't put the Danny I knew to the Danny on that computer."

"I haven't been in trouble in five years, Sarge...until today."

"I know. That's why it all made sense. A man like you—been in trouble his whole life—I guess you would get tired of fighting at some point. You didn't look to be afraid of Maloney. I figured that maybe you'd found a better way to live in here, and you didn't want to mess that up. Maybe you're a changed man."

He couldn't possibly understand me, but I didn't fault him for trying.

A convict quickly learns that the way men *should* live in life is not how inmates *must* live behind bars. Sarge had it all wrong. He looked to the convict as the cause of evil within the system. His officer's mind kept him from seeing how the system could be the cause of evil within the convict.

I told him, "I have always done what I needed to do in order to survive. Since I've been in prison, I haven't set out to hurt anyone who wasn't going to hurt me first. I'm no different today than I was the day that I came in."

He studied my face for a moment. "You got any family? Does anybody write to you? Does anybody send you any money?"

I shook my head. "All I have is me." He looked sad to hear that. To reassure him, I said, "I don't need much to get by. I've learned to do without."

An airplane flew overhead. My eyes followed its blinking lights from one end of the black sky to the other. I imagined that I was on that plane flying someplace. Anywhere but here.

Thinking of the trouble I was in reminded me that I didn't know what the inside of an airplane looked like, nor would I ever.

"When are you going to take me to the hole, Sarge?"

He raised his eyebrows. "Do you wanna go to the hole?"

I said, "I got caught fighting. I'm going anyway."

"Maybe not," he replied. "Maybe you've got some options. Maybe you have an ultimatum."

"*An ultimatum?*" He nodded. I shook my head slowly, "I'm not telling on anybody. I have to live in here, and I won't live as a snitch."

Snorting a laugh, Sergeant Thompson came out with it. "Maloney screwed up, Danny. He screwed up in a bad way because he hit you in front of outsiders. If you were to file a lawsuit, everyone in that room would be called to testify, and I don't think any of those people would support a cover-up."

"That's what the warden wants to do? Cover it up?"

"The warden wants it to go away. If it doesn't, his job will be on the chopping block too. Turds don't fall far from the asshole, Danny, and Maloney's actions are an indication of Broutal's leadership. Now as it stands, one of the state's inspectors has already filed a complaint with The *Department of Public Safety*. The department heads done called down here twice already. Warden Shelly has managed to smooth it over some, but he ain't out of the fire yet. His boss has explained that the inspector's complaint is not enough to launch a full-fledged investigation. For things to proceed they'll need a written statement from you, the victim." He paused to let that sink in. "So, you have two options. Number one: you write a statement saying that Maloney assaulted you..."

"What happens then?"

"First, our Internal Affairs will investigate it, then they'll turn over their findings to the *State Bureau of Investigation*."

"No Sarge. *What happens to me* if I write a statement?"

"Well, it's really an outside case, so they'll be careful. Protocol will be to isolate you from staff and inmates. They'll lock you up on protective custody, then ship you off to another prison—someplace as far from Broutal as possible."

I shook my head again. "I don't like option one. What's two?"

"You don't write a statement. You let bygones be bygones and we'll all pretend like none of this ever happened."

"What about Maloney? What happens to him?"

"He'll keep his job, but Warden Shelly will make sure that he takes a long, unpaid vacation. Maybe he'll quit anyway."

I didn't like it. They were in a bind, and the solution seemed too simple. There was a catch somewhere—something sweet for me, or something thorny and bitter.

"What about the fight I was in? If I keep quiet they'll bring the charges up once their troubles blow over. They'll turn the tables on me."

Sarge crinkled his brow. "What fight? I didn't see a fight. The warden didn't see a fight. Officer Maloney *claimed* to have seen a fight, but no one believes him." Sarge threw up his hands. "Far as we know, y'all were havin' a push-up contest."

I met his eyes, wondering if he was doing me the favor, or someone else.

"And Critter?"

"Look, Danny. No one saw a fight. That's the whole point. We can't charge any of you with fighting because there's no proof. Me and Captain Walker rolled back the camera footage, but we can't see inside the all-purpose room—which is why we suspect y'all go in there to fight anyway. But as long as no one tells us that there was a fight, then you're good to go. It works the same as if you don't write a statement against Maloney. Without you pointing a finger at him it all disappears."

Leaning deeper into the brick wall behind me, I stared up into the night sky wishing things didn't have to be so complicated.

The only benefit I saw in screwing Maloney, was just that: knowing that he would never work in a prison again. That was an outcome that could benefit the greater good of all inmates.

Personally, getting him fired wouldn't open the door for my release. I would still be serving a life sentence. I would be shipped to another prison; someplace where I wouldn't want to be. Life for me would become worse. Nothing would change for the better.

I took a deep breath and let it out, hating that I had to be the fulcrum between what was best for me or everyone else. Why did I have to carry the fate of everything on my shoulders?

I asked Sarge, "What should I do?"

He scratched his head. "It's not on me to decide. There comes a time in a man's life when he must think for himself. You have to live with what you choose, not me. You'll have to deal with what comes from it too. That's the hardest part of living—looking down a dark tunnel, not knowing if there's light at the end of it...or more darkness."

I sat for a long while, thinking in circles, realizing that I didn't have much practice in decision making. I was used to being told what to do. My life experience was too limited. I knew how to survive in prison and nothing else.

I closed my eyes. Sarge lit another cigarette. Crickets chirped. Wind rustled the leaves of distant trees. From the radio in the office, I heard a sorrowful woman wailing over a lonely guitar for her man to *stay*.

I wondered if Anderson was sitting in her chair thinking of me. I wondered if I could right the wrong I had done to her. She'd stepped-out on a limb by opening her heart, and I had disrespected her with my fear. *What is wrong with me?* Why is it so easy for me to fight and maim other men, but so hard to give into a woman's touch? *What is wrong with me?*

I thought of Maloney and all the jerks who had made my days in prison longer and harder than they had to be. I couldn't expect any better from them, but Anderson had already shown me that there was a beauty in life that I had never known. She showed me that in one moment of compassion. She was the best thing to ever happen to me, and I didn't want to give her up.

"I'm not writing a statement."

"You sure?" He didn't look happy to hear it. "Maybe you should think about it again, Danny. Give it some time..."

"I've thought about it, Sarge."

He stared at me, giving me time to change my mind. Finally, he nodded. "Let me go call Warden Shelly at home to fill him in. He's probably pissin' three shades of yella worryin' about it."

We both stood. Sarge went to his office while I closed the bay door and locked it. I had never been in the warehouse after dark. The only light came from the open office door. All else was pitch black.

Ms. Anderson walked down to where I was.

"Why did you stay so late?" I asked her.

At first, she stared at my chest. "Sarge needed help with the paper work, so I..." Her sad eyes rose to meet mine. "Danny, I know you didn't mean for me to read your poems, and I'm sorry." She held out my notepad.

I didn't take it. I reached out and held her hand instead. Stunned, she glanced down the hall toward the office, but she didn't let me go. Sarge could be heard yapping away on the telephone.

"Why did you leave me like that, Danny?"

I opened my mouth to apologize, but nothing came out.

She shook her head, frowning. "I think you've been in prison too long."

"It happened so fast," I tried to explain. "I didn't know if it was the right thing to do." A part of me couldn't believe that what I was experiencing was real. Even her hand in mine seemed like a fantasy. "I still don't know if it's the right thing to do."

""Well you need to make up your mind!"

"Are you mad?"

"Hell yes, I'm mad. You can't do that to a woman, Danny. You had me all hot and ready to kiss somebody, then you just up and left. The next thing I know, people are calling up here saying that you beat up six guys in the gym, and I couldn't help but think that it was somehow my fault."

"I didn't mean to hurt you."

"You haven't. Not yet," she said. "But you will if you don't make up your mind about what you want." She smiled a little. "I'm not going to wait on some man to decide if he wants to kiss me. You have no idea how hard it is to cool me off once I'm heated up—it's like throwing a cup of water in a volcano..."

I smiled, and I couldn't stop. Just to be near her set off sparks in my heart.

I said, "It sounds like you know what you want."

She squeezed my hand. "I do." She whispered, "I want you."

Sarge hollered out to us while squinting into the dark. "Come on, y'all! Quit standin' around greasin' farts, it's time to go! My wife Lulu done had a pot of fried cabbage and ham hocks settin' on the stove since three o'clock, and I mean to eat the whole thing! Y'all need to get a move on because my stomach is touching my back!"

I dropped her hand.

Smiling, she slid my notepad of poems into her back pocket.

After catching up with Sarge as he locked the office door, I asked him, "Now that it's all over, do you mind telling me what you would have done in my shoes?"

He faced me seriously. "I would've written a statement saying that Maloney assaulted me. I would've made sure that he got fired. I would've sued the Carolina blue off of the *Department of Public Safety.* I would have sued them for so much money that they would have offered to let me out of prison rather than pay me a settlement.

"Now don't get me wrong," he continued. "You made a safe choice for yourself, and I understand it. But sometimes you have to fight the bull in order to kill him. That's the thing about choices, Danny, every man needs to have his sights set on what he wants out of life. Once he's got that in his crosshairs, he'll die a happy man if all his choices help him to aim true. Be happy with your decision. It doesn't matter what I would've done. You are living for you."

Sarge walked ahead of Anderson and I.

I glanced her way, and the look in her eye told me that I'd done the right thing. My sights were set on her heart.

CHAPTER 6

Anderson told me, "My mom's Italian. She's my best friend. They say that my dad was German, but he died before I was old enough to remember him. I'm twenty-seven. Single. I have two dogs at home. Mickey is mixed with Beagle and Hound. Blue is a Black Lab." She pressed an index finger to her pursed lips in thought. "What else could you possibly want to know about me?"

It was Friday afternoon—two days after Anderson and I had come to terms with the way we felt about each other. We were walking the Seven-tunnel, alone. Behind me I pulled a flatbed cart stacked with microwaves. We'd been from tunnel to tunnel replacing old machines with new ones inside the employee break rooms. This was our last leg before returning to the warehouse.

We sauntered slowly to enjoy our time together.

I asked, "Do you have any kids?"

She stopped walking, so I did too. "Did you ask me that because you think I'm fat?"

"What?" I laughed, but she didn't—she was deadly serious. "You're not fat," I blabbered. "I asked because I wanted to know. It didn't have anything to do with how you look."

"Why are you avoiding the question?" She spied me through squinted eyes. "Do you think I'm too fat?"

My eyes took in the physical attributes that I liked about her, but my attraction went much deeper. Everything about her drove me wild.

I couldn't remember the horrible past before her. I only loved the delirium I felt while with her. I dreaded a devastating future without her.

What I hated most was the pressure of wanting to make her happy at all times. I didn't think that I should have to search for the right words, or run from the wrong ones when talking to her. *She wanted me too;* and if a pair of lovers truly shared the same burning interest, then the fire of one could only be used to warm the other—not to scorch.

I honestly told her, "I think you're perfect."

She bit her bottom lip as her eyes melted into mine. "You just passed your first test." She began walking again.

I fell in beside her. "Test?"

"Well...it wasn't really a test," she confessed. "But you passed. That was a good way to turn a negative into a positive."

I didn't understand. "I told you exactly what I was thinking."

"I know." She smiled my way. "You can't help it. That's why it's so special."

Talking in low tones, we kept our eyes alert for *ear-hustlers:* eavesdroppers who could hear our conversation and expose us. Appearing professional was a responsibility that went hand in hand with our affection, even though it proved hard to dampen the glow between us. Lingering glances and conspiratorial giggles were sure to give us away, but we tried as best we could to hide our growing bond.

Anderson never answered my question about kids, but I let it go. I asked, "What else?"

"What else *what*, Danny?" She rolled her eyes. "You asked me to tell you about myself, so I did."

"There has to be more."

"There's much more, but women don't like volunteering information. It's better when you guys trick us into revealing our innermost secrets. That way it doesn't feel like we're talking too much or giving up the goods before we're supposed to trust you with such ammunition that could be used against us at a later date. Then we can blame you—instead of ourselves—when we fall in love because you knew us so well."

I thought about it. "Women want to be tricked?"

"Does *convinced* sound better?"

I shook my head. "It doesn't matter how you put it, what women want is the opposite of the way things should be. It doesn't make much sense."

"Exactly!" She snapped her fingers and pointed at me. "Now you're learning about women!"

We'd spent Thursday, the day before, cooped up in the warehouse. Anderson and Sergeant Thompson had been in the office finishing up paperwork, while I sat out back reading Emily Dickinson and writing poems of my own.

While staring at the highway beyond the sally port, I thought of the cars that drove past. I wondered how it would feel to be able to go wherever I wanted, whenever I wanted. So I wrote:

just over the fence
through razor wire I watch cars drive by
on sundays I assume cadillacs drive to church
on mondays I guess trucks travel to work
occasionally someone honks or waves hi
some just stare with contemptuous eyes
you can tell who's rich by the collars of their shirts
you can tell who's in love by the way women flirt
i've learned lots about people, watching their cars drive by
why...sometimes I watch with nothing else to do
wishing I was in a car...driving past too
just over the fence

When Anderson was able to sneak away, she had sat on Critter's bucket and explained how men and women should get along.

It turned into a two-day conservation.

"So how do you like to be *convinced?*" I asked.

"First of all," she pointed out, "never ask a woman something like that. It's the fastest way to get left standing at a bar by yourself. You can't *ask* a woman what she wants to be *asked* about. That's cheating. You need to work for that knowledge."

"Well how is a man supposed to know about a woman he likes if he can't ask her?"

"Guess." She smiled. I didn't. "It's not as hard as you think. All you have to do is pay attention. Women tell men things about them without speaking a word. You'll know if she's loose or conservative by the way she dresses. You can tell her salary by her shoes. If she wears expensive perfume, then she doesn't mind spending money. You'll know if a woman wants you, or doesn't, by the look in her eyes as you walk by. Every woman wants a man that can figure her out, and a good man takes his time to discover the things that make a woman happy. We know when we've found the right guy if he can look into our eyes and think the same thing we do."

That was a lot to take in. "I've never been around women enough to know how to make you happy."

"You already have," she said. "Somehow you had me pegged from the get go. Reading your words was like seeing myself from the outside in. Even if the poem wasn't about me, it felt like you had written it to me—trying to help me see life through your eyes."

"It's not something I planned to do. One day I couldn't stop thinking about you, and I decided to write down what I thought."

"That's what makes me happy, Danny. That's what I want. Honesty. If you're true to yourself and your own feelings, then you'll be true to me and mine. That's all any woman should want."

I loved the easy way we were—the familiarity. Walking with her was like trekking a beaten path that I'd known in my past. It seemed as if we'd been together since before the dawning of time; when the miniscule Earth was but a grain floating in a vast pool of tar, and our two souls were shooting stars racing through the black of the nothing less sky.

I wondered if every man had a companion that made him feel free. For a moment, I allowed myself to believe that this was how life was meant to be—that maybe it wasn't destiny for some men to live and die without ever knowing a woman's heart, or how her presence could change him. I began to think that a life sentence didn't have to be a stigmata through the palm of love.

"I like talking to you," she said. "You know how to hold an intelligent conversation. It's a change of pace. Not at all what I'm used to."

"What do most guys talk about?"

"*Sex*," she hissed. "*Sex*, work, sports, *sex*, video games, *sex*, themselves...and more *sex*."

I didn't know anything about sex, so naturally, it was the last thing that I wanted to discuss. "Do you go to the movies?"

"I go all the time," she said. "There isn't much to do in Bonnieville. But the only thing I hate about the theatre around here is that they're always out of the candy I like. You know the little chocolate minty things?" I get those because I hate popcorn."

"Popcorn? Who hates popcorn?"

"I do." She shivered. "Can't stand the smell of it. Uh. Disgusting."

Her hair was pinned-up in an unruly clump by two onyx chopsticks. Twin locks cascaded from the crown of her forehead, framing her face. Her eyes were bright and glittery. Today she smelled of a warm waterfall and its enveloping mist. Her lips were as pink as a puckered pomegranate, juicy and glossed with sugary sweets.

"You can't hate popcorn. It's like lemonade or apple pie. It's American."

"*American*," she scoffed, "is freedom of speech. Democracy. The right to live how you want to live, not how a government tells you to live. For something to be *American* means that it has to be great. It's a state of mind, not a product. It can't be packaged and shipped across the globe. That's why our way of living doesn't work anywhere else. You can't take our constitution and apply it in a country that doesn't share the same ideals that developed it. You can buy popcorn anyplace."

I said, "This is definitely not a conversation about sex."

She didn't hear me. She went on. "I saw how people live in other countries. Everywhere that you go isn't a tourist attraction. Like when I went to the Shaolin Province in China. I wanted to..."

"*China?*" I stopped in my tracks. "You've been to China?"

"China...Tibet, Great Britain, Italy, Germany..." Anderson rattled off six more countries on two continents.

I couldn't believe it. I stood still until she gestured for me to keep walking.

"I grew up poor, Danny." Her voice slipped into a soft southern tone. "We didn't have anything—me and my mom. There were times that we had to live with family because we couldn't afford a place of our own. For a while we had a little old trailer in Bonnieville with nothing but woods and raccoons and bugs behind it. I used to catch cats because I didn't have many toys to play with. I went to the same schools that my mom went to when she was young. All of the stories I heard while growing up were of the same town and the same people doing the same damned things. I got an idea in my head that I wanted to get away."

"Sounds like you hated your life," I said.

"I don't know. I accepted it, even though I had dreams of other things. Ever since I can remember, I used to cut out pictures of faraway places from books and magazines. I pasted them in a big scrapbook and promised myself that I would travel to all of them someday. When I was little I used to thumb through that book, imagining that some other little girl was doing the same thing on the other side of the globe. My dream was to meet her wherever she was.

"I didn't get serious about it until I started working here at Broutal. I was young, green, and so naïve. It was crazy to meet inmates who had been in prison for thirty years. I looked at the dirty walls and the way you guys live, and it was hard to imagine someone dying here after all that time. It made me sad because I had the freedom to go anywhere in the world that I wanted to go, but I was wasting it.

"So I decided to stop dreaming. I saved up my money. I paid my rent three months in advance, and I took a tour of Europe and Asia. I crossed out a picture in my scrapbook for everywhere that I went."

"Do you still have a bucket list?" I asked.

"No, Danny. Not a bucket list. *A life list*. People don't enjoy anything when they're dead, and I don't want to think about dying while I'm having the time of my life." We stopped at a slider door leading to a long hallway of offices. "It's like being with you. I'm a daydreamer just like you. Maybe that's why I connect with your poems, because we're the same type of person. I don't think about the fact that we're not supposed to be building what we are, or that we could get caught. I only think about you, me, and how good I feel when we're together."

I imagined a plump little girl in pigtails flipping the stiff pages of a pasted scrapbook, staring in awe at the images she saw.

Next I pictured the gorgeous woman that I knew standing atop the snow-capped Himalayas—warm in a pink parka and goggles, smiling for the camera, triumphant and alive, fulfilling her dreams.

I knew that little girl. Trapped. Yearning for more than what she knew.

I too had stared and wondered at the exotic places in magazines.

But not from a kitchen table.

From a prison cell.

Listening as she went on and on about Buddhist monks in their orange robes and bald heads, I saw things as she had seen them. I admired her accomplishment. She'd been around the globe for us both, and I enjoyed living it through her eyes. A part of me wanted to tell her that she was a tough, courageous woman...

But I didn't say anything. I listened, swooning from the sound of her voice.

Once the slider opened, we walked down the hall toward the break room. Inside were four black, male officers were seated at a plastic table littered with crumpled sandwich wrappers and empty soda bottles.

Officer Johnson was the fat, pimply-faced one. Peterson was the jock, brown-skinned and muscular. Rynhold was older, early forties with a head full of wavy hair and a perfect smile. James was the youngest of the four; skinny, dark, and always cracking jokes.

I left the cart in the hall and carried in a microwave.

Peterson, the jock, snapped at me. "Ain't no inmates allowed in here!"

I ignored him. He started to say something else when Anderson stepped in through the door. Slack-jawed, they all stared as if the virgin mother herself had ridden into their village astride a milk-white unicorn.

She threw on her smile while walking to their table. "Hey fellas."

Assorted hellos and what-ups floated around the room.

Johnson, the fat one, said, "You don't ever leave that musty-ass warehouse to visit us anymore. You too good to go slummin'?"

"That ain't it," Peterson added, his eyes roaming over her hips and thighs. "Sergeant Thompson be tryin' to keep her all to hisself." He told Anderson, "You need to transfer back down to Dorm Three where we get all the action."

"No!" she declared, shaking her head. "Too many *gunslingers* in Three. Last time I worked up there I had to wear a raincoat while making rounds. They were standing naked in their cells trying to show me what they've got. I wish they would give them their sex magazines back so they would leave me alone. It's like they go crazy when they see a woman."

"Can you blame them?" Rynhold asked her. He licked his lips before tossing her a seductive smile. "I'm losing my mind just looking at you."

Anderson rolled her eyes. The others laughed.

She continued as if she hadn't been interrupted. "Besides, *the action* is why I transferred out of the dorms in the first place. We were breaking up fights every night. I got tired of driving home smelling like sweat and pepper spray.

"Now, I actually enjoy coming to work." She glanced at me for a smidgen, then turned back to them. "I only work eight instead of twelve-hour shifts. I can leave for lunch if I want, and I'm off on weekends and holidays. I'm right where I want to be."

"I don't blame you," James, the dark youngster told her. "I hate workin' around them nasty-ass inmates. The cell blocks smell like a zoo. They don't do nothin' but argue, fight, complain, and snitch on each other. Half of the time I don't feel like I'm workin' in a prison, I feel like a damn babysitter." The other officers nodded their agreement. "If it was up to me, I'd exterminate most of the institution. The only inmates that I would leave alive are the faggots and child-molesters. They don't fight, and they don't bother you. All they want to do is watch soap operas and fuck the shit out of each other."

The break room exploded in laughter. Even Anderson snickered along.

I tried not to ear-hustle, maybe because it was expected of me, or maybe because I didn't want to pay attention. I felt like the house-nigger slave performing his menial task while *Massa* lounged in the shade with his friends poking fun. Except in my time, *Massa* and his friends were just as black as me, which made me feel even worse.

Standing at a chipped countertop, I unplugged the old microwave. One of the cops told a joke and the place erupted again. They hooted and clapped as I silently placed the new machine in its spot.

I heard a couple complain that they had to go. As they rose from the table, Peterson knocked over a soda bottle, spilling its contents onto the floor.

James, the comedian, let into him. "Damn you clumsy! I can't take yo' lizard-lipped ass nowhere!"

Everyone laughed.

I glanced at Peterson. He was the only c/o who wasn't laughing. His face was a mask of embarrassment—embarrassment and rage.

"Wha'chu got all those muscles for?" James went on. "Yo' big ass can't even pick up a..."

Peterson swiped his arm across the table, knocking everything on its surface to the floor. James shut his mouth.

With veins bulging in his thick neck, he pointed to me. "Get over here and clean this up!"

I blinked at him, unmoving.

He shouted, "You heard me! Go get a mop and clean up my mess!"

"That's not his job!" Anderson told him. "Danny works for me!"

The break room fell silent. Their carefree laughter was now a whisper of the past—snuffed out by the deafening roar of pride.

All eyes were on me, waiting to see if I would move lickety-split or stand up for myself.

Before I could do anything, James, the instigator said, "I think Marlowe Graves is the janitor down here. He sleeps in Dorm Four. It's his job, so I'll call the sergeant down there and get Graves to come clean it up."

Peterson shook his head. "Fuck that." He moved toward me. "Why do we need to call another one? They're all janitors. Cleaning up our shit is what they're good for." To me, he said, "Ain't that right? I bet you'd lick my boots if I told you to, huh?"

Rynhold stepped in front of him, stopping Peterson five feet from me. He laid a palm on the big man's chest. "Calm down, bro. We were only playing with you. Forget about it."

Peterson shoved Rynhold away, but he took no further steps toward me. "Why y'all standin' up for this nigga here?" He asked them, pointing to me. "He wouldn't stand up for you! No inmates stood up for that sergeant that got her throat slit at Lanesboro Correctional! A whole cellblock stood around watching her bleed to death! I even heard they fought the paramedics so that they couldn't get in to save her! But y'all want to stand up for him!" Shaking his finger my way, Peterson said, "They aren't the same as us! They live in cages like animals, and they don't deserve any better than that! They steal, they rape, they kill! Why do you want to help him? Why would anybody want to help them?"

Softly, Anderson told Peterson, "You can't blame Danny for what someone else has done…"

Peterson wouldn't be swayed. "He ain't no angel. He's locked up for somethin', isn't he?"

James pulled out his walkie-talkie. "I'm calling Graves down…"

"No," I broke in, stopping them all. "I'll clean it up. It's no big deal, I've got it."

I stepped into the hallway feeling small. Alone in the mop closet, I was haunted by the strain I'd seen on Anderson's face. I hated that she'd seen me wallowing through the muck with hogs in a filthy trough, when I longed to stand tall and glorious like a stallion in her eyes.

While filling a mop bucket with water, I heard officers leaving the break room. I looked out and saw Peterson, James, and Johnson making their way toward the Seven-tunnel slider. I breathed easier watching them go.

It didn't bother me that an officer hated inmates. It didn't bother me to be spoken down to. Badges award insecure and powerless people with authority over others, and those who aren't worthy of that power quickly abuse it.

It was a fact of prison life that I had accepted long ago.

When I brought the mop bucket back to the break room, I saw Anderson leaning against the wall. Rynhold stood in front of her, running his finger down her cheek.

"Your skin's so soft," he told her. "You've got me wondering what the rest of you feels like." Anderson pulled his hand away. "Aw, don't be like that," he cooed.

The black hand of rage took me then. It lifted me onto its leathery back and carried me to a dark place of stone with pillars of fire and a dusting of sulfur over all that I saw. My hands squeezed the mop handle until my knuckles felt as if they would pop right off of my fingers. My teeth grinded against each other until I thought they would shatter. I wanted nothing more than to wrap that mop around Rynhold's head.

Yet I forced my eyes down into the soapy mop water below.

"Don't touch me that way," she told him, spotting me in the room.

Rynhold said something, but I couldn't make out his words. They continued talking with their voices lowered as I cleaned up someone else's mess.

Once finished, I returned the bucket to the mop closet. I saw Rynhold trying to hand her a slip of paper that I assumed to be his phone number, when I came back.

Anderson wouldn't take it. "I don't date co-workers. I tried it before, and it didn't work."

Rynhold hesitated before stuffing the slip of paper into his own pocket. "I didn't believe them when they said you thought you were better than everybody, but I guess seeing is believing."

"That's not it." She glanced at me, then back to him. "I'm not looking for anybody right now…"

"Whatever," he spat, and sat back down to his lunch.

Anderson left the break room in a hurry. I followed her out into the Seven-tunnel, dutifully toting my cart full of microwaves behind. Neither spoke. We were both caught up on a carousel of our own twisted thoughts; forgetting the fantasy fair we'd known before, only to reiterate the revelation of reality we had always been trapped in, but tried to ignore.

Once we made it back to the warehouse, Anderson went into the office where Sergeant Thompson was on the phone. I parked the cart near the twenty-seven cage where junk like the old microwaves were stored until they could be disposed of.

In the echoing atmosphere, I heard Sarge's bellowing laugh. Soon, the guffaw died down, but its robust tone told me that he was talking to his wife Lulu. He laughed differently for her. He laughed a laugh of comfort—a laugh of pleasure and abandonment of stress. She was his safe haven. His lifeline.

It occurred to me that Sarge was always talking about Lulu. She was forever the leading lady or spectator or innocent bystander in every one of his funny stories about life.

Anderson and I would never have a bond so complete. It didn't matter how close we became, we would always be strangers hollering from opposing cliffs across a wide ravine—able to communicate, but still distant. What I felt was tangible, yes, but it would never be as real as I needed it to be.

Never.

My body tensed as the rubber soles of her shoes squeaked closer. She sped around the corner, jiggling keys to the cages, eyes wide and searching for me.

She stepped close. Her cinnamon irises danced over my chest as she wrung her fingers together. Anderson's eyes rose to meet mine. Her pink lips parted to let loose a word, but she held back her first emotion. Instead, she said, "I'm sorry you had to go through that, Danny. They don't know you like I do, and Peterson...his brother just got shot to death in Raleigh, so he's taking out his anger on you guys. I know that isn't a good excuse, but it's the truth. I should have put my foot down, but I didn't want them to start thinking anything—you know—about us."

"You protected me the best that you could have."

"I should've done more."

She held my gaze until a realization washed over her eyes. "You're mad about Rynhold. I should have known it would upset you."

I envisioned his finger sliding down her cheek once again. I saw his wavy hair, crisp uniform, and his perfect smile. My fists became hammers at my sides. I wanted to find him. I wanted to beat him. I wanted to show him that he wasn't better than me, even though I knew that he was.

"I don't like him, Danny. I didn't ask him to touch me."

I raised my hand. "I know you didn't." She fell silent. The sadness in her eyes pleaded with me to let it go, but I couldn't. "If you were mine, I could have done something about it. But you aren't mine. You can never be. I don't know what we can do for each other besides bring heartache and pain."

The words poured out of me so quickly that I didn't have time to think about them. They were echoes of thoughts spoken in my mind— raw emotion, jealousy, and the truth as I knew it.

"What are we doing?" I asked her. "This is pointless."

"But Danny...isn't this what most inmates want? Don't you guys dream about a woman falling for you? Why can't you be satisfied with what little...?"

"That's what you don't understand, Anderson. I don't want a piece of you. I want all of you."

She didn't know what to say. It was in her eyes. Maybe she'd once thought that we could go along in some harmless way, stealing a few kisses for a couple of months, but now she didn't look so sure that she had a handle on the situation.

It was my fault. I was falling too hard, way too fast. I knew it, and I didn't like it.

"We should stop," I said. "We should have never began. I'm going to die in here someday, and you deserve better. I can't do anything for you."

"Danny..." She was careful to meet my eyes. "Whenever a woman is walked-out of here, the first thing officers say is: '*What did she see in him? He can't do anything for her. He can't pay her bills now that she's out of a job.*' But you need to know that sometimes it isn't about what one person can do for the other.

"I don't want anybody else. I want the man who dreams about me as much as I dream about him. I want the man who shows me how he feels with his vivid imagination."

"All I have is imagination." I took a step back. "We need to stop." I remembered Rynhold again. I saw his smiling face, lusting after her. "I don't want to tie you up. Sooner or later you'll meet a guy that you like, and I don't want to be the reason you make a mistake by turning him away for me."

She ran at me and snatched my hands into her own. "How come every time I tell you that I want you, you give me reasons why I shouldn't? You're making me crazy! One minute I'm crying, and the next minute I want to strangle you! I know you're in prison, and I don't give a shit! Stop feeling sorry for yourself!"

I tried to pull away, but she tightened her grip, drawing me closer until the after burn of her anger singed my heart too.

"You won't run from me this time!" She hissed in a whisper. "I know you're scared. You're scared, insecure, and self-conscious too. I would be the same way if I'd been living the way you have for so long. I get that, Danny. I understand. You've got your heart wrapped around mine and you think I'll break it. You think I'll meet some prince charming and run off to leave Danny all alone in his cell. That's why you're scared, but you need to get over it. Nobody wants to get hurt, so we hold back. It's a natural thing to do. But I will not let you walk away from me when I know you don't want to."

It was hard to look into her eyes. I felt the tender spots from my fight, days before, pulsating and alive. They were reminiscent of the same pain I felt when seeing her with Rynhold. She was right. I didn't want to be hurt, and I wasn't reassured by her words.

"This can't work, Anderson. I want it to, but…"

She shook my hands, forcing me to meet her gaze. "What do you see when you write, Danny?"

"What?" I tried to pull away again.

She pulled me closer. "Your inspiration. What is it? What drives you? Tell me! How do you see us? What do you see? Huh? What do you see?"

In my mind's eye, I stood alone in the center of an incomplete house. There was a roof and plywood floor, but the beamed walls were a skeletal ribcage of rotten two-by-fours that I saw straight through. Patches of mold grew on the floor beneath me. The stenches of death and mildew saturated the air. Some of the beams holding up the roof were cracked; some water-logged; some split in half.

To the right and left of my broken house were complete homes: one was a hulking Victorian manse, and the other was a white plantation with a white swing on its wrap-around porch. Those homes were picture perfect. They glowed with a luster—the luster of life.

I wondered why those homes were complete while mine was in shambles. What catastrophic even had destroyed my home but left theirs intact? Or maybe my home had never been completed in the first place.

What was wrong with my home?

It had a backyard—an endless ocean of lush, green grass. A deep valley lay far beyond that, cradling a silent pasture of violet flowers. For miles around were gargantuan hills and mountains stacked atop one another above a low lying bed of trees.

The beauty and wholeness of nature—the pride of man-made structures surrounded my incomplete home. It was as if the hands of the gods had touched all but me.

An open toolbox lay at my feet. Inside was a hammer, nails, a saw. It contained everything that I needed to work on my house. But as I looked around me, at the devastation. I figured that my ruined home was beyond repair. There was too much work to do. Most sections couldn't be salvaged. Most of it needed to be torn down and rebuilt.

My home wasn't worth the effort.

I didn't have the energy to build a newer, better foundation.

As I stood there feeling sorry for myself, I heard hammering in a distant room of my house. Soon, after, I heard the whine of a power saw. Wood fell on wood, and there was hammering again.

I followed the sounds through the hollow catacombs of my home until I ended up in a back room with the sun beaming in. She knelt on the floor with a nail in her teeth and a hammer in her hand. Sawdust sprinkled her hair. She smiled up at me.

Why was she trying to complete my house?

The more that I thought about it, the more I realized that maybe her house was incomplete too, and we needed each other to rebuild.

"I see you, Anderson."

"That's all I want you to see."

She stood on tiptoes and pressed her lips against mine. Her arms crossed behind my neck. I held her close around her soft middle. She trembled in my clutch, fitting right in, like an ancient memory that I wished to relive again. Our mouths crept open and I tasted the warm, wanting tongue of a woman for the first time in my life.

Leaning against the chain-link cage, I pulled her into me. She was a squirrely, squirming mess panting into my mouth.

I gave myself to her, but not for long.

I didn't hear Sarge laughing anymore. The fact that we could get caught overruled our pleasure, so I broke the kiss.

She smiled. "That's better now, isn't it?"

And it was.

She kissed me again, giggling. The next thing I knew, we were hugging—swaying side to side like old lovers cheek to cheek on a hardwood dance floor.

With my breath simmering her lobe, I whispered, "*tumbling in the blue from a plain long gone. falling for your right when what's left is all wrong. the lungs of my pains cry the same sad song. to be lifted by your wings as you sail, sail along.*"

Nibbling my cheek, she purred for me. Her thigh slid between my legs, massaging the hardness there. I closed my eyes, wishing to have her always, knowing that these were the feelings I'd been running from in the first place. I said," *suspended in time seems a worthless rhyme. like letters tethered as a mysterious sign. dancing 'round the heads of yours and mine. a tale of two talents, yet forever entwined.*"

She kissed my chin before pulling back. "When'd you write that?"

71

I nestled my nose into her hair. "I haven't been sleeping lately."

"Mmmm…" she kissed my lips. "Me either." We swayed a bit more. "It's lovely, though. So deep and cryptic…like a riddle. But what does it mean?"

"That I'm falling in love with you."

CHAPTER 7

i wish that I could lay awake, just to watch you sleep. staring at your lips, admiring your peace...

The words were born effortlessly. Their melodies fluttered around my mind like butterflies whose transparent forms danced in flawless harmony.

Words were my only perfection.

i got lost in the clouds today, thinking of how they seemed to sway. against a soft blue sky, as soft as your softest sigh.

The words.

Driving me crazy words.

Rhyming words. Constant companions. Welcomed lovers come to soothe knots from my twisted soul—as ever-present as the conscious thought sound tracking the vivid experiences of my five senses.

smell: for the scent of her hair.

sight: leads me inside her lair.

hear: her gasp into my ear.

touch: hands to draw her near.

taste: to let no pleasure go to waste.

Words.

Lonely words—black as a torrent of funeral tears. Sodden with love filled with pain and grief of new and old beginnings from endings of life as I had lived it before, and will live

it forevermore.

i want to know

is the birth of light the dying death of darkness? is the pact of lovers a mere horse's harness? is it destiny to die in a cell so cold? to never find purpose in this hell growing old?
i want to know
Paradoxical words.
Obsessive obsession.

Since beginning the poems, my notion of the realistic world waned. I began seeing all things from a poetic perspective. The sun was not the sun, it was an aurous orb of burning brilliance. A window wasn't a window, it was looking glass where I sat to watch the shadows of time pass.

In some ways, living in poetry was a deep convalescence that I used to ease the ills of the free mind within my confined body. In other ways, it was a nuisance that I couldn't get rid of.

My thoughts were only of her. I couldn't sleep. Didn't care to eat. Every sight, sound, or smell reminded me of her in some way. Of course, it added color to my colorless prison, but it all brought on a memory to make me smile stupidly or compose some new mental lyric to obsess over her with.

Nothing mattered except Officer Anderson.

I wondered if all men felt similar when they fell in love: happy, sad, focused, confused, wonderful, and terrible all at the same time. I couldn't steal my eyes away when near her, and I was consumed by a flame that burned hotter during the hour of separation. Despite how psychotic my emotions had me feeling, I wasn't sure if I wanted life to be any other way.

After all...*a dream is just a dream, should it fade. if the memories grow darker the longer you lay. when you open your eyes and the vision escapes. that dream was a dream wasn't meant to remain.* And I wanted her to stay.

Maddening thoughts ran rampant as I squinted into the Saturday sun, a golden eye, perched high in the cloudless sky.

I'd slept fitfully the night before, dreaming of her, waking in the day-mare of knowing that the warehouse was closed on weekends, and I would have to love alone until Monday morning.

On weekends, recreation is held in the gym and on its adjoining outdoor yard, for two hours, after lunch.

As a way to focus my attention on something else, I went to the yard and ran three miles. That didn't help, so I moved over to the pull-up bar and repped out set after grueling set until my back and biceps were as exhausted as my legs.

But still...*once upon a summer's noon, i dreamt of her beneath a moon. a feast for eyes and mine consumed, this flower of love—woman in bloom.*

beneath her toes grew patches of primrose...their petals, pillows, in rows of yellow. behold, from her mouth spewed riddles in code. but only the chose could decipher what she told.

you leprous slaves mistake messages you crave, for literal meanings of long lost days, but only her, my willing knave, knows the traps i lay are nothing but play.

The words would not leave me. I dared not write them down, because even I couldn't grasp their purpose. I told myself that they were words—just meaningless words streaming in and out of my thoughts with her image attached, but that didn't stop me from dwelling on them, or trying to figure out what the words were telling me.

I was on the grass doing V-up crunches when a group of men gathered near me. Ten or so guys stood listening to Roscoe, an eighty year old con, whose pitch-black skin was stretched taut over the jagged bones of his face like a tight leather glove straining against knuckles. His nappy hair glowed white in the sunlight, a cloud, above his shining forehead.

"We ain't no more than slaves!" Roscoe shouted, his old voice a growl. "I seen times when I's so tired, my homeboys had ta carry me from the fields to my bunk! Y'all got it easy compared to what we went through in the past! Look at my hands!" He displayed his gnarled and arthritic fingers for the group of cons surrounding him. "These here is the hands of black folk who been toilin' a white man's land since the first rising of the sun—that's how long they been workin' us!"

Kelly walked over and blocked the sun from my eyes. "What's up, Danny?"

Squinting, I noticed that he now wore a low haircut and a five o'clock shadow. I stopped the crunches at sixty and sat up. "How are you, Kelly?"

"It's, K," he reminded me.

I smiled, happy to have him as a distraction from Anderson. "What are you up to, *K?*"

He plopped down Indian-style on the grass beside me. "Not much. The Job Board assigned me to the kitchen yesterday. I had to wake up at three o'clock this morning. I got off at nine and took a nap. I was bored when I woke up, so I came out here to get some air. Maybe I'll play some basketball. There isn't much to do around here except work and watch TV."

I nodded. "It's designed that way. Less play, more work. You'll get used to it. You need to find a routine—something to keep your mind occupied. The time will fly past once you do that."

Roscoe's rising voice drew our attention. Hunched over his aluminum cane, the wizened old man told the men around him, "I been down fifty-seven years. That's back befo' most of y'all was born—back when they didn't allow a black man to be a chain-gang guard. If you hadda talk to the po-lice, you took a buddy into the office with you so couldn't nobody say you was in there tellin'. Us convicts ran the yard in those days, not the po-lice."

I spotted Critter meandering around the back of the crowd. He cradled a brown jacket, with something wrapped in it, underneath his armpit. He met with a Mexican who handed him something small. I saw men point at Critter and snicker behind his back. They made faces mocking the mentally-challenged while laughing at him.

The crowd grew. Roscoe spoke louder and louder with each new ear that appeared to hear. Soon he was yelling at the top of his lungs, curling his words like some fiery incarnation of Dr. King, pumping the cane high above his head like Moses roaring his sermon from the mount.

"They feared us once!" Roscoe told the men surrounding him. "Their fear was the reason y'all have weights and television and radios and telephones! They gave us those things to stop the killin'! We wuzn't 'fraid like y'all is! Naw! We wuz willin' to die for what we believed in!"

I'd known Roscoe for years. He had fallen in the sixties when cons lived by the *No Coal Burning* rule: meaning that blacks and whites didn't interact except to do business or to riot. Back then, it was a violation of the convict code to speak to an officer. It was a militant time when inmates policed and punished themselves.

Roscoe went on. "Now they takin' everything away 'cause y'all too scared to stand up for yourselves! You're scared to go to the hole, scared to lose a sorry ass job, you scared to die! You scared of your own shadow, 'cause they can't do no more to you that they ain't already done! I'm an old man—too old to work—but I ain't too old to fight for what I deserve! Y'all can't let them do this to us! You can't!"

Looking at Roscoe, I saw a future version of myself. He'd been in prison for over half of a century. I thought about the life sentence hanging over my own head, but I didn't want to admit that I was facing the same fate.

I closed my eyes, and for the first time that day, the recurring words about Anderson were welcome.

finish line

i run to you, when the pain grows too great. i run to you, to help my mind erase. i run to you, run straight for your embrace. i run to you, because all else is unsafe.

finish line

Memories of her took me from torture to refuge, swaddling me in a warm blanket of passion that chased away the cold-heartedness around me. For that alone I was thankful that my thoughts had somewhere beautiful to run.

Kelly asked me, "What's that old guy yelling about?"

I told him, "I don't know," and began another set of crunches to the words of a puzzling poem filling my head with nonsense...*why is their abstract pleasure in pain? like the tremors i get when someone utters her name? or the hot lightning streaking cool skies when it rains? maybe a freezing sensation before the scorching of flames?*

After finishing a set, I noticed two books resting on the grass by Kelly's side. "Are those library books?" I asked him.

He nodded and handed them to me. One was *King Rat* by James Clavell. I'd read that one four times.

The second sent a chill to my spine. It wasn't a novel, it was a nonfiction mélange of poetry, philosophy, and African-American history. It was *Be Unchained* by Woodrow Daniels. I turned it over in my hands and cringed at the author's photo on the back. I stared into his eyes until I couldn't stand it anymore. I had never read it, nor would I ever.

I asked Kelly, "Why are you reading this?"

He took the book and flipped a few pages. "Well, I saw it on the shelf, and I wasn't going to get it until I read the opening."

He handed the book back to me, and I read aloud:

"IN THE BEGINNING...MAN WAS ROBBED
BY A COLLAGE
OF PERFECTION
WITHOUT ARMS OR LEGS
A BEGINNING TO AN END, ABSENT OF PYRAMIDS
AN ORIGIN FOR MOUNTAINS, TREES, AND FLOWER BEDS
ANSWERS FOR QUESTIONS ECHOING IN HIS HEAD
DEVILS, DAEMONS, ANGELS: HOLY GHOSTS

PRAYERS, RITUALS, HOLIDAYS: POPES
ORNAMENTS, CROSSES, CRESCENT MOONS: CLOAKS
NO MORE THAN STAINED GLASS WHO'S EFFECTS MAKE ME
CHOKE
WE ARE ONLY REFLECTIONS OF THE MYTHS WE HAVE CREATED
AN ENTITY
IDENTITY OF POWER—OUTDATED
THERE IS BEAUTY IN THE LIFE MAN'S EYES PERCEIVES
AND THERE IS STRENGTH IN THE THOUGHT OUR MINDS
CONCEIVE
BUT WHERE IS LOVE IN THE LIE? TRUE HISTORY DECEIVES
ABOUT THE LEGEND OF ORIGIN AND HOW KNOWLEDGE WAS
RECEIVED"

Closing the book, I handed it back to Kelly.

"Deep stuff, huh?" He asked.

I nodded with a sigh, wishing I hadn't read it at all.

He said, "The name of that one is '*CREATION*'. He's written a lot more. There were like thirteen books of his in the library."

I didn't reply. I started another set of crunches, hoping to forget Woodrow Daniels and his cryptic books.

Critter appeared standing over me. I sat up as he dropped the bundled-up jacket he'd been carrying between Kelly and I. "Hold this here a minute, Danny. I gotsta go handle a thang or two." He disappeared back into the crowd.

Kelly eyed the jacket. "What's in it?"

I shrugged, looking at it too. "It doesn't matter. It's not mine." Kelly reached for the jacket. I clamped my fingers around his wrist to stop him. "It's not yours either."

He snatched his hand away, then massaged his skin. "It could be something dangerous..."

"I don't care what it is, it's not ours to touch."

Kelly looked away from me after I'd seen the childish hurt in his eyes. I wasn't used to having kids around.

Back tracking my aggression, I said, "You'll save yourself a lot of trouble if you learn to mind your own business and keep your hands to yourself."

Kelly didn't reply. He pretended not to hear me. He stared off in space, silently fuming.

Over at the gathering more men spoke up, voicing their own opinions.

A white man told Roscoe and the crowd, "They only pay me fifteen-dollars-a-week in the print plant, and we work a mandatory fifty-hours in five days! I run the five-color press, the most expensive machine over there! If I worked for a private company on the street, I would be making twenty-five-dollars an hour! So you're damn right it's slavery!"

"Yeah!" Added another. "We make nine-cents-an-hour in the cannery, but we work just as hard! We sweat like dogs while the supervisors sit on their fat asses and pull in a sixty-thousand-dollar salary! The state saves millions because of the work we do, and how do they repay us? By taking the cable TV! Taking coffee at breakfast! And now this!"

I pumped-out sixty more crunches. Kelly got over his anger and stretched out on the grass too. He tried to copy my movements, but he was weak and uncoordinated. I could tell that he'd never worked out before. He was a fragrant hen in a wolves den, and I hated feeling the responsibility of having to save him from harm.

Critter came back and went straight to his jacket. He squatted over it, slyly peering all around to make sure no one was watching him. He told me, "Hawk the man, Danny. I cain't afford no c/o's catchin' me unawares. This here's the best batch I done made all year."

I cut my eyes around the yard to search for any officers in our vicinity. The four C/O's that I saw were caught up in their own private conversations, paying us inmates no mind.

Kelly's young eyes bulged when Critter unwrapped four soda bottles that were filled with a muddy, reddish liquid. Critter removed one bottle, then wrapped-up the remaining three.

Kelly asked him, "What's that?"

Critter snapped, "It's called: *none yo' damn bidness!*"

"Calm down, Critter. He's okay," I said. "Critter, this is K—K, this is Critter."

Critter nodded along for my sake, but he kept an eye on Kelly as he sat with us and opened a bottle. First, he offered me a drink. I turned it down with a shake of my head. He shrugged and put the bottle to his own lips, drinking until it was all gone.

When finished, he stared at the empty bottle wearing a proud smile. "That there'll knock the hair off a bear's nuts!" He laid the empty bottle on the grass and contemplated his bulging jacket through greedy eyes.

My line of sight drifted over to Roscoe and his gathering. A hundred or so men now stood around listening. I asked, "What are they talking about over there, Critter?"

He licked his lips, his eyes still on the loaded jacket. "Somethin' bout how they gon' start feedin' us two-meals-a-day instead of three. I heard Warden Shelly talkin' bout it to Cap'n Tubelow down to the tool room, but hell Danny, I was so busy humpin' sacks of mulch that I ain't pay much mind to it. I'ont thank 'bout eatin' too much no how. I just goes to chow when I git hungry. I reckon they can feed ol' Critter whenever they want—as long as they feed me."

Two-meals-a-day? When had this happened? Had I been so caught up in my tender affection that I'd lost touch with the concrete and steel world around me? Falling in love had opened my eyes to so much...and shut them tight to all else.

Is that an ailment of love? To only see that which makes you happy?

My eyes looked over the vast prison yard, soaking up the environment I'd been neglecting. I saw an ocean of crabgrass and red clay-dirt enclosed by three razor-wired fences. Inmates were everywhere, from the entrance to the gym, to the farthest point out from any building. This was the only rec yard at Broutal, and it accommodated over one thousand convicts at any given time.

I spotted eight officers on post. They roamed in pairs, mostly caught up in their own conversations. Two white perimeter trucks were parked in the grass on the free side of the fences. The drivers sat on the trucks' hoods with Mini-14 rifles strapped to their shoulders.

Pockets of prisoners were scattered, most groups segregated. Blacks played basketball. Mexicans played soccer. Whites played volleyball. Old men tossed rusty horseshoes. Gays kept to themselves. Gang members rarely strayed from the pack.

We were oil in water.

I saw heated arguments, dancing, running, walking, rapping. I saw smooth drug deals and drug usage. Two black men fought next to the basketball court. A player went up for a three-sixty dunk and made it. When the spectators yelled, I wondered who they were cheering for, the ball game or the men tearing each other apart.

It was an ordinary day, and I saw the things that I always saw on the yard.

Everything was usual. Everything except the ever-growing mass of men gathered around Roscoe. Over there was something I had never seen in prison before.

Unity.

Critter asked Kelly if he wanted to get drunk. Kelly asked me if I had a problem with it.

I told him, "You're a grown man. I'm not your father." He nodded along as if I had given my consent anyway.

As Kelly unscrewed a bottle, Critter leaned in close to his ear. "This here's my special brew. I calls it *Ruby Red*. Mm-hm. I cooked this 'un slow so's the 'gredients mix in real good."

Kelly ran has nose in a circle over the mouth of the bottle, frowning at the odor. "Do you make this stuff all the time?"

"Sho' the hell do! I'm from Franklin County, Virginia—the eastern piedmont. We's moonshiners by trade. My kinfolk been cookin' since before honest Abe freed the slaves. My pa learned me when I's knee-high to a grasshopper. Cookin' prison wine ain't nothin'. I made hooch with 'tatoes, corn, peaches—hell, I can cook outta anythang you put in my hands. One time, when I's at Odom Work Farm, all's I had was a banana and half-a-head of rotten lettuce. I did the best I could..."

I nudged Kelly. "He'll shut up if you go ahead and drink it."

He gulped down the bottle until it was empty and he was blue in the face.

Huskily, Critter asked him, "You like it?"

Kelly wheezed while coughing and spitting in the grass. "That's the nastiest shit I've ever drank in my life! What are you trying to do? Kill me?"

Critter took the bottle from him. "I ain't had the best 'gredients. All's I could get my hands on was tomato paste, some canned pineapples, and an onion...but she'll git you there. Stick 'round awhile and you'll see." Critter's eyes were swimming in his own brew. There was no telling how many bottles he'd downed before showing up on the yard. He told Kelly, "You just let that'un settle, and if you 'ont puke on me, I'll slide you one mo'. I done sold all I needed to sell to pay my debts off so..."

"If I don't puke?" Kelly glanced at me as if I'd betrayed him.

Critter confessed, "I only made one lethal batch—and by *lethal* I 'ont mean it would kill you, but you'd have the shits so bad that you'd wish you was dead.

"I's only thirteen and 'xpirimentin' with cauliflower and soy sauce. I knowed it was bad when I smelt it, so I th'owed the bottles away.

My auntie Billie Ann seed me and thought I's try'na hide somethin' so that I wouldn't have to give her a taste. Billie Ann was a half-breed, Cherokee and cracker. She was the ugliest woman I ever seen in my life. The best time to git it on with her was in the pitch-black of night—when it's so dark that you'd slap yourself try'na pick a booger. Mm-hm. She had one brown nipple and one pink one—that's how we knowed she was a true half-breed. The bush of black hairs on her cooter had a white stripe down the middle like some kind of skunk—smelled like skunk too if you caught her after a week-long drunk spell—course she was sixty-nine when she first dug her claws into me, so I'ont 'xpect she could wash too good.

"Now when she got her hands on that one bad batch of 'xpirimentation I done concocted—ooooo-weee—you 'ont ever never wanna whiff on no stank like what come from 'twixt her legs, boy I'm tellin' you! And she was horny as hell too! She chased ol' Critter up and down the holler, smellin' like an outhouse on the day after a good Thanksgivin'! I avoided her for three damn hours 'til she got smart and waited on me in the kitchen, 'cause she knowed I'd be hungry after all that runnin'. When I finally gave in to her charms, she wouldn't turn me loose. And to be honest, it won't too bad 'til she got to fartin' and carrying on..."

I laughed and listened and laughed a little more. Kelly's puckered lips spread into a grin as the hooch worked on him, and he ended up laughing a lot more than me. They drank two more bottles together, and soon my laughter died away.

Roscoe's crowd had grown even larger than before. Their voices drew my attention. I felt a disturbance there. It was like smelling rain before seeing clouds, or feeling faint vibrations before a deadly earthquake.

Someone over there yelled, "How do they expect us to survive on two meals-a-day when we're forced to work fifty, sixty hours a week?"

Another agreed and added, "If you refuse to work, your ass goes to the hole for fifteen days! So they'll get something out of you either way it goes, work time or hole time!"

Finally, a young black man declared, "What we oughta do is write the newspapers and tell them about what's going on in here!"

A splattering of *yeahs* chorused around.

I saw gang members hovering near the edge of the crowd. I thought they might cause trouble until I realized that they held prison jobs too.

Roscoe said, "Them fuckin' newspapers don't care about you!" A few men didn't agree with him and tried to shout him down, but Roscoe wouldn't be shushed. "Don't get mad with me, get mad with the truth! Ask yourself: What do those *good* folk out in that world wanna hear about some *bad* killers and rapists for? Half y'all in here for messin' with kids anyway!" Those who had once spoken against him were now silent. "You ain't nobody for them newspapers to care about! You is a burden to them people out there!"

Another man yelled, "Tax dollars are a burden too! That's what the people care about—how the government is spending their money! Those politicians are raising taxes, telling the people that we're in here living on the high horse, when we're really eating scraps and wearing rags!"

Roscoe's eyes lit up with laughter. "And what do you think the people gonna do once that grand scheme you talkin' about comes to light? Do you think they would happily take money from a senator to place it in your hand? Is you crazy? That's like snatchin' a T-bone from a lion to turn around and toss it in with a tiger—everybody gets a bite but the provider! *The People* gonna get robbed anyway!

"But y'all don't care about *The People*, even though you want them to care about us. All y'all want is a fireplace in your cell so a big-booty boy can feed you cookies from the canteen while you got your feet kicked up in a recliner chair! And you think *The People* care about you enough to fight for it!

"Wake up! *The People* hate us the most! They were your jury! They convicted you! They voted in the politicians that wrote the laws keepin' you locked up! *The People* don't care how we live in prison, as long as we're *in prison!* That's why they pay taxes!"

Roscoe met the eyes of as many men as he could. "Who do they think of when some crazy shoots up a shopping mall, or some nasty kidnaps their kids? Who? It might as well be your mug shot shown on the news—yours or mine, 'cause they gonna blame us anyway! You ain't nothin' to people who ain't doin' time! They don't care about you getting' up at the crack of dawn to work for pennies on a farm or in a plant! They don't hear your heartfelt prayers as you beg the Lord's forgiveness of what you've done! They don't see that you cry tears of pain like they do! To them, you ain't a man...you is a crime! A killer, rapist, lost cause! So go on and write your newspapers! See if they write back!"

No one responded. Maybe because he'd spoken the truth, or maybe because those men had been surviving on a false sense of hope that a savior would drop from the sky to rescue them when injustice became too great...and Roscoe had jarred them back to reality.

No one would help us.

We were alone.

Roscoe said, "If we're gonna change something, we do it ourselves!"

Critter hopped up and walked away.

I asked Kelly, "Where is he going?"

Kelly was happily drunk. "To throw the bottles away." Then he asked me, "Is Critter autistic?"

I looked out and spotted Critter talking to a con who held an acoustic guitar. "He's definitely *something*, isn't he?"

Kelly laughed. "I like him. He's one-of-a-kind."

Critter came back toting a battered, black guitar with duct-tape holding it together at the seams. He sat down indian style and twisted the guitar's tuning knobs while plucking the strings.

"You play guitar?" Kelly asked him.

Critter nodded. "Only when I'm drunk. We used to cook shine out on a mountain, and we'd camp there overnight. I played the gi-tar, my uncle Earl played his banjo, and my granpa Earl played a man-do-lin. My granpa Earl played so fast that some said he must've fingered the devil's wife to git so good, but he ain't never owned up to it. My pa was a fiddler, but mostly he just sang and watched the fire to make sho' it didn't git too hot. Now shut-up, and I'mma play us a song. You like Bluegrass music?"

Kelly shrugged. "I've never heard of it."

Critter's jaw dropped. "You ain't ever never heard of Bluegrass?" He scrutinized Kelly through narrowed eyes. "Where you from? You ain't Mexican is you? You 'ont look white, and you ain't black neither. I'ont like nothin' Mexican—not since my tenth birthday when my granpa Earl bought me a piñata that I couldn't bust. I hit that thang and hit that thang 'til my arms like to fell off, but I couldn't bust it. I ain't liked nothin' Mexican since—not pinto beans or senioritas or sushi or Telemundo or karate neither! I'ont like nothin' Mexican at all!"

I said, "Play your song Critter."

He went silent in contemplation. His lower lip sagged. As his distant gaze got lost in a patch of crabgrass, I imagined his focus as the blank, weightless space between planets.

After a minute or so, his fingers began plucking the strings with a gentle expertise that made Kelly gawk with astonishment.

The song he played had a slow soul—the makings of a sad, sad ballad. Its melody ascended higher and higher as each note climbed single steps up an endless stairway to heaven…only to come crashing down all at once with a deep-throated strum of misery.

He said, "This 'un here is *Ginger Blue*. My great-granpa wrote it.

"*She was a beauty who lived down Sugar Creek Road*
Her hair was aglow like spun threads of gold
Her pa was the preacher, her ma, the town seamstress
But Ginger Blue was known as Marshal Bill's mistress"

Critter sang with a clear, beautiful voice. He held the Bluegrass sustain in perfect harmony and timing. When he shook the auburn hair from his face I saw that his scrunched, rodent-like features were relaxed and almost human. His eye was still black and ugly from our fight, but the peace of his song seemed to ease his pains. Besides drugs, music was the only thing that could make Critter happy.

"*Her husband left to fight the North, they gave ol' Tim no slack*
He willed his Ginger Blue a cabin, with an endless holler out back
'Twas a lonely life for one so young, a girl and a widow
'Til she glimpsed the Marshal's spotted mare, trottin' up Sugar Creek Road"

A commotion made me look toward the gathering of men.

Nasir, the inmate *Imam:* spiritual leader of the prison's Muslim community, pushed his way to the center of the crowd, overshadowing Roscoe. "The problem," he began, "is that you all are too complacent. There are far greater causes abroad to waste time bickering over food and television. This is exactly what Broutal's administration wants, for us to be concerned with petty grievances and ignore what *should* be foremost in our minds—freedom."

"*The marshal'd come to pay respects for Ginger's husband Tim*
But the lawman's grief was led astray when Ginger fell for him
Now Marshal Bill had fear of God and rebuke for devils too
But his old heart just couldn't resist the charms of Ginger Blue"

Nasir was a black, mid-westerner who had introduced The Nation of Islam to Broutal. Tall and light-skinned, he wore his mustache and goatee in the fashion of Malcom X. Whenever I saw Nasir, he stood confident in polished prison boots, pressed brown prison pants, and a white Kufi atop his head. He spoke with the *proper* English of a pedantic who had once spoken the improper patois of an American ghetto. Stains of his pinched upbringing seeped through the whitewashed words he used, no matter how intellectual he tried to sound.

Six of Nasir's black, Muslim converts created a semi-circle of protection around him. "No one has complained that we have no law libraries in North Carolina institutions," he said. "I know of a man serving a sixty-year sentence for shoplifting a microwave pizza to feed his three-year-old daughter after he'd been laid off. How can he hope to be freed if knowledge of the laws binding him is forbidden?" He rotated in a constant circle so that all could hear his message. "They stole our law libraries and replaced them with a state-contracted *Prisoner's Legal Service* that refuses to help ninety percent of us. Open your eyes gentlemen. The problems you fuss over are infant figs on an elderly tree. If you truly want to fight for something, join us in the fight for freedom."

"He split his time 'tween Ginger and work, neglecting his old life
the good townfolk began whisperin' round his broken hearted wife
so Mary crept on Ginger's cabin and saw the two in bed
when the Marshal left, in the still of night, Mary kilt Ginger dead"

A man from the crowd shouted to Nasir. "And who is gonna give us this freedom you talkin' about? The Moo-slims? Allah? I don't follow nobody but Jesus! He's the only Shepherd I'll ever follow!"

Nasir smirked. "That's another problem—too many *sheep* in line for the slaughter, and not enough *shepherds* to lead the flocks toward greener pastures!"

Some men booed him. Others walked away.

"A day went crawling past 'fore the preacher found her gone
And late that night, a mob of men, stormed the Marshal's home
They took his badge and chained him up, they had no mercy left
Judge found Bill guilty of slaying Ginger and sentenced him to death"

Nasir's voice rose above the unruly men. "We will never achieve anything if we do not adhere to one accord! No one is asking you to join The Nation or to become a Muslim! I want to focus our priorities on the one thing best for us all! Freedom! Why work so diligently to change our situation in hell when we can fight for our place in heaven? How many of you are serving life without parole? How many expect to die in prison? How many of you were railroaded by a corrupt justice system because you are black or poor or ignorant of the law, or you trusted a lawyer who was only looking out for his own interest? This is not a question of which God to follow, it is a question of which injustice to address first! I say that we should band together to change *Structured Sentencing* laws!"

North Carolina enacted *Structured Sentencing* laws in 1994 under a *GET TOUGH ON CRIME!* banner. The new law assigned felons two potential release dates—a maximum and a minimum date: meaning that the total time a convict served in prison could not exceed the maximum date, nor could he work to undercut it any lower than the fixed minimum. It created a definitive end to his sentence, eliminating the old parole system that rewarded convicts early release for hard work and good behavior.

Structured Sentencing gave no incentive for a man to better himself while locked-up. It didn't matter if he lived like an angel behind bars or a demon; his time was etched in stone.

Under a system of parole, a man worked toward personal goals. He worked because he knew that his fate was in his hands. He worked hard to get out of prison, and once freed, that work ethic of earning what he wanted in life, instead of stealing it, carried over to create a productive citizen.

Under *Structured Sentencing*, a man worked because he would be punished if he didn't. He learned to resent the long hours and little pay. He learned to hate those who supervised him and loathe the entire experience of working.

Since enacting *Structured Sentencing* laws North Carolina's prisons have become a cesspool of drugs and violence—a breeding ground for hollow men who only know the fruitful side of punishment instead of change.

"Now I did not come to preach," Nasir went on, "but the Holy Qur'an says: '*Without hope, man is but an animal.*' Maybe we can all agree that something needs to be done."

"*One Sunday, the howling winds gave voice to some old ghost*
The townsfolk showed, after church, and laid a noose 'round Bill's throat
And there, in the very front row, his guilty wife Mary cried
she shed her tears, blew her nose, and watched an innocent man die."

Critter finished his song. Kelly clapped and laughed and patted my friend on his back, declaring how great it had been.

The crowd around Nasir began to disperse, but that didn't stop him from going on and on... "I and my brothers have drawn up a petition stating that no man housed at Broutal will work unless..."

Critter tuned-up his guitar again and began another song. "This 'un here's by Steve Earle. It's called, *Copperhead Road*."

I tried my best to listen to him and nothing else.

As he began the opening riff, I smiled to myself, realizing that because so much was going on around me...I hadn't thought about Anderson for fifteen whole minutes.

CHAPTER 8

The flaming sphere of sun hovered at its highest peak in the azure wash of clear sky. It was murderously hot—so hot that sweat evaporated before leaving my pores.

We three sat in the same spot on the yard. Critter absent-mindedly strummed the guitar as he and Kelly spoke of different things, while I stayed silent.

I couldn't get Anderson off of my mind...

you and me

pancakes and bananas topped with strawberry cream, aren't sweeter than your kisses, but oh how I dream; that earths would quake and tumble steel beams, crumble gaoler walls that lie in between...of...

you and me

delusions of your touches consume until i scream, phantoms of your lips crush mine to smithereens; has me praying for the day when our lusts will convene, and we lay-up in the fantasies i have clearly seen...of...

you and me

please...let this infinite loneliness cease, so i may rest my head on your cloud, a small peace; white cotton of the sky, bedded with silver sheets—will be the texture of my breath when our bond is complete—the bond...of...

you and me

I thought of her so much that I had to give in. When the poems and rhymes appeared, I meditated on the feelings they brought along, enjoying the creative company of their spirits until they packed up and moved on.

Wandering words they were.

Removed but never forgotten, my thoughts always left behind a multi-colored trail of lower-case letters—like refrigerator magnets—for the next family of traveling poems or rhyming words to follow and find me in my most vulnerable state.

happy trails
comets and horses, even snails leave trails
but so does a mind when scrutinized in detail
lava and airplanes, leaky pails leave trails
but so does a heart when its love is derailed
poodles and wagons, boats with sails leave trails
but if you discover their origin most mysteries unveil
happy trails

Critter nudged me with his elbow. "You hear what he said, Danny?" His eyes were alight with glee...drunken glee.

I hadn't heard anything. "Hear what?"

"K said they got cell-a-phones where you can watch movies—even porn! I wish I had one. I know 'xactly what I'd watch too, *Desperately Seeking Susan*. That was my third cousin Bethany's favorite movie—on account of her lovin' Madonna. Mm-hm. I love Madonna too. You ever seen that black and white movie where she had them cones on her hooters? Er'body said that was a new style, but hell Danny, my auntie Sally Mae used to walk 'round with her hooters pointy all the time—the tips was so sharp they'd poke out yo' damn eye if you wasn't careful. I could always tell when she wasn't wearin' a bra, 'cause her tits would drag the floor..."

I said, "I read about cell phones all the time. The newer ones are called Smartphones. I've never seen one in person, though."

Kelly's eyebrows raised. "You two have never seen a cell phone?"

Critter told him, "Danny's been locked up almost as long as me. The onliest time I seed a cell-a-phone was when the IRS man came to the house askin' how my Pa bought a new single-wide and diesel truck in the same day, but he ain't held no job for ten years. That fool ain't make it past the front stair. Pa came out the screen door with his thirty-aught-six and rammed his barrel down the revenuer's throat. The man ran off with a brown stain spread across the back seat of his britches. He left er'thang he had on the porch. That's when I seed a cell-a-phone. It was grey, as big as a brick, and I had to use two hands to hold it. But now you sayin' they so small that a man can fit one in his pocket?"

"Yeah," Kelly said. "You can do everything on a phone that you can do on a laptop or computer. You can play games, pay bills, go on Facebook, and fly remote controlled airplanes and helicopters..."

Critter asked him, "Do people still talk on 'em?"

Kelly nodded. "Most people don't talk much anymore. Everybody texts. I think it's easier than talking."

Critter thought long and hard before asking, "What's text?"

"Texting is like typing, except most people don't text a whole word. That way you can text faster."

"You gotsta know how to read to text?"

Kelly looked at Critter like he was crazy. "Of course."

Critter didn't reply for a good while. He just sat, strumming his guitar in a blank state. Without confessing to Kelly that he was illiterate, he said, "Well I guess I won't be textin' nobody, but I sho' would like to git my hands on one them cell-a-phones to watch a porn or two. Mm-hm. That'd be nice right now. Last time I seed a porn—I walked in on my grandma Nadine with the TV blastin' and her feet kicked up in the air. She had her stockin's rolled down to her ankles and her bloomers pulled to the side while her fingers..."

Kelly cut him off, probably realizing that the only way to keep Critter quiet was to drive his conversation. "What's that song you're playing?"

Critter stared at him, dumbfounded. He looked to the guitar next, as if it had a mouth and would give him the answer. Without stopping, he listened to the music..."That'un there? That's *Beautifully Broken*."

Kelly listened intently before declaring, "It's nice. Who's it by?"

"Gov't Mule. My kinfolk only played Bluegrass, but I play anything. All's I gotsta do is listen to a song a time or two, and I can play it. Learnin' the words takes longer." He stopped playing abruptly. His eyes got stuck on a patch of grass for a minute or so, then he asked Kelly, "You ever listen to any Led Zepplin?" Kelly shook his head no. "Damn shame. Y'all kids don't know shit. Listen to this here and don't forget it. This'un is called *Babe I'm Gonna Leave You*."

As Critter plucked the strings, I imagined a fire-haired angel straddling a harp beside the pearly gates of heaven. I closed my eyes as he began to sing, but instead of his voice, I heard my own whispering haunting things that tortured me.

love is just a dream

a wisp in the clouds it seems
the force of a stream

Some black guys called to Kelly and asked if he wanted to play basketball. He told us goodbye and ran off to have fun.

"Want me to play you a song, Danny?"

I thought about it and nodded. "Do you know any Stone Temple Pilots? Can you play *Atlanta?* "

He went silent on me. I imagined his thoughts as a million scraps of paper swirling in a windstorm as he worked to grasp only one. He said, "I can play the music, but I'ont know the words."

I smiled a little. "The words make me sad anyway."

He began the song, and over the hypnotic music, he asked me, "Why come folks cain't never 'gree on nothin'?"

"What do you mean?"

"Them men arguin' with Roscoe. They was s'posed to be talkin' bout one thang, but like to git to fightin' over somethin' else. How they 'spect to git anythang done like that? My uncle Earl used to say that two fools don't make one wise man—now that I thank 'bout it, my granpa Earl used to say the same, 'cept he said two *black* fools."

The gathering of angry men had long since departed. I glanced over at the spot where they'd been, seeing and hearing their voices again.

I told Critter, "That's just the way people are. Everyone has something to say, but no one wants to listen. It doesn't matter if it's in here or out in the world, we all think that what's in our mind is more important than anything else. That's why we have so many wars. People are always trying to prove somebody wrong, but if they could realize that there is some right in everything, we wouldn't have half the problems we do now. Instead of focusing on the argument, we could actually find ways to build up our world...not tear it down."

Critter zoned-out on it for a moment. "I reckon you're right, Danny. You the smartest black man I know, and trust me, I done met some dumb ones—some dumber'n me."

I laughed while using my tee shirt to swat flies.

Soon after, I paused to watch a middle-aged Asian convict teaching a twenty-something black kid some crazy form of martial arts on a worn patch of grass in the center of the yard. I'd been watching them spar for a couple of years, and although the kid had learned some serious skills, his teacher gave him no quarter.

The taller kid crouched low—so low that one of his knees barely hovered an inch above the ground. At first, he curled his fingers like claws and danced around his teacher like a tiger, a jaguar—some kind of cat. The Asian crouched just as low, but he held his hands flat and open with the thumbs tucked. He moved more gracefully, like an owl, a crane—some kind of bird.

The kid went at his teacher with lazy blows that the Asian blocked easily. Quickly, the master spun and swept the kid's feet from under him, laying the student flat on his back.

The kid climbed to his feet and dusted himself off. He and the master bowed to each other and squared off again.

"I been thankin', Danny."

I said, "Don't hurt yourself doing that."

"Wha'chu mean?"

I shook it off. "What have you been thinking about, Critter?"

"I'ont want to only eat twice-a-day neither. Seems like a man needs more'n that to git by. I mean, hell Danny, I don't git no money orders from home, and I'm damn near starvin' on what they feed us now. I ain't seed no real beef since the last time it seed me, and that's a fact!

"They ain't payin' us nothin'. I only make five-dollars-a-week. I cain't git high and eat off that too—no sir, it just ain't happenin'. Sheeiit, I went to the canteen to buy a stick of deodorant yesterday, but the price done went up to three damn dollars! That's more'n half my check! I smeared toothpaste under my arms after I got out of the shower last night, and that worked just fine. Mm-hm. It tickles a lil' when I sweat, but other'n that it's okay. It sho' smells good, and it's cheaper too..."

The Asian slung a high kick. The kid ducked it, then countered with a lightning fast kick of his own. The teacher caught the foot mid-air and twisted it hard, flipping the kid onto the ground face first.

I snorted a laugh. *Nice try kid.*

After watching the teacher help his student up, I turned to Critter and asked, "Why are you so worried about it? You're going home soon. How much time do you have left, anyway?"

"I'ont know. A hun'ert days and a wake up. Somewhere's 'round there if I make my minimum sentence."

My heart dropped to hear the news.

It was great that he was getting out...but why was he able to go home while I wasn't? I had never asked Critter why he was in prison, but I wondered if the crime I committed was so much worse than what he had done.

I took my eyes back to the kung-fu fighters so that he wouldn't pick up on my pain.

I said, "You don't seem too excited about it."

Critter stopped playing and held the guitar—he held it tenderly as a father would cradle his own child after birth. "I been locked up seventeen years. I'ont know 'bout nothin' besides gard'nin and moonshinin'. What I'mma do for work out there? I cain't even read. My granpa Earl used to say I's dumber'n a box of rocks with an afro, but he ain't try to teach me no better. He told me what to do, and I did it. Same as with the C/O's, I guess. I'm so used to folks bossin' me 'round that I ain't sho' I can think on my own enough to survive."

I watched the student and master go a few more rounds, each time the teacher won. Once, he kicked the kid in the head, and the kid went out for the count. When he came to, the teacher helped him to his feet, then knocked him out again.

Each outcome offered no change.

There was no question about who was better than who.

Prison life is the same—so repetitive that the monotony makes weak men kill themselves. We become creatures of bad habits—dependents. We pay no bills, have no responsibilities; but we have beds, food to eat, and clothes on our backs.

Our lives are seemingly easy.

Repetitive, but easy.

The system fails most because it doesn't teach a convict to hold his own in the way that the Kung Fu master teaches his student.

Prison knocks you down and holds you there.

I thought about news stories I'd seen depicting the lives of people who had fallen down in the screwed-up economy. I thought of the college students who'd graduated into debt, unemployment, welfare—begging for a hand-out because the hand-out was all that kept them afloat. I thought about how hard their lives were, and how difficult my life would be if I graduated into society as an ex-con.

I asked Critter, "Are you afraid to be free?"

Critter began strumming his guitar as he thought about it. Eventually he nodded. "I reckon so."

With my eyes locked on the fighters, I told him, "Me too."

I wondered what Anderson was doing at that moment—if she was as stuck on me as I was on her? Was she alone? Or was she spending her weekend with someone else?

Needing to change my train of thought, I said, "You'll be fine. Any place has to be better than this, no matter how hard it is out there. Just don't give up, and send me a postcard when you get to where you're going. That way I'll know you made it okay."

Critter smiled his rat-teeth at me. "You got my word on that—just as sho' as my name is James James James Jr!"

The old Asian attacked the kid swiftly with a blurring barrage of kicks and punches that flew so fast, even I had a hard time tracking them all. Somehow the kid held him at bay. The master went harder, but the kid stayed calm and waited for his opportunity. When the time was right, the kid weaved inside and swept the teacher off of his feet, slamming him to the ground.

"I'll be damned," I said to myself. "Maybe things do change if you never give up."

The old man wore a proud smile as he climbed to his feet. He patted his young student on the back before they bowed to each other and squared off yet again.

Behind me, a deep voice asked, "Are you Danny?"

I turned and spotted the Black Muslim, Nasir, standing cross-armed, flanked by six of his Muslim converts.

I stood quickly, and Critter did too. "Who wants to know?" I didn't know what to expect, but I was ready for anything.

Nasir gave me a wide grin. "I don't mean you any harm, brother. I just came to talk."

I saw Nasir stare down at my belly, counting the veins crisscrossing my eight-pack. "Talk about what?"

He cast his eyes toward Critter. "We should talk *alone*."

Feeling Critter by my side, I told Nasir, "I don't keep secrets from my friends."

"I don't expect you do," he said, smirking as if he wasn't used to people rebuking his orders. "You can tell him whatever you want...when you and I are finished talking. He's your friend. Not mine."

The tone of Nasir's voice told me that it was a serious matter. To be sure he didn't have anything against Critter, I gestured to the guys standing behind him. "What about your Muslim brothers?"

Without looking their way Nasir mumbled something in Arabic, and the six black men walked away quietly.

Put in my place, I looked to Critter. "Catch you later?"

He gave a cautionary glance toward Nasir, then he offered me his fist to bump knuckles. "Reckon I'll see ya." He sat back down with the guitar across his thigh and began a song by Soundgarden...*Blow Up The Outside*.

After shrugging into my tee shirt, I turned to Nasir. "You have my undivided attention."

The Muslim nodded and began walking toward the inner fence line where a beaten, dirt path ran parallel with the yard's perimeter. I followed silently, assuming that Nasir wanted to keep moving as a way to ensure no one ear-hustled on our conservation.

He didn't say a word until our boots were crunching rocks embedded in the rusty, clay walking track beneath our feet. "What happened between you and Hernandez?"

I drew a blank. "Who?"

Nasir walked softly with his hands clasped behind his back. "The Mexican with TS-16 tattooed across his forehead."

Hernandez. I thought about the guy I'd fought down in the gym and how fast his hands had been. I almost cracked a smile thinking of how I'd beaten him.

"We had a misunderstanding," I said. "Why? Is he still mad about it?"

"He is nursing a broken rib. Maybe he will be upset once he has healed and can fight again, but for now, he is happy that he did not end up in segregation for fighting. He is wondering how *you* made that happen."

Nasir had kingly airs about him. He looked older up close. Crow's feet perched in the corners of his eyes. Wisps of silver hair peeked out from beneath his kufi and throughout his goatee. He walked and talked like an educated man, as most black Muslims did—priding himself in seeming brighter and more informed than everyone else—but the spice of his inner-city upbringing seasoned the flavor of his bland speech in ways that made him sound fake.

Among his peers, Nasir was a leader of men. And like most leaders, he felt entitled to his peers' most private information.

But he wasn't entitled to mine.

I said, "It's none of your business."

"No, it is not," he admitted.

Examining Nasir's eyes, I got the feeling that he hadn't approached me about Hernandez. "We fought. So what? Everybody knows about it."

He nodded, moving it along. "What about Officer Maloney? Tell me what happened between you and him?"

So that's what it was all about. The yard had heard about our showdown in the aftermath of my fight with the Mexican men, and suspicious minds wanted to know how we'd avoided the fallout. I imagined inmates gossiping about me—calling me a snitch.

I didn't care about that. I hadn't done anyone wrong, and I didn't owe any explanations...especially not to Nasir.

"A wise man tends his own garden," I warned, "lest he be bit by a spider."

He smiled at my words. "You strike me as a smart man, smarter than the other young brothers around here. You are also smart enough to see that I already know the truth. The man assaulted you, and the fact that no one has seen him at Broutal since it happened tells me that he is in serious trouble."

I hadn't thought about Maloney's rage since I'd been submerged in Anderson's tenderness. I hadn't thought about him at all.

Nasir continued, "I am guessing that Broutal's administration offered you some sort of deal to let you all stay out of the hole if you did not file a written statement against Maloney. I am willing to bet that they sent a staff member you like and trust to talk you out of it—someone that you respect."

Sergeant Thompson's jolly guffaw rang in my ears.

"I know how the system works, Danny. I have been in prison for a long time, young brother, and I know how crooked they are. We do not matter to them. They believe they can treat us any way they want because we do not take the necessary steps to prevent their abuse, nor do we speak out once we have been wronged."

I asked Nasir, "What does it have to do with you?"

"It is not about me, Danny. I bring this message for you and all of the men you have seen slain at their hands. Think about the beatings, the unjust confinements. They do not treat us this way because it is right. They do it because they can—because we allow them to. You need to file a written statement against Maloney. Do not sacrifice your justice to appease the tyrants who would not sacrifice for you."

I stopped walking, and so did he. We turned to face each other. Beyond the dark oracles of his eyes were the shades of men I had long since forgotten.

I didn't need Nasir to make me feel guilty.

I had seen men die.

As a child who had grown into a man behind prison walls, the odious face of human atrocity was a familiar beast that I would always know. So common is he that I can predict his arrival in moments of anguish and mounting violence. From prison to prison I have heard his hooves pound concrete floors like drums before a funeral pyre. His accompanying odors of fresh fear, burnt sulfur, hot blood, and death dried tears have brought bile bubbling up the back of my throat. His roar is the myriad screams of those who had once cried out for mercy, but received agony instead. His laughter is the law protecting him from moral punishment on Earth.

"Are you my judge and jury?" I asked him. "Are you going to tell me that I was wrong? Are you here to say that my life has a greater purpose than to serve myself?"

Nasir took a serious step closer. "Yes." His eyes never left mine.

Noise was sparse on the yard, but in the distance I heard Critter belting out another Soundgarden song. He sang *Rusty Cage* as if his life depended on it.

I remembered Anderson and the kisses we'd stolen in the warehouse.

A grain of regret blew in beneath the jamb of my soul.

Nasir was right. I had made a selfish choice that would only benefit me. I couldn't write a statement against Maloney and still expect to remain at Broutal. An investigation would mean giving her up, and I didn't want to do that.

Not yet.

Not ever.

If other men had to suffer for my comfort, then so be it.

"I can't change the world, Nasir, and I won't try. Nobody had to trick or *convince* me not to write a statement. I didn't want to. I haven't survived in here by making trouble, and I won't start now. I don't complain. I don't ask anyone for anything. I like my job. I like my cell. Sometimes I even like this prison."

"The devil must like hell as well, especially after being forced to live there for so long. But none of those comforts will satisfy the hunger for justice that you will feel for the rest of your life, Danny. The same thing happened to me. While serving time at Central Prison I was beaten mercilessly. At the time I wanted to do something about it, but I was too young to know how to fight the system. But you...you do not have to worry about that. I can help you file the proper legal motions that will force the **S**tate **B**ureau of **I**nvestigation to prosecute him. It is not too late, brother. We can shed light on the dark ways we are treated in here. First, you will need to..."

"Nasir, you aren't hearing me," I said. "I'm not writing anything. I made up my mind a long time ago. I've looked past it, and that's what you need to do."

Nasir peered all around to make sure no one else could hear him.

"Look man," he hissed through clenched teeth. "Do you know how long we've been tryin' to get rid of that devil? You don't know the power you hold. You could get Maloney walked-out of here! You could file a lawsuit, and you would win!

"I told you, Danny, you're not like the rest of these young, black men in here. They call each other *nigger* and *bitch* like it's the thing to do. They walk around with their pants hangin' off their asses. They look at being locked-up like it's a rite of passage. They wear their prison time as if they're proud to be here—like rotting away in a cell makes somebody a man.

"The future of our race is dismal, my friend. I used to think it was the white man's *conspiracy* that had us fucked up. But it isn't the Europeans. It's us. We hurt ourselves because we don't want to face the fact that we commandeer our own destiny. We blame our problems on everyone else, because we refuse to fight for what we want.

"But you, Danny...you're different. You're smart, well-mannered, you speak well. Why can't you see that you can help us all? Why? *You had witnesses!* Listen to reason! Hernandez told me himself. Those women—those inspectors will stand up for you."

"How would you know?"

He stared into my eyes. "How do you know they won't? Or more importantly, why are you afraid to try?"

I looked over the rec yard, past a thousand hollow men living even emptier lives. My gaze traveled down to the weight pile where the youth relied on brute strength to determine their masculinity. Next, my sight graced two old men patiently thinking their way through an intense game of chess. I saw two men kissing in a corner. A crowd had gathered around Critter as he hollered Black Sabbath's *War Pigs* at the top of his lungs.

I wondered why Nasir felt that the fate of their safety should be a burden on my back.

His eyes followed my gaze. "Aren't you sick of places like this? I've dedicated my life to educating my brothers so they don't make the same mistakes I did. I love my black people, but you have no idea how it feels to be mistreated by the same folks that I want to see succeed...only because we are here. They're out in the community screaming that there is no unity, then they strut up in here with their noses thrust into the air like we ain't grapes from the same vine."

I told Nasir, "I don't look at a man's race to judge him."

He kind of smiled, but not really. "A c/o told me that he felt like he was in prison whenever he came to work. He'd said: *I'm locked up too. I can't go home until they let me go*'. I wanted to knock his head off of his shoulders. There hasn't been a day made when he could ever feel what we feel. He can quit when he gets tired. He can find another job any time he wants. But not us. We have to put up with their shit. We have to endure.

"Well I'm tired of enduring, tired of seeing young men leave prison even more bitter, angry, and violent than when they came in simply because they've been beaten down and enslaved."

His eyes were full of fire. Calmly, I said, "We're different men, Nasir. I don't hold any anger toward people."

He shook his head as if I wasn't catching on to his message. "Danny, I don't know what you believe, but the Holy Qur'an tells me that: *'Disorder and corruption have prevailed on land and sea owing to the evil which people have wrought. The result will be that He will make them taste the fruit of their misdeeds'*..." Nasir wrapped his hand around my forearm. "Help me serve them the *rotten* fruits of their misdeeds, Danny. Help me shove it down their fucking throats."

To myself, I muttered, "*Surah* thirty, *Ayat* forty-one," thinking of the chapter and verse he'd recited.

Surprised, Nasir asked me, "You know the Qur'an?"

I said, "...'*their deeds are like a mirage in a desert, the thirsty man assumes it to be water until he comes up to it and finds nothing at all*'."

Nasir whispered, "*Surah* twenty-four, *Ayat* thirty-nine."

I snatched my arm from his grip. "That's what you are, Nasir. A mirage."

"What are you talking about?"

I said, "You wear so many masks that even you don't know who the real Nasir is. You say that you only want to help me, but you really want to help yourself."

He put a palm over his heart. "Myself? I have nothing to gain."

"And neither do I."

"I'm here to help you, Danny. I'm here to help us all."

"If you were really in my corner, you would hear me out when I ask you to back off."

He shook his head as if I had it all wrong. "Danny, the Qur'an says…"

"I know your Qur'an and the Bible, the Tao, the Catechism, the Dhammapada, and the Bhagavad Gita too. I know them better than you, so don't quote me the meaningless words of dead men and ghosts as a way to convince me to do something that I don't want to do. It's my ass on the line, not yours. I am my own man, and I make choices because I want to make them."

"You don't understand…" Nasir reached out and grabbed my arm again, digging his fingers into my flesh.

I jerked free, raising my fists with murder on my mind.

Nasir threw his hands out, palms flat in surrender. "Why are we always so ready to fight each other? I'm not your enemy! Maloney is! The system is!"

I made no move toward him. His eyes were wide with fear and he threatened me in no way. I unclenched my fists and dropped my hands.

Nasir let the air chill between us before he said, "Why are you protecting him?"

I thought of Anderson and how I longed to be in her arms, chasing the fiery tail of a comet called *Happiness* wherever it led. I would have given years of my future to be with her for one single moment.

"I'm not protecting anybody." Nasir stayed quiet, listening to me. "We're all human, and we all make mistakes. I made a bad one that landed me here. Sometimes I think about the changes I've made in my life, and I'm proud of the man I've become. It doesn't matter if I never make it out of here. I wouldn't be who I am if I hadn't made that mistake. And those mistakes…they shape us—our failures mold our futures so much more than our triumphs because we can't forget how we failed. They are the black shadows that follow us wherever we go, and those mistakes make us want to be better people. No amount of remorse can change what I did, but sometimes I wish someone would see the changes in me and give me a second chance."

Nasir cocked his head at an angle. "Is that what you did for Maloney? Did you give him a second chance?"

I almost laughed in his face. "Let it go. You've asked me *why* a thousand times, and I gave you an answer good enough to satisfy them all."

Nasir grit his teeth. "Do you think he would give you a second chance? What if you climbed over that fence right there? Do you think the cop on the other side would think twice about killing your black ass? Hmmm?" His narrowed eyes bore into mine. "Wake up! You are a lone man of morals in a pit of heartless savages. You talk about mistakes...why can't you see that you are making the biggest one of all?

"We are at war, whether you want to be or not. It is *Us* against *Them*. The battle is raging all around us. We must fight in any way we can, and you have the best chance at winning that I have ever seen—yet you choose not to use it."

"No, Nasir..." I took a deep breath and let it out. "*You* are at war. Me? I'm done fighting." I turned to walk away.

Nasir called out, "I wish you the best, Danny, I really do! And I'll pray that you never come to regret your decision! Peace be unto you, Danny! Peace be unto you."

I kept walking

CHAPTER 9

Slow Sunday showers kept me locked inside my cage.

I didn't go out to eat.

I didn't go out to do anything.

Reading the morning away, I bounced between Ernest Hemingway's *Old Man and the Sea* and the *Tao Te Ching* by Lao Tzu.

Though my eyes roamed over the lines, I found it hard to focus on what I read. There was another book on my mind...

After leaving the yard the day before, I had taken a trip to the library. Recalling my conversation with Kelly, I'd chosen a book by Woodrow Daniels entitled *From Monkeys to Madmen: The De-Evolution of Humanity* to check out.

I had never read his work, and I always swore that I wouldn't. Why I brought it back to my cell was a mystery. But there it sat silently on the bed beside me: a collection of radical poetry and deep philosophical thoughts.

Through the course of the last night and the long morning, I had reached for it several times. I had almost picked the book up to read once, but as my eyes locked on the author's picture my hand paused inches away.

I knew his face better than I knew my own.

The sight of it made me tremble.

I can't read it. I can't.

So I stood and paced the five by nine cage, avoiding the book on the bed. I glanced at it each time I walked past. It beckoned me—begged me to examine its contents.

The twisted mind of my father. Woodrow Daniels.

Wet tears trickled down my cheeks as the eyes of his still image bore into mine.

I couldn't do it. I couldn't read it.

To collect myself, I leaned against the back wall of the cell and stared out of its six-inch-wide, Plexiglas window.

Black clouds blanketed the noon sky, offering a picturesque reflection of the darkness in me.

The storm had reached a furious fury. Hard rain drove down in slanted waves across the ocean of Broutal's immense farmland. While staring out at the endless rows of crops, I saw lines upon lines of inmates weaving between, slopping through the mud in state boots and black rain slickers, digging sweet potatoes destined to be canned and shipped off somewhere else.

They were slaves who wouldn't receive a share of the profits they harvested.

The futility of their task was the same as the futility of my love. Anderson and I were plucking soggy sweets from clumped mud only to enjoy their feel while it was within our grasp, knowing that our pleasure couldn't be cherished forever.

Inevitable demise lay in wait like a poacher poaching love birds.

The impermanence of our affair made it more precious than if we were able to care for each other openly, but the intensity of what I felt was so strong that I knew it would kill me in the end.

I wished our time would creep slower than wet sand clogging the lazy eye of a hazy hourglass, but one more hour of our future together wasn't guaranteed.

blinding light

daydreamer, you dream of evermore days; forgetting your future...your future of decay—when a body turns cold what words are left to say? When the casket is dropped, tearful mourners walk away.

daydreamer, you fool, you live in those dreams; ignoring reality...your reality screams—the horror that fate is nothing like what it seems; and your dreams of tomorrow aren't what you want them to be.

daydreamer, she dreams of poetry as flowers; but your tokens of love truly hold no power—for, hand-held flowers wither within an hour; if not blessed with the flood of a continuous shower.

*what water can you bring from a cloud of dry dreams? when the feeling isn't some**thing**, it is really no-**thing**! in essence, we get* *nothing from our evermore feelings. so tell me, what's the purpose of those foolish daydreams? blinding light*

The storm outside my window was the raging tempest in me. Low rolls of distant thunder was the moaning of my heart when it wanted her close. Fat raindrops were hot tears watering my grief and helping it to grow. Howling wind was sorrow whispering words of uncertainty.

Haunted by her face imprinted in my mind, I turned back to the book on my bed and cringed from its sight as well. Being caught between my two struggles was like running from the monster of misery into the arms of anguish.

For a good while I wondered how the two were connected—my love and my pain. Ever growing *love* of Anderson. Ever dying *pain* of my father. They were past and present but completely relevant.

The only way to figure it all out was to read his book.

I found myself walking to the bed. I sat down, staring into his eyes. With tears streaming down my face, I picked it up in trembling hands and began to read.

I remembered my father in death as I had known him in life, hunched over some ancient manuscript in his gargantuan study. He was always at his desk scribbling notes in preparation for his next lecture, his next book, or the next speech he was scheduled to give.

He'd loved his work in ways that he had never loved me.

My father had been in his late fifties when he met and married my twenty-five-year-old mother.

I never knew her.

He said that she died giving birth to me.

He was my only family. Tall and slim, my father had skin blacker than coal. He hardly ever combed his wild, white hair; he wore it in a thick bush atop his head, causing his students to dub him *Black Einstein*.

In his lifetime he'd been a writer, civil rights activist, and regarded as one of the most brilliant minds in the world. He'd published nineteen books—critically acclaimed insights into the human experience, spanning from slavery to Silicon Valley. His talent had brought him fame, fortune, and precedence as a black intellectual in an otherwise white world.

My father had been a very important man.

As Dean of Philosophy at Chowan College in Murfreesboro, his light workload allowed him to travel and write at his whim.

Whenever he left on an intellectual excursion, he hired a live-in nanny to cook and clean for me.

When he was home, he could be found seated behind his big oak desk, mumbling the dusty words of wisdom from some shriveled-up scholar. In his study, music played constantly. A burning cigarette usually idled in a full ashtray beside a glistening decanter of bourbon. He was always in his study. Early to rise, he'd be working in the wee hours of morning as I left for school. Late to retire, he would be seated at his desk when I climbed into bed at night.

During my childhood, I didn't do normal things with my father. He wasn't into sports or watching Tv. If I wanted to go to an arcade or an amusement park, he would give me a handful of money and drop me off at the front door. Most of the time I stayed at home, reading books, mimicking him. The professor. The philosopher who had his son more familiar with Plato than Play Dough. Aside from going to school, I barely left our *Becker Farms* home in Roanoke Rapids.

Despite the fact that I'd never met my mother, our home was filled with photos of her. She was only twenty-nine when she died giving birth to me.

Whether or not my parents had been happy together was a mystery. I don't remember my father ever being happy. I only remember the sour-faced old man who rarely spoke to me.

Judging from the pictures of my mother, she'd seemed happy. A bright smile was all I ever knew of her. I spent years looking at those pictures, staring into her eyes, falling in love with her, wondering about the woman she'd been.

Tall like my father, she posed confidently on long legs. Her pecan skin glowed, regardless if she'd been soaking up the sun at Myrtle Beach or waiting for a taxi on a snow-covered street in New York City. She had a pretty face with a little pug nose and Asian eyes. Her lips had been perfect. Her eyebrows, perfect. Everything about her had been perfect.

The only time I ever saw a glimmer of love in my father's eye was when I spotted him admiring a picture of the two of them all dressed up for a night out on the town. In the picture they didn't look like a couple. He looked more like her grandfather. When he caught me staring at him, hollow holes burrowed into his heart, changing him back into the frost-haired recluse that I was used to.

He hardly ever spoke of her. Of course I asked questions, and my questions were ignored. The mention of her brought so much pain into his face that I'd grown up with the belief that she had done him wrong in some way, and he hated her because of it.

The first time that we seriously spoke of her was on my eleventh birthday.

He had summoned me into his study where he sat at his desk. As a present he gave me a well-read copy of Danté, *The Inferno*. He explained that it had been my mother's favorite book next to Zora Neal Hurston's *Their Eyes Were Watching God*.

I had read *The Inferno*, but holding what had once been my mom's copy made it feel different, and I knew that I would read it again and again.

I was turning the dog-eared pages when my father said, "I asked her to marry me, right here, in this study."

Glancing up, I noticed him staring at the floor, his eyes lost in some distant sight that only he could see.

"I was married before," he went on, "years before. But my first wife and I divorced. We were too young when we'd fallen in love—too young to know that it wouldn't last. After her, I swore that I would never marry again."

Some time passed before I gained the courage to ask, "Why?"

Without meeting my eyes, he grumbled, "*Why?*"

"Why didn't you want to get married again?"

He sighed long and heavily. "*Why* is the sky blue? *Why* is the moon white? *Why?*" He smiled a little. "Because love hurts. We spend every waking moment wishing for it, and when it finally arrives, it's as welcome as the shining sun after a fierce hurricane."

His gaze slowly rose to meet mine. "But the problem with love is that once you've found it, you want it to last forever, and it never does. It dies like everything else.

"And once it's gone, the aftermath of love is far worse than the loneliness before it. A single person finds strength in their loneliness. A single person works for their own happiness, and not the happiness of another. There is balance and self-sufficiency in being alone. It's so much easier to fulfill simple pleasures because you only have to please yourself.

"But...*to love is to sacrifice*."

My father stared down into his lap, wringing his hands. His lips were tight from whatever frustrating thoughts troubled his mind. He looked as if he would cry.

He said, "When you love someone—when you want that love to work—*yourself* must die away. You must be willing to give all that you are, and much more.

"You see, the emotions between lovers are collective. They are like two stone pillars holding up one roof. Personally, you are dependent on the other pillar. Without it, your foundation would not be whole—the fragile roof of life would come crashing down on your head.

"Your dependence is so sensitive that you feel the slightest imbalance within that other pillar, and you know when their happiness is fading; you feel their unease as if it were your own. To keep the harmony of balance, you love harder. You give money, space, gifts, and freedom. You give more and more until you're drained, used-up, and just plain tired.

"Then eventually you realize that you cannot make her happy, because you are the cause of her sadness. The veil begins to lift from your eyes. You look up and see the roof collapsing, but there isn't a damned thing you can do about it.

"Instead of hating her, you hate yourself. You once thought that all you did was to make her happy, but that wasn't entirely true. We are selfish by nature. Your joy depended on her joy. So in essence, you begin to understand that everything you did for her...was actually to satisfy your own needs. You wanted to see her smile so that you could smile.

"When the feelings of love finally leave, you realize that you were better off alone in the first place."

We sat silent and still for a long time after that. I opened the book again and read a handwritten inscription: *To Angel. From Woodrow.*

I asked, "It was my fault that she died, wasn't it?"

My father looked at me. He looked me straight in the eye. "In time you will learn that everything has a purpose. Life in itself is an unsolvable riddle. Often, the things that prove hardest to understand hold the deepest meaning, if you ponder them. Every word in a poem. Every star in the sky. Every *confusing* thing has an origin and a purpose. Rain falls to replenish the Earth. The lioness murders to feed her young. An elephant's shit fertilizes the soil. We even have dung beetles to clean it all up. Everything in life has its purpose, no matter how puzzlingly horrible...even death."

Renewed youth flickered in his eyes as the philosopher came out.

The philosopher.

Not the father.

"But don't think you're the first to think such a thing," he said. "Clarence Darrow once said: '*Just think of the tragedy of teaching children not to doubt.*' How can you receive answers if you don't ask questions?"

I looked upon him with tears in my eyes, loving him for his uncanny lessons; hating him for teaching me like an adult when I only wanted to be his son.

"Death is natural," he told me, "and so is the grief that goes with it. Without grief, how can you know how much you truly loved? And so there is something to be learned from that too. James Allen tells us that *'wisdom is mainly recollection of all that was learned by sorrow'* ..."

With a book that my father had written in my hand, I leaned against my cell wall, staring through the narrow slit of a window, watching summer rain pelt puddles and slither in slender streams through the muddy tracks left by overworked prisoners. I struggled to push away the past. As much as I hated the memory of my father, I had to admit that I was his spitting image.

I stared at the dedication of the book. I hadn't been able to read beyond it.

It read: *"To my son.*
"WATER YOUR WISDOM TO NOURISH ITS SOUL.
'TIL IT'S ALL USED UP, AND THE GROUND HAS GROWN MOLD.
SO WHEN YOU DIE AWAY, YOUR WATERS STILL FLOW.
GIVING LIFE TO OTHERS, WHERE YOUR STORM HAS BLOWN."

My tears came then. Images of dark days with my dad flooded over my bright bond with Anderson.

I hoped that what he'd said about love wasn't true.

I needed love.

I needed her.

I need.

I.

Closing my eyes, I saw blood and lust. Kisses and tears. Hatred and fear. A photomontage of purple violets and crimson violence.

I thought of Anderson and how much I loved her.

I thought of my father and how I had killed him.

CHAPTER 10

Monday.

Dawn was a beaming butler carrying robust rays of morning to my cell on a silver platter of buttery delights. Anderson was the first thing to cross my mind. I couldn't wait to see her. The prospect that her presence could calm the black hangover of yesterday's thunderhead had me eager to face the day.

I slid out of bed at six-oh-seven. While heading to the shower, I saw other inmates wandering in waking stupors, mixing cups of instant coffee, and preparing for work.

In the shower I imagined how it would feel if my hands were Anderson's soaping my body. I imagined making love to her, giving every inch of the raging passion I had to offer...

Five minutes later I stepped out of the shower in nylon shorts and flip-flops.

Down on the main floor of the cellblock, six or seven inmates were gathered in a far corner. I noticed that they were all gang members. Two black cons argued in the center of the group. As I began walking toward my cell, their voices died away and were replaced by the smacking thuds of knuckles pounding flesh.

The silent spectators backed up to give the men room to fight.

This was no evenly matched tussle. One of the men jabbed at his unarmed opponent with a sharpened, steel shank. The unarmed fighter didn't run. He eluded the attack at a safe distance until his assailant extended his knife hand too far. When the unarmed man saw his chance, he caught his opponent's wrist and wrestled the sharpened, steel rod away from him.

With the homemade weapon in hand, he stabbed the other man in the eye.

The wounded fell to the floor, clutching his face. The other guy straddled him. I should have turned away, but I didn't. I watched him raise the shank high above his head, then ram it into the guy's chest over and over again.

Some inmates stepped out of their cells searching for the origin of the commotion. Others peered through the windows of their cell doors to see what was going on. Hundreds of eyes were transfixed on the violence as it happened, but no one made a move to stop it.

Not even me.

An officer ran into the cellblock screaming into his radio, "Code blue! Code blue! Dorm Four! C-Block!" But even he kept at a safe distance while awaiting help to arrive.

Fingering water from my ears with a corner of the towel, I continued on to my cell. I went inside, and I locked the door.

I heard dozens of officers flood the cellblock as I sat on the edge of the bunk drying my toes. Their stomping feet sounded like the running of the bulls in a shoe box. Over the concerted racket of their radios cackling all at once, they yelled at the inmate stabbing the other. "Let him up, Jimmy! You're going to kill 'im!" And finally, "Hit him with the pepper spray for goodness sake! What the hell are you waiting for?"

I stuffed my wet towel into the crack at the bottom of my cage door so that pepper spray wouldn't waft into my cell. I didn't bother to look out of the door's window to witness what went on below.

I didn't want to see it.

Too often I had seen the sight of one man lying half-dead, while another was hauled off in handcuffs; both of them thrashing from blood and mace stinging their eyes.

I didn't bother to get dressed for work. I knew that the stabbing would cause an institutional lockdown. We would be locked in our cells until the administration determined whether the fight had been an isolated incident, or the beginning of a gang war.

I laid on my bed knowing that a lockdown could last for two hours, or two weeks.

Closing my eyes, I thought of Anderson. Her smiling face was the narcotic I used to take it all away. Addicted to the peace she brought, my every vein cried out for the needle of her love to slide beneath my skin and help me escape misery.

and the blood-red sky weaved thin threads of golden clouds throughout the fabric of its unfathomable expanse. half of a flaming sun peeked over the edge of the world as it rose. she lay naked on a flocculent fleece, white as milk's froth, in the center of a field of soft green grass. the tail of a glowing rainbow was pitched in the ground at her feet. the thick air was littered with floating souls of those who had once loved and now lost. they were faceless white orbs dancing like leaves in a worrisome wind—faceless, but as alive as I, giggling, "It's your time..."

she beckoned me closer with arms wide open. her skin, sprinkled with an angel's dust, sparkled like the treasure she was— illumined by the rainbow's radiance.

i knelt between her legs. my mouth watered at the tuft of curly brown...

"Lockdown cleared!" Was shouted over the intercom at eleven-nineteen. "All inmates are to report immediately to their assigned work detail following chow!"

Jitterbug, the cellblock's janitor, was mopping up the dried blood where the stabbing had taken place as I was leaving for work. I nodded a silent greeting to him.

He said, "That boy died up in here this mornin'. I'm tired of this shit."

Sighing at the brown stain beneath Jitterbug's feet, I admitted the same. "I'm tired of it too."

The tunnels were abuzz with news of the stabbing. Rumors had the death toll at one c/o, three convicts, and the fatality count was steadily rising. Each ear perked at any new development, no matter how outlandish it was.

Taped to a tunnel wall was a memo notifying us inmates that Broutal would begin serving two meals daily on August third. No one seemed to care about that. Everyone was too busy regurgitating lies about the stabbing—ignoring the substantial for the sensational. Most cons walked past the memo without giving it a glance.

The Black Muslim, Nasir, was holding court in *The Center.* Surrounded by his Muslim brothers, he passed out photocopies of a petition he had drawn up.

Three white officers, who stood on post in *The Center,* watched with nervous eyes as he shouted at the passing inmates. "Listen to you all! Listen to your gossip! A man died today! He was a gang member, and you all slander his name even further because you don't think the same thing can happen to you! Let me be the first to inform you all! You do not have to be in a gang to be killed in prison! They are about to starve us to death!"

A Black Muslim tried to hand me a copy of their petition. Nasir met my eyes as I declined to take the paper. He turned away as if he hadn't seen me at all and went on ranting. "Yes! We are criminals deserving of punishment, but at what point should men willingly accept discomfort? How much is too much? When is it okay to submit to wrong? I will tell you when! Never! The man who lays down on the tracks and holds still for the train to run over him is a damn fool, and he deserves to die! Do not be that fool! It is one thing to recognize the wrongs done to us, but it is quite another to ignore it! Stand up and be heard! Stand up and use your voice against injustice! Stand up and let them know that we won't take this lying down!"

The white c/o's told Nasir to move on and stop causing trouble. His Muslim brothers made a forceful stand by shouting at the cops. They were still arguing as I walked past.

When I entered the warehouse, I heard a country song playing softly in the office.

Her scent filled the main corridor. Today she smelled of shooting stars and crystalline moonbeams.

Pausing outside of the open office doorway, my breath came in ragged bursts that I struggled to keep even and calm. My moist palms trembled with an overanxious need to set eyes on her. I took a moment to pull myself together before stepping inside.

Sergeant Thompson sat to my left, typing and talking on the phone at the same time. A mug of coffee steamed at his side.

Anderson was a bedazzling beacon in my peripheral to the right. I swallowed the urge to ogle her even though I knew that's what she wanted. Her hot brown eyes sizzled the side of my face, but I forced myself not to look her way.

Not yet.

"Good afternoon, Sarge," I said after he'd hung up the phone.

He grunted as an answer, reached for his coffee, and spilled half of it on his desk when the phone rang again. "Damn it to hell! Nothing is goin' right this morning!" He answered the phone.

Anderson was laughing, but looking my way—laughing and squirming in her seat as if she wanted to run to me. Our eyes met. Her laughter sputtered to a halt. She squeezed her thighs together while looking me up and down. She asked, "Where are the lawn mower blades?"

My knees were butter. It was a challenge for me to stand so confidently in her presence. "They're in the fifteen-cage."

Anderson nodded, then cut her eyes toward Sarge. He was wrapped up in his telephone conversation, staring at his computer screen.

She said, "Go and wait for me."

Our knowing eyes locked for the whisper of a second before I pulled myself away and went to the fifteen-cage.

I waited impatiently against the chain-links, still shaking from the sight of her. I thought *...it feels like I've been waiting all my daze, for a sensual savior to conquer my maze. to cut a clear path through complicated ways, and lift the fog of my murky haze.*

Jangling keys and squeaky shoe soles announced her arrival well before I saw her. When Anderson raced around the bend, she was all business. No smile. No hello. The ring of cage keys clattered at my feet as she dropped them to cradle my face in her hands, kissing me. Her lips were soft and cool, her tongue a strawberry sweet soothing me. She let out a moan when our mouths began their dance. My hands slid down her body, sinking into her little love handles.

*Finally...*to have her body against mine seemed well worth the wait. It felt like I had scaled nine levels of hell to reach the prize of her heavenly embrace, and I would gladly do it again with a smile upon my face.

She pulled back, still cupping my chin in her palms, her lambent brown eyes swam in mine.

I tried to kiss her again. She stopped me.

"Let me look at you," she whispered. "Please...just let me look at you."

And so I stood still as her eyes traveled over my face again and again. You're beautiful," she said and leaned in to hug me with her head against my chest. "I was so worried about you. Everyone was calling about the stabbing this morning, and I almost lost my mind when I found out that it happened on your block."

"I didn't see it," I lied, not wanting to begin the day dwelling on something horrible. "I slept through the whole thing."

She hugged me tighter, maybe realizing that I was there in one piece and nothing else really mattered. Softly she whispered, "*stolen moments. i closed off the world so my heart could open. thinking the words that need not be spoken. in the end, words are just miniscule tokens, of feelings i felt when lost in stolen moments. stolen moments."*

She pulled back and stared up at me with a quivering smile. "I get it," she said. "*This* is a stolen moment. It's a time when we shouldn't be together, but we are."

We kissed again. Her thigh brushed the hardness between my legs, and when she realized what it was, her flesh went in search of it again.

With our lips still touching, she said "I have been thinking about you all weekend. You're the only thing on my mind. I've been thinking of things I want you to know about me. I'd been planning to tell you so much, but now that I'm here in your arms, I can't think of anything at all." Her eyes bounced between mine. "Do you think I'm crazy?"

I laughed some. "No more than me." It was a comfort to know that she felt the same things I did—that I wasn't alone in my misery. I said, "I wish I had woken up next to you this morning."

In my mind's eye I saw the two men fighting again. I saw the glistening steel shank plunged into the man's chest.

"I do too," she confessed. "It's no picnic on the outside either."

We swayed together. We were two silks of seaweed sliding with a current that only we could feel.

I told her, "I'd rather be out there. You can get up and go someplace whenever you please. No one is breathing down your back, telling you what you can or can't do."

She squeezed my neck in her arms. "Seems that way doesn't it?" We rocked back and forth, riding the rhythm of our bonding hearts. "Everything is so expensive. I mean, nobody tells me that I can't do something, but if I don't have the money for it, I can't do it. Gas is so high. The only place that I can really afford to go is work. The only things I do is work, pay bills, buy stuff I don't want, and go back to work."

"But you're still free," I reminded her.

"There's no such thing as freedom, Danny. Not today. Maybe people were free when they didn't have to pay taxes on their caves or mud huts, but they had to worry about dinosaurs and saber toothed tigers eating them when they went out, so even they weren't free.

"I was born into debt. I've paid every note on my house for the last seven years, but if I miss paying taxes on it just once, the IRS will take it. That's not freedom. That's slavery. No matter how you look at it, you always owe something –you owe time, and I owe money. Where is the freedom in that?" She laughed to herself, and I felt the tremors throughout my own chest. "Sometimes I wish that I could be locked up in here with you..."

I said, "You wouldn't wish that for long."

"No, really! Think about it. What if I slept in your bed? Showered with you? What if we ate every meal together? What if we could make love all day and night without ever having to worry about starving or being evicted? We wouldn't have to work. We wouldn't have any bills or responsibility—that's what ruins relationships, you know—it's the outside problems that usually push people apart. Life would be so much better if all we had to focus on was the act of love."

I shook my head. "There's more to life than love."

"But nothing is more important," she added. "Don't you feel the electricity when we're together? It's like a magnet. I've never felt that with anyone else. I can only imagine what it would be like if we could express our feelings without having to sneak around and hide. Love isn't supposed to be this way. I keep telling myself that...but I'm still falling for you, and I don't want it to stop."

Her compliments made me feel unworthy, as if I didn't deserve for someone to feel good about me. I was used to being the bad guy. I said, "I wish that I could do more for you."

She put a finger to my lips and whispered, "*like a feather fallen flat against my palm. or a breeze through trees rustling my calm. is how she sang into my life upon the tongue of a psalm. and stayed, like a sage spreading love as her alms.*" A low purr rumbled from the back of her throat. "Keep doing what your heart tells you to do, baby, and I'm all yours."

I ran my fingers through her hair. "Did you memorize all of my poems?"

"I can't help it, Danny. I wake up with them in bed beside me as if they were you keeping me warm at night. Some are confusing, but the more I read them, the more I understand about you. I'm beginning to see your vision." As an afterthought, she said, "But who knows? Maybe I will memorize them all."

I kissed her softly, wishing we could sway this way forever, like two willows whose wood was twisted at the trunk, weeping and wallowing in the wind together.

But our time was limited. Even the few moments we had together were dangerous. So gently, I pushed her away.

"Danny, what's wrong?"

"We have to be smart about this. Sarge could come back here at any time."

She shook her head. "He's buried in a mountain of paperwork. Besides, he's leaving at one o'clock to take his wife's car to the shop."

My eyes searched hers. "He's leaving? Why didn't you tell me earlier?"

"Because it was supposed to be a surprise." She slunk into my arms again. She kissed me, just once. "We'll be alone until five o'clock."

I couldn't believe that we were going to have the entire warehouse to ourselves. "Are you sure you want to be alone with me? I'm a hardened criminal."

She pressed her thigh into my crotch. "You are, aren't you?"

"What about the truck?" I asked. "One will be here in ten minutes."

"You'd better unload it quickly, huh?" She bit her bottom lip. "But don't you get any dirty ideas." Her thigh slid up and down my erection. "I have lots for you to do today, so conserve your energy. You'll be lucky to leave here in one piece."

I couldn't stop smiling. The calm way that she was gave me confidence that we could pull off whatever she had planned. "Just don't hurt me."

She whispered, "I'm gonna break your back."

We kissed again, both of us knowing that she needed to get back to the office, yet still caught up in a stolen moment.

we embraced in a shallow pool at the foot of a modest waterfall raining over our heads in a translucent sheet. warm water lapped against the crest of my chest. beyond the bubbling brook was a short cliff of jet black rock that gave way to a dense forest of white-bodied trees—their bark the color of old ash—with scarlet leaves as their red hair.

Her hand slipped between my legs. Her fingers dug inside my pants and curled around the ridged rod there. My mouth went slack as she pulled it out into the open air. I didn't care if Sarge was in the office, it didn't matter if we waited until he left. I was willing to go wherever she wanted to take me.

golden clouds hung heavily in an orange sky. two suns sat at opposite ends of the endless horizon—a purple sun set to the west, a blue sun rose from the east. her fist glided along the dark staff in her palm, stirring warm waters between us. her fervent stroking had me yearning to move past the point of no return.

I licked her teeth. One hand cupped a cheek of her round ass while the other palmed a plump breast through her shirt. She was all mine. Lonely days and nights would come and go like low and high tides, but for this moment, she was mine...all mine.

tribal drums beat on a far off shore. a trio of pterodactyls glided overhead, cawing at our love. her fingers tugged and twisted. the water grew hotter, boiling and steaming. little convulsions were a prelude to my mounting pleasure. every muscle in my body tensed as i was about to explode in her hand...

"Y'all got them lawn mower blades? I told Cap'n Walker that I wasn't 'llowed to come up in here no more, but he sent me to git 'em anyhow. He say he don't care who or what don't want me in the warehouse, he said to git 'em, so that's what I's doin'.

"I ain't wanna come down here. I's down to the operations building trimmin' my Spanish Bayonets—that's what I do here at Broutal. I'mma gard'ner. That means I plant rose bushes and rooster combs and sunflowers—hell, sum' them sunflowers grow bigger 'n me. That's how good I am at growin' thangs. Mm-hm. One time I hadda hide in some sunflowers 'cause my great-aunt Merle was in heat! She done tried to climb in bed wit' me, and when I tried to run..."

CHAPTER 11

The truck's load was light. I inventoried in three pallets of boots, inmate uniform pants, and a dozen boxes of socks in less than forty-five minutes.

Anderson told me to leave for lunch so that Sergeant Thompson could get his affairs in order with as little distraction as possible.

Expecting her to be alone when I returned, it was strange to hear a man's laughter coming from the open office door as I reentered the warehouse.

Hugging the wall outside of the office, I crept on the doorway to spy inside without being seen. Officer Rynhold slouched in a swivel chair with his polished boots propped on Sarge's desk. I remembered him from the past Friday when his friend, Peterson, had embarrassed me in a staff break room. He'd hit on Anderson that day, and she'd turned him down.

Rynhold was fortyish with dark, peanut colored skin. His close-cropped, wavy hair shined beneath the fluorescent lighting. From where I hid, I took note of the crisp creases throughout his neatly ironed uniform pants and shirt. Slim and well built, Rynhold was a handsome man that many women would be attracted to.

The fact that he was in the office with Anderson bothered me.

I couldn't see her from where I stood, but I heard her say, "I appreciate you walking your supply order down here, but you didn't need to do that. You could have e-mailed it to me, like everyone else does."

Rynhold's bright smile threatened to blind me. "Now you know that I didn't come down here just to drop off a supply order."

Anderson let a pause still the air. I imagined her staring at him, blank-faced and blinking. "Why did you come down here then?"

His smile widened. "To give you a second chance," he said. "And...to apologize for coming on so strongly last time. But in my defense, I want to say that you are a very attractive woman, and I couldn't help myself. I was hoping that you would let me apologize the right way, you know, over dinner."

She sighed loud enough for me to hear. "I don't mean to hurt your feelings, but I don't date men that I work with."

Rynhold kept on smiling. "Who's talking about *dating?*" He laughed a little to show that he was joking.

I wanted to run in there and knock his teeth out.

She said, "You're gonna get me in trouble."

He raised an eyebrow. "Trouble? With who? Sergeant Thompson? You don't need to worry about him. He's my main man. We used to work Dorm Three back in the day. He owes me big. I had to rescue him once."

"Rescue him?"

The curiosity in Anderson's voice made me want to leave. Eavesdropping felt wrong, and the longer that I stood there, the harder it was to pull away. My loyalty demanded a respect for her privacy. My pride begged to know how she was with other men.

Rynhold went on. "Me and Sarge were slumming on third shift. The prison was a lot rougher in those days. We had a stabbing at least twice a week—fucking fights every day. It was hard work, but better too because we had more leeway to keep the inmates in line. Back then, if you had a problem with one, all you had to do was take off your badge and invite him into a mop closet. Nobody snitched on each other. There were no cameras. We all had a sense of pride in who we were and what we had to do to keep order."

He paused in thought, staring at the floor with a half-smile across his face. Finally, he asked Anderson, "Do you remember *Sugah?* He used to be housed here at Broutal, but he was shipped to another prison a few years ago."

"Big ol' white boy with blond bangs?" She said quizzically. "Wasn't he the one who stood at six-feet-eight with double-D breast implants?"

Rynhod nodded. "That's him. Who could forget Sugah, right? *The Amazon* was what the young bucks called him. But anyway, it was a cool New Year's Eve, and we'd caught Sugah in another inmate's cell giving out midnight kisses below the belt. I'll spare you the grizzly details."

She chuckled. "I appreciate it."

"We took him down to the Sergeant's office in handcuffs, and the next thing you know, Dorm One called in a code for a gang fight. Well we all ran off, leaving Sarge and Sugah alone in paradise."

Anderson sniggered again. "Oh no. I don't think I want to know how this turns out."

Each inflection of her laughter was a knife in my heart. To feel possessive of her was an odd experience. Why didn't I want her talking to him? Why was it so easy for him to make her laugh? Did she like him more than she liked me?

"Don't be fooled," Rynhold continued. "Just because he tucks his peter doesn't mean he's soft. Sugah was one the toughest convicts to ever walk this yard."

"He just happened to be gay," she added, giggling.

Rynhold shrugged. "Like I said, gay doesn't mean soft. Think about it. You've got to be one tough mother fucker to take it up the brown eye and like it! He's a tougher man than me, I swear!" Anderson laughed long and hard. Rynhold gave her time to recover before continuing. "We all knew about him. There wasn't a C/O this side of North Carolina who hadn't heard about Sugah knocking out guys so he could suck them off. It was common knowledge."

Anderson snorted a laugh. "I thought that was a joke!"

"You don't own a penis. It's a joke to you because you're safe. But those of us who pee standing up have to take things like that seriously. Sugah was strong as a damned bull. He'd knock your mustache off if you let him. I once heard that he'd been raised on a hog farm in Alamance County. Freaks like him are the reason that I quit eating pork."

"That sounds so nasty."

"Tell me about it. But that's prison. It's never the way you want it to be. Have you ever looked up some of the inmates' crimes?"

Anderson said, "I don't get into that."

"Why not?"

"Because I don't want to judge them. They're locked up for something bad, but that doesn't mean they're bad people. I don't want to think differently about somebody because I know what crime they committed in the past. I've done bad things too, and I don't want someone looking down on me because of a mistake I made. So I don't think about their crimes, I take them as they are to me."

He regarded her with penetrating eyes. "That's noble—noble and naïve. We work in a dangerous place. Take a guy like Sugah. He's in here for raping a man. It helps you to understand how he thinks if you know what he's in here for. Of course you wonder why he did that. Had he been raped before? Were his actions a learned behavior? You know something is wrong with him..."

"You can look at him and tell that," Anderson added. "He's got titties."

Rynhold nodded. "He's out in the open. What about the inmates who aren't out in the open? What about the ones who are hiding? And I don't mean gays. I mean crazy mother fuckers. Sure, they appear normal enough. Their cells are always clean. They shower. They work okay. They give all the signs that make them appear normal, but the guy that you're around every day could be a psychopath."

"That's why I don't want to know about the crimes they've committed."

Rynhold crossed his arms. "I do. I look'em up every chance I get—I sure do. An inmate's file is there so that we are aware of the level of danger we face when interacting with them. It's not good to go around stumbling in the dark—which brings me back to my story about Sergeant Thompson." He snickered a little. "Sarge knew about Sugah, but to this day, no one knows why he let him out of the handcuffs. It's like he was asking for trouble."

"What happened?"

"Well, we stopped the fight in Dorm One, and when we made it back to the unit, Sarge was knocked out cold on the office floor. Sugah was hunched over him with this lusty look in his eye. We got there right in time too, 'cause Sugah was just beginning to unbutton Sarge's trousers."

"Uh-uh!" Anderson stomped her feet while laughing.

"When I pulled him off, Sugah didn't even put up a fight. He turned to me and said, *'I wasn't gonna hurt him, baby. All I wanted was a little taste. You can't blame a girl for that, can you?'*"

Anderson laughed so heartily that I imagined her falling out of the chair as she heaved for air.

"Sarge was out for so long that we decided to teach him a lesson about trusting inmates."

"What'd you do?" She asked, hanging on his every word.

"We pulled down his pants and drawers, strapped 'em tight around his ankles with his belt, and we left him lying there."

Anderson sucked in a gust of air. "You didn't?"

"We sure did—left his pink willy leaning to the side and everything."

"My god, that was so mean."

"Yeah. Then we hid out in the hallway. When he came to, we ran in there hollering: '*What happened, Sarge? Where'd he go?*'

"He was so confused that it didn't register at first—not until he saw his pee-pee waving at him. Boy did he raise hell, flapping like a wet fish, trying to pull his pants up! We had to restrain him from running to the arsenal to get a pistol to shoot Sugah!"

"I will never look at him the same!" She declared.

"Me neither," Rynhold mused. Every time I see him I remember his hairy ass rolling around on the floor, trying to cover his pecker and pull his pants up at the same time."

Anderson laughed for a long time.

Rynhold remained silent, staring at her with the same lusty look Sugah must have had while staring at Sarge on that long ago New Year's Eve.

I hated him.

I hated him because he was a free man who would never share the miseries that I knew. I hated him because he could marry, breed, and love like a normal human being—while I had to steal trinkets of joy like a thief. I hated him because he could possess a woman in each and every way that I couldn't. But mostly, I hated him because I knew that Anderson deserved someone better than me.

lipstick on a toad
a princess shouldn't be forced to accept
the pauper who knows nothing except
regret, sorrows of perpetual rain
a princess needs a sane prince to reign
for fame, of the camelot her heart will raise
but i bring war, catapults that raze
insane, miseries of a lovely illusion
non-profit promises of poetic allusion
confusion, is all that my intentions elicit
when our love is a drug, smuggled and illicit
an explicit, tryst for a princess isn't fair
she deserves much better; can't pay his own fare
compare, the lover whose love leaves a hole
to a prince with powers to make her life whole
bold, were those little handwritten presents
but words can't bless her with a palpable presence
lipstick on a toad

After clearing her throat of the last little giggles, Anderson told Rynhold," It's time for you to go. My helper will be back in a few, and we have lots of work to do."

"*Helper?* You're running me off for an inmate?"

"No," she said, "I'm running you off because it's time to work."

Rynhold studied her, stern-faced. "Your helper—he's the tall inmate who got into it with Peterson the other day, right? Young guy? Dark-skinned with a bald head and goatee?"

Anderson didn't reply verbally.

Rynhold asked her, "How much do you know about him?"

"Not a lot. He isn't very talkative, but he works hard. If it wasn't for him, nothing would get done around here."

"What does he do when he isn't working?"

"He sits on the loading dock and reads."

Rynhold threw her a crooked smile. "Has he ever hit on you?"

"He's still able to walk, isn't he? If I won't date officers, what makes you think I would go for an inmate?"

"I don't mean anything by it, Anderson. You need to be careful, that's all. I've heard about him. You say he reads at work? They say the same about him in the dorms. He doesn't talk, he's anti-social..."

"That doesn't make him crazy."

"Maybe it doesn't. But it's hard to figure a guy like that. Most convicts wear their personalities on their sleeves. You can peg their strengths and weaknesses a mile away, but this guy..."

"Danny," she informed him.

"*Danny.* He's the one you need to watch."

"Trust me," she said, "*I keep a close eye on that one*. I don't let him out of my sight."

The easy way that she'd said it stilled my heart. It was a reassurance that I was in her thoughts, no matter whose company she was in.

"Have you ever looked him up? Do you know about his crime?"

"No. I don't care. He's a good worker. It doesn't matter."

"He killed his old man, Anderson. Stabbed him thirty-eight times."

The office went quiet for a long time. After hearing him, my body stiffened, but I felt more defeated than angry. I wasn't the same person I had been seventeen years ago. I didn't expect Rynhold to see that. I only hoped that Anderson could.

my facade

124

is it you hiding me or me hiding you? ever since i've been hidden, i still feel blue. even though there's no lie if you haven't asked for truth. even though there's no why without when, what, or who.

the past is the greatest scapegoat of all. steep stairs up the platform from which we stand tall. fickled failures find purpose, passion not to stall. a perseverance to erect, the foundation not to fall.

this blood on my hands is why i am who i am. the remorse of my youth upraised a stronger man...in ways the pure of heart will never understand. sad yesterdays are wise waves that saturate my sand.

so why...do i...still wear...this facade?

because for you i couldn't remove my carnival mask. i didn't want you to run from the love we have amassed. i knew that if you saw me as the boy from my past. the future that i need, with you, won't last.

my facade

When Anderson finally spoke, her voice was strained—choked. "He did what?"

"He killed his father, and he never told anyone why. He didn't say a word when interviewed by the police. He just plead guilty to First Degree Murder like it didn't bother him at all."

"Wait a second," she said. "How do you know all of this?"

"It's no secret. This guy had a high profile case. It's all over the internet. His daddy was somebody rich and famous. I'd never heard of him, but he was a man that a lot of people respected."

"But why did you look Danny up? What did he ever do to you? Why?"

"Because that's my job. It's yours too. We aren't inmates. We don't have a code of loyalty to uphold with them. We have a duty to protect ourselves and each other from harm.

"And if that isn't good enough, think about it this way: if he killed his own daddy, what do you think he would do to a pretty little thing like you?"

I didn't hear Anderson reply.

Rynhold continued to stare her way as he stood up. "I like you," he told her. "I don't want to see you get hurt when it could have been avoided."

Anderson was still quiet. Rynhold walked slowly toward the door.

He asked her, "Is it always so peaceful up here?" He paused in the threshold with his back to me. "It's so quiet that I can hear my heart beating."

"It sure is. That's how we like it."

Rynhold stuffed his hands into his pockets. "I heard that the warehouse has a job opening. I would love to get out of the dorms to work up here. Would you put in a good word for me?"

"No."

He laughed some. "Aw, come on! Don't you want someone working around here that you can trust?"

"*Trust?*" She scoffed. "Sarge trusted you, and you left him wiggling around on the floor with his ass and privates hanging out. Do you really think I would let you do the same thing to me?"

He grinned. "I was hoping you would. But you might like it. I'll be wiggling on the floor with you."

She pushed him in the chest. "You need to leave."

He laughed and smiled like it was all a big joke. "Why do you keep turning me down? What is it about me that you don't like?"

"It's not about you, Rynhold."

"Well what is it about?"

"I have somebody," she said. "I have a man who makes me happier than I've been in a long time. I don't want to mess that up, and I don't want anyone else."

Rynhold paused to think about it before replying, "I can't argue with that. It sounds like you're in love. Do I know him? Who is he?"

Rynhold backed out of the office and came face to face with me.

"Son-of-a-bitch!" He shouted as our eyes locked. Startled, he tripped over his own two feet and fell flat on his back. He hopped up quickly with his fangs bared. "How long have you been snooping on us? I oughta lock your ass up!"

Leaning against the wall with my arms crossed, I kept quiet. I let my eyes tell him that I'd been standing there long enough.

Anderson poked her head out into the hallway, smiling at me. "Hey, Danny! You're late. It's one forty-five."

"Sorry about that boss." My eyes stayed still on Rynhold. "I'll get right to it." But I didn't move.

Rynhold's gaze pivoted between Anderson and I. Maybe he sensed the sensuous energy in the air...maybe not.

He told Anderson that he would call about his unit's supply order as he walked around me. She told him not to bother.

Once he had disappeared through the exit, she said, "I wish you had shown up twenty minutes ago! I've been trying to get rid of him forever! I hate the way he looks at me! It's like he's got x-ray vision and he can see through my clothes!" She let out a long sigh while staring into my eyes, and then she asked, "Did you catch up with Critter?" I nodded. "Well what did he say?"

It was my turn to sigh. "Not much. First he told me about this kid named Kelly who got here a few weeks ago. Some guy ran into his cell and tried to rape him. Kelly beat him half-to-death with a lock on a sock."

"Kelly? Was this guy your friend?"

I thought of Kelly's young face and the talks we had.

I shook my head. "No. He was just a guy that I knew. He'll be okay. He'll do a year in the hole, but no one will try to rape him again. That's for sure."

Anderson nodded. "But Critter didn't see anything?"

"I don't know. I didn't ask him directly. I don't think he saw it…"

"I was massaging your penis, Danny. How could he have missed that?"

"Your back was to him," I said. "Besides, Critter doesn't see things the way we see them—you know, normal people. Half of the time he's too caught up in his own thoughts to pay attention to anything else."

She cocked her head to the side. "I hope you're not trying to comfort me with *that*." I shrugged. She asked, "Do you think he'll tell anybody? If he does realize what he saw?"

I wanted to tell her that it wasn't Critter's fault we'd been careless. It was our own. To paint him the bad guy because of our mistake wasn't fair.

But I didn't say that. "He's not a snitch. He just…"

"Blabs incoherently," she finished for me.

We were quiet for a minute, staring at each other. She wore a fresh smacking of lip gloss, and I had the urge to suck it off, but I didn't know where we stood on the Critter issue.

She went into the office and came out with a ring of keys that I'd never seen. My eyes followed as she strutted toward the warehouse's entrance.

I called out, "Where are you going?"

Over her shoulder, she told me, "To make sure we don't have any more surprises."

She put a key into the door of the main entrance and locked us inside.

"Why did you do that?" I asked, once we were face to face again. "What if somebody comes up here?"

"Nobody comes up here, Danny. You know that."

"Rynhold just left."

She put a hand on her hip. "That was one time out of a million. No one else has come up here in a long time, and today will be no different."

I didn't want to admit that she was right, but she was. "What if someone does show up? Wouldn't it be strange if the door is locked?"

Anderson stepped close to me. "I don't care. "She searched my eyes with less than a hair's breadth between our lips. "You're afraid, aren't you?"

It was hard to meet her stare. "Yes."

Her hand caressed my forearm. "Why?"

I wanted to embrace her—to pull her close and shut my eyes tight as I held on for dear life. "Because I don't want them to take you away from me."

She smiled and kissed me. "Go in the office and sit down. I have a surprise for you."

I did as told. I eased down in Sarge's chair while she went to her lunch bag next to the microwave.

"Did you eat?" she asked.

I thought of the grey soy burgers the kitchen had served for lunch. I thought about their leathery texture and the prized chunk of gristle in every bite. "No. I didn't eat."

She smiled. "Good. There's nothing better than a hungry man."

Anderson dug into her lunch bag. She placed three plastic bowls into the oven and turned it on. Next, she went to her computer. Seconds later a slow country song began to play softly. As some soulful singer sang about traveling across the land in a beat-up van, she said, "I hope you like *The Zach Brown Band*. Every song they sing reminds me of you." She went back to the microwave and waited.

I stared her up and down. There was a tingle pulsating throughout my body. I was warm and sweaty and nervous.

"Anderson, what are we doing?"

She smiled over her shoulder. "Quit being a scaredy-cat and you'll find out." She opened the microwave and removed a bowl of mashed potatoes to stir before putting them back in to cook a little longer. She told me, "I wanted to bring you two juicy steaks, but I couldn't think of a way to get a steak knife through the metal detector out front. I chopped up four T-bones instead." She pulled out all of the bowls and began sliding hot food onto a plastic plate. "You'll have to settle for steak and broccoli stir fry."

Craning my neck, I peered around her. My mouth watered at the sights and scents. "You didn't have to do this, Anderson."

"Yes I did. Why can't I make you feel as good as I do? You work hard so that I don't have to, you write for me, and you've never asked me for anything. It's not in me to take and take without giving, sweetie. We're in this together."

There was a light in her eyes that I'd never seen in a woman. She seemed to enjoy preparing the food even more than I was eager to eat it.

I knew nothing of the give and take balance that made a relationship work. I only knew the raw emotions I felt inside and an overwhelming need to get them off my chest. But by watching her...

i learned that a man and woman are a lot like the hot and cold currents of a funnel cloud. alone we are weak and aimless, drifting down dusty desert plains, tumbling over icy tundras—no more than whispers whistling against jagged crevices and cracked tree limbs.

but together, when the push and pull of one against the other is perfectly harmonious, two winds become one to create an unstoppable force strong enough to crush any obstacle in its way. that power cannot stand alone.

love's duality maintains its intensity.

if one current loses steam, the raging storm dies... and so does the passion it once created.

What she cooked made me love her even more, if only because she was trying to show how much she loved me.

I shoved chunks of steak into my mouth as soon as the plate hit my hand. A slow trickle of grease slipped from my lips. I licked it up and kept on trucking. I hadn't eaten much in days. I'd been living off of love and nothing else.

Anderson smiled down at me as I crunched fried onions and bell peppers between my teeth. I marveled at neon green broccoli with their fat heads still attached. Buttery mashed potatoes melted on my tongue.

"Is it good?"

My mouth was too full to talk. I should have been embarrassed, but I wasn't. I gave her a firm thumbs up. She giggled and handed me a cold bottle of water.

After washing down the food, I asked her, "Aren't you going to eat something?"

She smiled, but it didn't hide the sadness in her eyes. "I wanted to see you happy. I don't need anything else."

I stared up at her knowing that to a man on the outside an evening meal was an insignificant occurrence—an expected, everyday thing. I appreciated her sacrifice because she'd put her job on the line to bring me dinner. What made it so extraordinary was the looming fact that it may never happen again.

She felt it too.

Impermanence.

That's what I'd seen in her eyes. It was easy to recognize because the same fear dwelt in mine.

We were having a great day together, yet we were just two kids playing house over empty plates and bone-dry tea cups. Sooner or later we would have to leave our make-believe world.

Reality was an anvil suspended over our heads by a shredding thread.

Although our days were numbered, I asked myself: *Why waste time worrying over troubles darkening tomorrows?* To constantly live in fear for the rapture of future was as pointless as counting down to a prophesied apocalypse.

Life is a precious gift, and love is a present that should be cherished in every way.

Tomorrow will be a nightmare haunting the missed opportunities of what could have been a beautiful today.

I sat my plate on a desk and stood up.

"Aren't you going to finish eating, Danny?"

I took her in my arms and kissed her. "After..."

"After?" She asked.

My hands sank into her soft bottom and pulled her into my growing erection.

A lazy smile spread across her lips as she wrapped her arms around my neck. "Yes..." she purred. "*After...*"

CHAPTER 12

"The twelve-cage," she panted.

I had Anderson firmly by the hand, pulling her quickly through the labyrinth of cages. "Why the twelve-cage?"

"Mattresses, Blankets."

She was right. Along with an assortment of clothing items, the twelve-cage also housed brand-new inmate mattresses, pillows, and dark blue wool blankets.

Once there, her hands trembled while unlocking the gate. I was all over her when we stumbled inside. I shoved her against a shelf and stuck my tongue in her mouth. Her fingers fumbled between my legs, molesting me through my pants.

We stood there kissing, gasping for air, fondling each other through our clothes for what seemed like a long time.

I was trying to unbutton her uniform shirt when she stopped me. "Hurry up and get a mattress, Danny. I'll get a blanket."

She ran to one corner of the cage. I ran to another.

A pile of brand-new, polyester filled mats were stacked neatly on pallets that rested against the chain-links. I snatched one down and slung it to the concrete amidst a square patch of sunrays beaming in from the skylight above. She rushed over, ripping open a plastic package containing two brand-new blankets.

Together we knelt on the mattress facing each other. Miniscule particles of dust drifted between us. Streaks of sunlight lit the crown of her hair like a halo—bathing her in a white aura of perfection.

Smiling at me, she said, "It's not *The Waldorf*, but it'll do."

She laid back. I tumbled down between her spread legs.

My body molded into her open arms.

Her lips were silk sheets sliding against mine.

Her tongue, a honeycomb drenched in dangerous delight.

and in my heart, all time stood still. frozen as flakes outside my windowsill. is this a newfound love, or an ancient prophecy fulfilled? a sacred gift, or tainted curse—like man's sense of free will?

Her hands tiptoed between us, tugging at the tail of my tee shirt. Before I knew it, she had the garment up and over my head. I watched her wet tongue circle her soft lips as she feasted her eyes on my tight body.

I'd been working out all of my adult life, but never had I imagined that a woman would appraise me with such wanton lust in her eyes.

Her fingers were searing pokers branding my flesh wherever they probed: ovaling my dark nipples, tracing solid crevices between my abdominals, skipping their way down to my belt. She open my pants and shrugged them down past my hips—just enough to set my cock free to fondle as she had hours before.

I leaned over, twirling my tongue around her earlobe. She gasped while jerking me with one hand and massaging the heavy sacks beneath with the other.

Slowly I unbuttoned her uniform shirt. Boiling breath caught in my throat as her heavy, braless breasts spilled out. I scooped them up, worshipping pink nipples with my teeth.

She pushed me back. Her eager hands struggled with her own belt buckle. I slid her fingers aside and unbuckled it myself. She lay docile while I yanked off her shoes and pulled her pants down over plump hips and thighs.

My eyes locked on her patch of brown curls below. She hadn't worn panties or a bra. I loved thinking that she'd planned this all along.

I threw her pants halfway across the cage. I left a trail of kisses from her ankles to her knees. I nibbled the soft flesh of her inner thighs.

She coaxed me on top of her.

I kicked off my boots and shimmied out of my pants and boxers.

My overactive mind tried to conjure up some vivid daydream to flavor our moment. For a time I imagined us together beside a marble fireplace; the shade of its raging flame colored her buttermilk breasts pumpkin orange, but the reverie faded as soon as my lips closed around a pert nipple.

I didn't need to imagine anything.

No fantasy compared to our reality.

Her undulating hips acted out her frustration. "What are you waiting for, Danny?"

Butterflies of anxiety filled my belly. I had seen the frozen act of sex in still photos before the prison system had banned pornography. Over the years I'd even heard about it from more experienced boys and men. But to be poised above an eager and impatient woman was a far cry from the manual stimulation that I was used to.

Anderson cupped my face in her hands and stared deeply into my eyes. "You've never done this before, have you?"

I couldn't answer.

She smiled softly as her hand dipped between us and guided the head of my penis to the mouth of her vagina. "Start out slow," she said. "Very slow..."

Slipping inside was like traveling through time. Breathless, I closed my eyes tight and cradled the underside of her shoulders, pressing my chest to hers.

"Mmmm," she whispered. "Yes. Just like that. Exactly like that."

Her simmering abyss was wet and slippery. Silent gasps gave me the confidence to press on. Her legs spread wider. Fevered hands sprinted up and down my back. Finally, she cupped handfuls of my ass to pull me in deeper, inch by maddening inch.

Soon, I burrowed in as far as her body would allow. "Danny..." she whimpered. Her hands pushed my hips out, then pulled me back in deeper than before.

> precious. my precious keepsake. let me dig down deep to
> bury it safe. inside your warm, wet, most cherished place.
> is where i will stay, never to be replaced.
> mine. in your belly i tattoo my sign. i will live in you as two
> lovers entwined. never forgetting the feel of your divine.
> prolonging the magic of loving our first time.

This was no new love. I had to admit that. It had existed for months. Images of the past flashed in hues of red, yellow, and blue — violent bursts scattered across the black nothing of my closed eyelids. Our love had begun with casual glances, eye-batting smiles, and short snippets of conversation. We'd been attracted to each other light-years before we'd acted on it. Destiny led us hand in hand on a journey down a dark tunnel of uncertainty. The mysteries ahead were faint and shapeless. The past, a ghost. All we possessed was a present moment of pleasure...for even the wonders of the world must someday crumble to dust.

so share with me a piece of your heart. a tiny token of which you will part. so you'll be with me always, whether near or far. and i can view your memory as treasures in a jar.

Beads of sweat trickled down my back. The cage grew thick with heat and the scent of passion. She cried out for more and more of me until I was pounding so deeply that it hurt. I wished that I had eight arms and hands to fondle her in devious ways—to worship every place at once and make her experience so much better.

loveliest lovely. i have only dreamt of the day when you would touch me. when the bright of your light would overshadow my uglies. when the eruption of your climax would beautifully corrupt me.

Abruptly, her body stiffened. Her back arched high off of the mattress, and she let out a slow wail punctuating her pleasure.

If we were to stop right then, with my own peak lost in the glow of her limelight, I would still have been pleased, knowing that I had given her the greatest gift a man could ever give a woman.

After she'd calmed a bit, I buried myself deep inside of her and held it there, feeling the aftershocks of her orgasm gripping me.

in these moments we abandon ideas of tender. making way for the freedom of sweet, sweet surrender. not knowing all along that our restraint was a pretender. we can't hide who we are when true passion is rendered.

When her eyes met mine, I'd never felt more alive.

"Danny…"

Coated with the slick of her love, I kissed her cheek and whispered, "*you are my burning sun and glowing moon. a shimmering horizon threatening to consume. the dead, black catacombs of my lonely tomb. the reason i live, the only reason I DO.*"

She clung to me, dipped her hips to slide me out, then scooped her pelvis to plunge me back in.

I kissed her lips. *i will want you tomorrow as much as i need you today.* I kissed her forehead and eyelids. *i want you forever as i have wanted you always.* I kissed her throat and chin. She picked up the pace beneath me, grinding her belly into mine. *i want you silently sighing with nothing left to say.* I licked her lips from corner to corner. *valentine, i want you as mine until the end of days.*

She kissed me hard, and when I pulled back, my lips were soaked with the salt of her tears. More flowed from her eyes, melting streaks down her cheeks.

The strain of our forbidden affair was all over her face. Never had I seen someone so sad...yet so happy.

Though I enjoyed being with her, I hated love for what it was doing to us.

loved

inconsiderate, uncompromising,

love

miserly and selfish.

demanding, it expects much more than it offers.

love

it possesses.

it embodies.

it becomes.

you are never in love.

love commandeers and lies within you.

loved

In her tear-stained eyes I saw the unspoken truths of our relationship that I wished to forget. A dark and turbulent future lay ahead. For each day that we could make love, months would pass when we could not.

Obsessing over thoughts of losing her was like dreaming a recurring nightmare. I wanted it to stop.

I couldn't enjoy our moment by dwelling on a suffering that had not yet come to pass.

So I kissed her tears away. I told her that I loved her. I cradled her in my arms and made love to her like it was the last time we would ever see each other again.

CHAPTER 13

Beneath the blanket I lay on my back, naked. Anderson nestled against me with her thigh thrown over my belly. Her calf flirted between my legs. While combing my fingers through her hair, I noticed her open eyes staring at her own hands dancing slow circles over my chest.

in a pure world of perfection

all of our days and nights would be petrified in the still afterglow of loving ardor—each moment frozen in a serene portrait of peace, respect, and admiration that knows no bounds. we'd have no fear for the ills of tomorrow, the day after that, nor the sorrows of yesterday's gone past. all our memories would be of slow kisses and soft utterances of love.

in a pure world of perfection.

Her voice was soft and flowery. She spoke with the sound of satisfaction. "Are you still hungry?"

After grunting, I whispered, "Not for food."

Gentle giggles bubbled from her throat to mine. "Just let me know when you're ready for more, and I'll give you all that you can handle."

My eyes closed with a smile across my lips. I wished to lay with her forever. I wished to know that the sun had risen and set a million times over, and she had not left my side. I wished to live in a timeless blur whose infinite hours brought me closer to knowing heaven in a cage.

"Maybe we should go," I said. "We've been back here way too long."

Stirring beside me, she glanced at her pink wrist watch. "It's not even three, Danny. We've still got a little time." Her calf sawed against my crotch.

I couldn't hide my body's growing excitement. "How long do you think...I mean, how long can we stay?"

"How long do you want to stay?" Her teeth nibbled my throat until my Adam's apple was sore and stinging. "I don't ever want to leave." Her hand stole between my legs and wrapped around the hardness there. "What's this? It feels like you don't want to leave either." Anderson raised up on a propped elbow to kiss me. Her fist pistoned up and down in long, slow strokes.

I admired her boldness. Her strength. When she made up her mind to do something, she went all the way. She was dangerous, and I loved her for it.

She tossed her leg over my waist and straddled me. My penis was smushed between her lower lips and my belly. She grinded against the stem, masturbating me with her clit. We kissed here and there. Sweaty and tangled hair hung over her head like straw peeking out of a scarecrow's hat.

"Why are you so afraid, Danny?"

"I'm not. I...I just don't want to get you in trouble."

her lips crushed mine in a deep, deep kiss. i held not the will, the will to resist. her passion, wild, wildly senseless. her love so pure, so purely endless.

Her pelvis slid back and forth, drenching me with her mounting pleasure.

"How do you think I feel, Danny? If we get caught, they'll just walk me to my car and tell me not to return. I'll still get my last check on the first of the month. I can go on with my life like nothing happened." She kissed me, then pulled back to let her brown eyes bounce between mine. "You're the one who will pay for it. You'll suffer the most. That's what I worry about."

My hands sank into the pillowy globes of her bottom. Hungry fingers found the nest between her legs, and I slid one inside.

Shivering above me, her body pressed hard against my finger, driving it deeper. "Danny, I don't know what I would do if something happened to you. I've seen people that I work with torment you guys in ways that soldiers aren't allowed to torture enemies in war."

I asked, "If it's that bad, why don't you tell someone?"

"Tell who?"

"Newspapers. A magazine. They would listen to you before they'd listen to a convicted felon."

"I can't do that. We *work* by the same codes that you guys *live* by. We don't tattle on each other. No one wants to work around a snitch. We face life or death situations in here, you know that. I clock in not knowing if I will live to clock out. Sometimes we're forced to do things we don't want to do. I'll admit that some take it too far, but the same officer that broke an inmate's arm yesterday could be the one who stops another inmate from raping me tomorrow. There are two ways to look at every incident. The worst of it is having to turn a blind eye to something that I know is wrong. It makes me feel guilty of what I've seen and didn't report."

"So why do you work here?"

"Because my bills won't pay themselves."

"Can't you find another job?"

"Where? There's no place to work in Bonnieville. The nearest mall is over an hour away in Salisbury. This prison is the biggest industry in town. Look at how many different types of people work here: young, old, Black, White, and Hispanic. Do you know how many people would be jobless if criminals decided to quit committing crimes? Broutal Correctional is the best thing that ever happened to Bonnieville. The only other industries here are farming, schools, and construction."

"You could move," I said.

She laughed. "Can't do that. Then I'd be too far away from you." Anderson reached between us and slid me into her slick passage. Time stood still as she eased me all the way in. "Losing you isn't something I want to think about right now."

I didn't have anything else to say.

She rode me at a snail's pace—fucking me as slowly as sap dribbling down the bark of a Sycamore tree.

"So many women are waiting for a man like you, Danny. They live, pray, and die without ever knowing your name—without ever crossing your path. Some live out their days alone and miserable. Others don't think you'll ever come around, so they marry a convenient substitute for stability—but they can't love him like they would love you. For years they sip coffee or tea or wine while sitting on porch swings, wishing upon the stars, crying their eyes out because they haven't or won't ever find the man they've always dreamt about."

Anderson sighed in my ear. "Not me, Danny. I've found the man of my dreams, I swear I have. I may have found you in a prison, but at least I found you."

I cradled her in my arms. She buried her face in the crook of my neck, and soon after, she sniffled as her tears wet my skin.

"I know our situation isn't easy, but I want to play house for just a little while longer...just until life forces us to grow up and be adults again."

Gradually her movements sped up. Her tears of agony turned into throws of passion. Her dancing hips felt so good that nothing escaped my lips but clipped puffs of air as she impaled herself with long strokes of violent love. Soon, my own pleasure arrived, and we shuttered together. Her muscles were squeezing fingers milking me dry.

When the tide calmed and peace lapped softly against our sands, she slunk down on my chest, limber and lazy. Her head rested against my heart with me still raging hard inside of her.

"I love you." She said. "I haven't said it before, even though I've been feeling it."

"You don't have to say it." I buried my hand in her hair and scrunched the wild strands between my fingers. "It shows."

She kissed my lips and then smiled mischievously. "There's something else you should know about me."

"Like what?"

"I'm a painter." She smiled as I raised an eyebrow. "*Really*, I am! I'm good at it too."

"A painter?" I kept my hands in her hair, not wanting to let go. "What do you paint? Apples? Bowls? Scenery?"

She kissed me again. "I paint you."

"You paint *what?*"

Anderson laughed and laughed as if she'd been dying to tell me and it gave her pleasure to finally reveal such a secret.

Her eyes examined the contours of my face as her giggles died away. "They look just like you, Danny—right down to the nose and eyebrows. It's amazing..."

I asked, "How did you do it without me being there?"

"Have you ever noticed me sitting on my stool while *supervising* you stock the cages?"

I nodded.

"I was *studying* your beauty. Lusting. Memorizing. Taking mental notes of your complex details. I was sketching you in my mind."

Her fingers traced my lips with the delicacy of a brush stroke.

"I've painted you sitting on the loading dock with your pants rolled up your calves and your head propped against the brick wall behind. Your notepad is in your lap, and your pen is poised, ready to write something down. I finished that one a whole week before I knew that you were writing poems about me.

"I've painted you sweaty and unloading pallets with your muscles bulging from the weight of a heavy box. I've painted you leaning against the twenty-seven cage with a sexy smile while waiting for me to open it."

She gazed deeply into my eyes. "I painted you fucking me. We're doing it on an intricately carved canopy bed in some ancient castle with tall stone walls and a fire blazing in the corner. You're wedged in between my legs. I've got this twisted look of painful pleasure across my face. I painted the balls between your legs and the sweat-soaked muscles of your broad back. The contrast of my pink skin against your milk chocolate is fucking phenomenal. I get wet every time I see it. I have to keep that one in the closet under a tarp."

I kissed her hard. She tried to pull away, but I held on tightly. I dipped my hips and then brought them back up, fucking her from the bottom—fucking her as slowly as silvery sparkles settling in a snow globe.

She whispered, "We're two artists creating with the same heart. How rare is that?"

While staring into her eyes, it dawned on me that she had been attracted to me for as long as I had been attracted to her.

"When did you start?" I asked. "The paintings, I mean."

"I've been painting all my life, but working and responsibility got in the way for a while. It's not easy to become a successful artist. It takes patience, and patience is the one thing I don't have. I guess I got frustrated. Maybe I lost my hunger, I really don't know. I stopped...for whatever reason. I hadn't drawn or painted a thing for three years when I began working here with you."

Steadily I slid in and out of her—fucking her as slowly as a trickle of hot lava bubbling down the crust of a volcano.

"I was inspired the first time I laid eyes on you, Danny. You were so quiet and respectful. You didn't leer at me in creepy ways. You didn't hit on me. You were a man among savages, but I have to admit that your manners began to irk me. I always had this feeling that you wanted me, but you didn't pay me any attention. At first I thought you were playing some game and eventually your true colors would come out. I found myself wanting you to stare at me, or brush against my breast. I wished you would say something dirty and inappropriate, but you never did.

"I drove home every night wondering why you were so reserved and disciplined. I would lay down at night and think about you. I imagined what you were doing, if you had been thinking of me too, and even what you looked like naked.

"There came a point when I was tired of imagining, and I wanted to *see* you. I drew your face first, but of course that wasn't enough. That first drawing was just a gateway drug driving me closer to more dangerous things...sensual things..."

Closing my eyes, I pictured her at an easel. Her fingers were speckled with rainbow colored freckles—each hue: an element depicting lust unsettled.

pinta mi
with her practiced eye she paints me a surprise
red lips across my belly, pink handprints on my thighs
she paints lipstick on my penis
in oh's that make me squeamish
she paints teardrops from my eyes
so that i hurt when she cries
she paints stitches across my heart
where anguish broke it apart
she paints her name over my soul
mated with shades remaining bold
she paints my body with a sensitivity seldom seen
she paints my portrait with love, because true love paints me
pinta mi

"It's become an obsession, Danny. I don't know how to stop it. Most days I can't wait to get home...just to sit before a blank canvas and smear it with your image. It's crazy sometimes." She smiled a little. "Painting you is like foreplay. I'm always in a hurry to finish myself off afterward."

I thought of her restless nights expressing true emotion through art. She'd spent hours alone at her easel constructing pictures of her heart's desire.

We'd been creating together: the misery of infatuation.

She in her world, me in mine: the misery of loneliness.

I wondered if our souls had known all along—if our metaphysical beings had been guardian angles guiding our hands from opposite ends of the same maze so that we could meet and find our true path together: the blessing of fate.

She said, "Sometimes I can't separate the two. When I see you in life, I see your skin in dabs and swirls. When I look at the paintings, I see your flesh..." she let out a long sigh. "My work of you is my very best. Nothing holds a candle to them."

I gripped her hips in my hands, pistoning up and down until my legs cramped and the pain was unbearable, but nothing would stop me. I kept on, glad that she'd happened onto my poems that day—glad, not for the sex, but because I truly loved her.

Anderson latched on, clawing at me. She moaned my name in ecstasy.

We came together.

Afterward, we lay silent. I held her close, still raging hard inside her.

Softly she asked, "Why did you kill your dad, Danny?"

My penis went flaccid and slipped out of her.

I wasn't surprised that she'd asked. I was surprised that she hadn't asked sooner. How could she see so much good within me and not question the obvious evil?

Of course many had asked the same when I was a child. Adults wanted explanations for an act that I didn't even understand. When I failed to tell them what they wanted to hear, they called me crazy.

They wanted to know why I killed him in order to judge me. They did not feel my grief. They did not know about my sleepless nights or the heavy hand weighing down on my heart. They didn't care about my guilt. They cared about the crime, not my father.

So I told them nothing. I didn't fight when I went to court. I took a plea bargain for life without parole. I didn't want their mercy or their judgment. To them I was a murderer—a flaw within their perfect society. I felt that I didn't owe them anything.

But Anderson...I owed her the truth. We couldn't move forward without it.

While combing knots from her hair with my fingers, I told her tales about my famous father and his accomplishments.

And then, I explained his shortcomings. "I grew up believing that my mother died while giving birth to me. That's what he told me. I never had reason to believe otherwise..."

She rolled off of me. We curled into each other, legs and arms entangled beneath the blanket. Her breath was warm and sweet against my lips. I longed to kiss her again, but the time for kissing was over.

"I found out that my mom was alive by accident, really. My father usually beat me home from school, so most days he brought the mail in. For whatever reason, he was late getting home one day. When I pulled the mail out of the box, a few letters fell to the ground. I noticed that one of the letters was for me, and my mother's name was scribbled in above the return address."

Anderson rested her palm against my ear and slid her thumb back and forth over my cheek.

While recounting what happened, I remembered opening the letter with trembling hands. At the time, I didn't know if someone was playing a joke on me or not. I read the letter ten times before it sunk in that my mother had actually written it.

With dry eyes I recanted my mother's apology for abandoning me. "She explained how terrible their marriage had been before she left. She admitted that she was the blame for most of their problems. My father had been more of a father figure to her than a husband, and she'd felt trapped while with him. When she left, she left me with him because she thought that he would be more of a stable parent.

"At the end, she asked if I had received the other letters she'd written over the years, and if I had, why hadn't I written her back?"

Of course I was too young to comprehend the truth. I figured that she must have written to the wrong address, or maybe the mailman had delivered my letters to the wrong house. My imagination came up with millions of excuses for why I had not received her letters.

I never once suspected my father's betrayal.

"I was at the kitchen counter writing my return letter when my father came home. I told him about the letter and that I was writing a response. At first he stared at me with a blank look on his face, as if what I'd said didn't make any sense. Then he snatched the letter I'd been writing and tore it up.

"He was furious, and I couldn't understand why. He called me a mindless twit who had no business checking the mail in the first place. He slammed his fist on the countertop and demanded that I give him the letter she'd written."

I saw compassion in Anderson eyes as she lay listening.

Now that I knew love, I couldn't imagine life without it. The feeling was so deep in me that I didn't want to let it go. In some ways, I felt that I would rather die than lose her.

It didn't matter that I was in prison. It didn't matter that a lonely night awaited us both. Yes, the clock ticked on. Love could not stop the sun from traveling across the sky. We both knew that we would soon separate. She would drive home, and I would be locked in my cage. There was no comfortable way to prepare for that detachment, but even alone—within the confines of my lonely cage—I knew that she loved me, and that was all that mattered.

The affection that we shared helped me understand the mysteries of my past. Why had my father been so upset? Why had he been so hurt? Why had he taken his anger out on me?

Maybe my father had been so attached to my mother that it crushed him when she left. Maybe her departure had been so devastating that he'd tried to make me forget her too.

"I begged him to let me write to her. He refused. When I cried and asked why, he told me that I was too young to understand. He said that I was better off thinking that she was dead—that way I couldn't be hurt by her absence. Then he asked if she'd written about the man she had run off with. He wanted to know if they'd gotten married. He asked why hadn't she shown up on our doorstep instead of sending letters like a coward. He said that she didn't love me—that she'd only written to satisfy her own guilt for leaving, and if I let her back into my life, she would only leave again."

He told me those things to gain an ally in his bitterness. I understood that now, after my time with Anderson—after laying down with and learning about love.

My father had never let my mom go.

He'd loved her until the day he died.

"He was selfish," I said, "He never thought of me. He told me that she was dead and that it was my fault. Even now I wonder how different my life would have been if I had grown up knowing the truth. We wouldn't have argued. We wouldn't have fought. I wouldn't have killed him."

Every muscle in my body was tight and trembling.

Anderson stroked my arm, whispering, "Calm down, Danny. Please calm down."

"No. He should have allowed me to make my own choice. He shouldn't have lied. That's what hurt the most, the lie. He could have said that he was sorry or tried to make it work, like a good father would have done."

Instead, he demanded that I hand over the letter she'd sent. He wanted to see the return address. He wanted to read exactly what she had written about him—*about him*—it had always been about him, never about me.

"The letter was in my back pocket, but I refused to give it to him. He approached me with his hand out. When I didn't give him the letter, he slapped me. He wrapped his hands around my throat and tried to choke me."

I don't remember grabbing the knife. Sometimes it seems as if it had magically appeared in my hand—long and slender with a well-washed wooden handle.

It had never been my intention to hurt him. I had only wanted him to stop attacking me.

"It angered him more to see the knife in my hand. He yelled for me to put it down, but he didn't remove his hands from my throat, so I stabbed him in the belly. I stabbed him again and again until his eyes were wide, and his hands were grabbing at the knife.

"By then, he had let me go, but the action of stabbing him didn't seem real. It wasn't just a reaction to immediate danger, it was some built up rage that I'd never known until then. I never realized how much I hated him until I felt an inkling of power over him. He'd controlled so much of my life...in a crazy way, the knife made us equal."

The blood is what I remember most. There was blood on the floor, on the cabinets, blood on the ceiling...blood on my hands.

"Somehow the knife slipped in my grasp and I cut my own palm. The stinging pain woke me from the trance...it was the reason that I stopped stabbing him."

Heaving for air, I had stood over his limb body as he lay bleeding on the floor. I saw him then for what he truly was—just an old man. Small and frail—powerless. I looked at the rips torn through his clothes, and I realized that he couldn't have hurt me.

"He stared up at me with tears running down his cheeks. He apologized. With his very last breath, he apologized to me for what he'd done...but I never got the chance to apologize to him."

We lay silent for a moment after that. Anderson wiped my tears, kissed my lips, and I was happy that I had finally told someone after all those years.

My voice was hoarse and deep. I said, "I was only thirteen, so they put me in a training school. I was held in solitary confinement until the courts decided to try me as an adult. I plead guilty to first degree murder when I was fifteen years old."

The cage around us was still and quiet. The only sound I heard was Anderson's soothing breath beside me.

"During my first five years in prison, I wrote my mom constantly. I must have sent two hundred letters to the address she'd written from, but I never heard from her. Not once. Maybe my dad had been right about her the whole time. Maybe she never cared for me at all."

Anderson asked, "What about your other family?"

I shrugged. "I don't have any. My dad had two older brothers who died before I was born. I never knew anyone on my mother's side." I took a deep breath. "Sometimes I wish I had killed myself when I killed him."

She cradled my face. "Don't say that, Danny."

"He didn't deserve to die like that. No one does."

"You can't let your guilt destroy you. I know your past hurts, but you can't take it back. It's already done. You're a good man, and you need to move on. Be grateful that you have a heart that helps you to feel when you've been wrong, and get on with your life." She kissed me. "There's always hope."

"Hope? Hope for what?"

"That you'll get out of prison someday."

I thought of old men who had served well over forty years in North Carolina prisons. I knew dozens of them. I thought of the war stories they told: the pretty cars they once drove, their nice clothes, the girls, the music they once loved. Those men had survived on hope. Maybe they even had faith—a dream of strutting through to the good side of some penitentiary gate.

But they never had.

They were still serving life...serving it with me.

I wondered if they still had hope, and why?

"Don't you want to get out, Danny? Don't you want to be with me?"

I thought of those old men. Those bald, toothless, walking with a cane old men who had once been young and vibrant like me. They had hurt someone, and the wasting of their lives was the punishment.

Anderson didn't understand that it wasn't a *want* situation.

I was in prison because I deserved to be there.

She asked, "Do you think they'll ever release you?"

I shook my head. "No. No I don't."

CHAPTER 14

She was the first thing on my mind when I awoke two days later.

No longer was joy an evanescent idea that I had always sensed but never felt. What she brought to my life was a real and tangible sweetness whose robust bouquet was meant to be savored like a dying man's last wish.

When I sat up in bed, I spotted the letter resting on a stubby steel table that was bolted to the wall.

The Letter.

It had arrived yesterday. I stared at it, blinking sleep from my eyes, thinking about what it said and all it meant for my future—our future.

I had not received mail in ten or more years. Amazed that it actually existed, I reached for it to read again:

'Dear Mr. Daniels,

'My name is Herbert Schoenlieber, and I am an attorney with *The Juvenile Justice Group of America*. As you may already know, The U.S. Supreme Court has recently ruled that it is in fact a form of Cruel and Unusual Punishment to sentence a juvenile offender to life without the possibility of parole without considering a lesser sentence.

'Because of your age at the time that you committed your crime, the life sentence that you were serving has been abated. I have taken up your case *pro bono*, and I will represent you in any proceedings following the court's ruling.

'Although your sentence has been removed, you stand convicted of murder, and you will not be released immediately.

'Because of North Carolina's Structured Sentencing laws, we are now awaiting newly formulated sentencing guidelines from the state legislature; however, with the amount of time that you have already served, I hope to see you released by this time next year.

'I will contact you as needed. Feel free to write about any...'

I sighed while staring at the words—not reading them, just staring. So many things shuttled in and out of my mind. The thoughts that didn't center on Anderson drifted toward the outside world that I'd lost sight of long ago.

As a lifer, I found it better to forget the outside—to be immersed in everything *behind* the walls, so that what went on *beyond* them wasn't an affliction. No matter how violent or oppressive life was on the inside, a man's infatuating thoughts of the world could be much worse on the sanity.

My time was easier to handle than most lifers'. I had no ties binding me to the free world. I had no wife, kids, or family to be concerned about. No one depended on me. I rose each morning ignoring shadows of the past. For those same reasons, I had never planned on a bright future.

I'd accepted my fate.

Buddhists strive for *Nirvana*. Christians, *Heaven*. Muslims, *Paradise*. Students study for degrees. Entrepreneurs seek wealth. Entertainers strive for superstardom. There is a goal to be reached in every ideal known to mankind; an end to one's suffering on earth; some promise of glory motivating its faithful practitioners to fight through the struggles they face. For most convicts, that goal is release and the opportunity to begin with a clean slate.

Not for the lifer.

There is not much difference between the lifer and the death row inmate. The recompense for our past deed is death. The reward for positive changes made in our lives is death.

Death.

Death.

DEATH!

Death was what I'd been looking forward to for fifteen years. I had no faith. No hope. I'd never thought about a job or family or car insurance or equity. I'd only thought of dying in prison.

How do I suddenly change that frame of mind?

I sat on the edge of my bed hanging my head. I didn't know what fate awaited me in the outside world, nor how to prepare for it.

As more and more questions arose, my peace traveled to Anderson. I had not told her about the letter, but I was sure that she would know what to do. I needed to talk to her. I needed her guidance.

I needed her.

After climbing out of bed, I began my morning routine of showering, shaving my head, and getting dressed.

Breakfast was cold scrambled eggs and soggy toast. After forcing down enough to survive on, I went to work.

While entering the warehouse, I ran my fingers across my back pocket to make sure the letter was still there. Goosebumps dotted my skin as I neared the open office door.

She wasn't there.

Sergeant Thompson sat at his computer with his reading glasses on. Upon spotting me in the doorway, he stopped what he'd been doing. Lines of worry creased his forehead. His lips were a pencil line of frustration. He looked at me as if the sky was falling and the biggest piece was on a course for my head.

He gestured toward Anderson's chair. "Sit down, Danny."

I tried to read his eyes, but they gave no clue as to the nature of what he had to say. My heart beat triple time. The first person that I thought of was Critter. I imagined him blabbing about what he'd seen Anderson and I doing, and I wanted to kill him.

Gritting my teeth, I told Sarge, "I'm good standing."

After removing his glasses, he let out a long sigh. "We got a new officer working in the warehouse with us."

My heart dropped to the pit of my belly. "W-what happened to Anderson?"

"Nothing. She's in the back showing him around. She's going to be training him for the next couple of weeks."

For a moment I breathed easier knowing she was safe.

But then, I remembered the precious hours Anderson and I had spent swaddled beneath a warm blanket in the twelve-cage.

An extra set of eyes meant that the comfort we had was gone.

Fingering the letter in my back pocket, I knew that I would soon be free, and we would have the opportunity to love each other openly. Realizing this gave me confidence and hope for a beautiful future.

Shrugging, I leaned against the door's frame. "So what? That means we'll have more hands to help."

Sarge shook his head. "You don't understand. It's Maloney. His suspension ended yesterday. Warden Shelly *personally* assigned him up here with us."

I felt a tightness in my throat where Maloney had wedged his forearm into it. My lungs struggled for air as I recalled the murderous look in his eyes as he'd raised his baton to strike me.

"Why did Warden Shelly do that? He was in the all-purpose room too. He saw the man assault me."

"It don't make a damned bit of sense. I called him, and he said that since you didn't file a written complaint against Maloney, then you must not have a problem working with him. Maloney has been in a lot of shit with inmates, and putting him up here is a way to keep him out of the dorms where he would really do something stupid."

Damn. It was my own fault. I should have spoken up for myself when I'd had the chance. Now it was coming back to haunt me. *Damn.*

Sarge said, "I'm going to speak with Warden Shelly again to see if we can't get this fixed. It may take some time, but bear with me. You're the best worker I've ever had, and I don't intend on letting anything happen to you. To be honest, I don't think we should be stuck with the asshole neither. They oughta fire his dumb ass..."

"Fire who?" Maloney asked from behind me.

I spun around and stumbled into the office.

Maloney was just as huge and menacing as I remembered him to be. The scowl on his face bragged that he'd heard all we'd said about him and he didn't care one bit.

Anderson stood sheepishly behind him.

For a moment we all paused in the uncomfortable silence.

Finally, Maloney smiled at me. "Don't I know you from somewhere?"

CHAPTER 15

Maloney told his friends, "I was a Gunnery Sergeant with MEF when I served in the Corps."

One of the other officers asked him what MEF meant.

Maloney puffed up his broad chest to say, "I was with the 2nd *Marine Expeditionary Force*. He then peered into the eyes of those surrounding him. Their silence said that no one had a clue as to what he was talking about. He explained, "In Iraq we ran support for large missions. We were the jack-of-all-trades unit. We were called in on smash and grabs, recon, hostage extractions. We did it all, and we did it well. We were usually sent in to open doors where there were no doors before. If we entered a combat zone at midnight, we lit the night sky like a showdown at high noon. For us, every day was the Fourth of July--- fucking bombs and bullets flying everywhere."

I glanced at the out-of-shape c/o's listening to Maloney with wonder in their eyes. They sat in a half-circle on plastic lawn chairs while eating their lunches, hanging on his every word, immortalizing him.

"We were based at Camp Lejeune in Jacksonville before nine-eleven. My unit was one of the first called to duty. Most of us had been training for years but we'd never seen any action, so we were all gung-ho and eager to go to war. We thought we were so ready, you know, but protocol can't prepare you for the atrocities of combat. Death has a way of changing you..." Maloney smiled a bit. "In basic, I had a drill instructor who'd been to Vietnam. He was this old fart who was on his last leg of retirement. We always laughed at him because he used to say kooky things that never made any sense. One of the things he said was: '*Only battle can prepare you for battle*.' But those words stick with me even today, because I never knew how right he was until I saw so many of our own killed in action."

Maloney went silent. No one else spoke. Within that hush I heard the legs of a plastic chair scrape against the concrete floor. Someone gulped a drink. Another officer cleared his throat.

He said, "We were sent into Fallujah two months into my second deployment."

By observing Maloney from a distance, I had learned a lot about him in the week following his arrival to the warehouse. I studied him like the zoologist studying a wild animal in his natural element. If he was a ticking time bomb, then I wanted to predict the moment before he exploded so that I could take cover.

I noticed that his green eyes were sometimes vacant—he had a tendency to stare off into space—but when a person held his undivided attention, his gaze delved beyond their outward appearance in search of something deeper. He looked through people as if he trusted no one and each new person that he encountered was a potential enemy waiting to do him harm.

Among his peers Maloney was an alpha-male who exuded confidence in all that he did. He walked taller than most with his gait rolling stiff and strong shoulders. Despite his basic rank of officer, he spoke with an air of authority, every word drenched in resemblance of a barked command.

Though callous, Maloney's co-workers flocked to him. He was the brute they all feared and respected. Once word spread that he was working in the warehouse, C/O's from all over the prison came to pay homage. Our workplace was no longer a quiet rabbit hole hidden within the jungle of a wild prison. His presence made it a town square where groupies came to fellowship with their idol.

On his first day, two officers showed up to eat lunch with him. Three came the next day. Four arrived the day after that. Sarge's office was much too small for them to squeeze inside, so they set up a semi-circle of chairs twenty-feet from the open bay door where I sat on my bucket.

He told them, "We were leading a convoy hauling supplies to a make-shift base just inside the city. What I remember most about Iraq was the heat. It was always so fucking hot. The sand got in your boots and eyes, but the heat was murderous. You couldn't hide from it. We toted eighty-pound rucksacks in one-hundred-and-fifteen degree weather sometimes. People look at me funny when I talk about the heat. Most people think that violence is the worst a soldier faces in war, but a lot of times it's the conditions. The violence was sporadic. We might go one, two weeks without an engagement. The heat though...the heat was constant."

I sat on my bucket at an angle, not facing the officers, but so that I could see everyone clearly if I cut my eyes in their direction.

In my lap I held a pen and a brand new notepad. On the first page I had scribbled: *scattered pads of green. does ink chronicle her dreams? is her soul like mine? a voyeur of our time...*

I wrote absentmindedly while listening.

Over with the officers, Maloney sat center stage. While the others dipped their hands into clear, plastic lunch bags he ate nothing at all. Occasionally he sipped from a bottle of water, but mainly he told stories as they ate and listened. At times someone else would join in, talking about cars or hunting or something funny that their kids did. They always spoke of things outside of the prison where they worked, never about Broutal or the inmates they watched over. It's like they wanted to forget where they were, and they were enraptured in Maloney's stories because his exploits took them as far away as possible.

"Fallujah," he muttered, staring off into space, lost in thought.

"Some of our troops had been there for a week or more." His eyes were downcast, focused on the concrete floor. He didn't seem to be telling a story. He spoke as if he was only describing sporadic memories that crossed his mind in no particular order. "We got there in the thick of it. Some pencil-dicked commander underestimated the insurgent's strength, so the few units before us had went in unprepared for the bloodbath that had them in over their heads.

"My unit wasn't on a combat mission at the time, we were armed escorts. Our orders were to drop the supplies and hightail it back to base, but somehow we overshot the rendezvous point. By the time we realized that we were lost, we were so deep into Fallujah that it was too late to turn back.

"I rode shotgun in the third Humvee from the front of the convoy. Staff Sergeant Romlin was driving. Corporal Johnson was in the back yapping on the Sat-Phone while trying to figure out where we were on the GPS. I had Lance Corporal Sucier on top of the truck, manning the fifty-cal in case things got hot and heavy."

Of the three men besides Maloney, I only knew Officer Rynhold— Anderson's constant admirer. I suspected that he had come to the warehouse seeking her attention, not Maloney's.

Pender, an obese white guy, ate a turkey on rye to Maloney's left.

Jenkins, another white c/o, nibbled pepperoni pizza to Maloney's right.

Anderson sat outside of their circle munching carrot sticks, staring at me.

I was an island to myself, listening and learning.

Before biting into his sandwich, Pender asked Maloney, "How long did you serve?"

"Sixteen years," he replied. "It took me nine to rank-out at Gunny."

Anderson's eyes were all over me. She bit a corner of her bottom lip. I almost lost my mind wishing that it was my teeth sinking into her flesh. Feeling the black beast stiffen awake inside my boxer shorts, I turned away and gazed through the open bay door where I watched a hawk swoop down to snatch a pigeon right out of the air.

Maloney's hoarse baritone droned on. "The fucking camel toes were everywhere inside of the city. They lined the streets like rats at a garbage dump. The whole place was war ravaged. I saw signs of heavy fighting on every building. Cars were shot up, storefronts burnt out, and there were huge gashes on the sides of homes where mortar shells had punched through.

"It was hard to believe that people actually lived there. The saddest part was the kids—kids everywhere you turned. They ran beside our Humvees in bare feet and rags begging for money or candy or anything that you had to give them. Little girls offered themselves for marriage in order to escape that godforsaken place.

"Most of the Iraqis hated us. You could see it in their eyes. They wished death upon us as we rode by. They didn't understand that it wasn't our fault we were there. We had a job to do. But that didn't stop them from looking at us as if we were Satan in the flesh.

"While riding through the city I told Lance Corporal Sucier to keep his eyes peeled and let loose with the fifty-cal if he had to."

Rynhold was stunned. "What if he'd killed an innocent bystander?"

Maloney shook his head. "Nobody's innocent in war, especially not over there. All they know is war. They offer Morning Prayer to the cadence of bombs bursting overhead. Their children learn to shoot before they can read or write."

Pender said, "You make it seem like they deserved to die."

Maloney shrugged. "They aren't like us. We are diplomatic. We would rather negotiate than go to war—that's what I mean. I've been there, you haven't. You're looking at it through the eyes of a civilian. Ask yourself this: *How do you reason with somebody who thinks he'll go to heaven if he kills himself, and you too?*" He waited for someone to reply. When his question was met with silence, he answered it himself. "You don't reason with a terrorist. You kill him."

Jenkins asked, "I saw a story on the news where the troops spoke to community leaders about alternatives to…"

"That's bullshit!" Maloney stated. "That's for the cameras. Soldiers aren't politicians, if we were, they would have taught us to write instead of to shoot. Politics don't matter on the battlefield, just your brothers beside you. My job was to carry out orders and get home in one piece. Nothing else. If they weren't wearing rank or camo, they were a target. You never knew who had the boom-boom. Was it the kid kicking a can down the street? How about granny whose burka was too bulky in front? The enemy was everywhere. If you let the wrong one get too close, you wouldn't get a second chance to try it again."

My gaze fell on Anderson. She was staring at me, waiting to capture my attention, fucking me with her eyes. She smiled when I looked and then turned away, teasing me. I watched her awhile longer, letting my lust slither over her thick thighs and on up to her deep brown eyes. It was a chore to peel my sight away, but I had to. Maloney was no fool. To broadcast our affection in front of him would be our undoing.

She and I hadn't been alone since his arrival, and it was wearing down on us. Anderson had been training him for his warehouse duties, and he was her constant shadow.

I had been forced to carry the letter for days while waiting for a chance to tell her the good news. So far that opportunity had not come.

I glanced over at Maloney. He had the other officers captivated with his war story. "Lance Corporal Sucier spotted the asshole even before the gunner in the first vehicle—that's how good my guys were. He gave a shout down to us, and I saw a towel-head crouching behind the crumbled corner of a brick wall. There was no sure way to read his intentions, but as we neared him, the look in his eyes told me that something wasn't right. I saw a cell phone in his hand, so I gave the command to stop the convoy as I raised my rifle scope…"

Anderson gasped. "You were going to kill him for having a cell phone?"

Maloney grunted. "I would've killed him for less than that. On an American city street a man with a cell phone is no big deal. Not in Iraq. Cell phones are used to detonate *Improvised Explosive Devices*. For all I knew, the whole street could have been lined with roadside bombs. What looked like a regular guy with a phone could have been the next bin Laden."

She rolled her eyes. "Sounds like you were just paranoid to me."

Maloney narrowed his eyes toward her. "If you ever go to war you'll see how paranoia can be your best friend. Only fools wait for an enemy to show himself. I knew plenty of honorable soldiers who went to war with godly morals, and they died ungodly deaths. Maybe I'm wrong for wanting to take the first shot, but at least I'm here talking to you...and my enemies are not."

Years ago I'd read an interview with Charles Manson, the mastermind behind a forty-year-old slaughter. When asked if he considered himself a paranoid schizophrenic, he'd replied: *Paranoia is a heightened state of awareness*. Thinking about that, I recalled flashes of fights I'd been in and how the feeling of absolute terror kept me ducking and dodging blows while swinging my own fists with everything that I had. I too knew the voice of paranoia, and because of that I identified with Maloney's logic. His stories of war sounded a lot like doing time. Inmates and soldiers alike faced life or death situations. A person's perception of what is going to happen before it does determines whether they will survive an altercation or not.

Maloney's experience overseas said a lot about his no nonsense character. I didn't agree with his personality, but listening to him speak helped me to understand him better.

He said, "To be honest it didn't matter if he turned out to be the bomber or not. *Someone* detonated an IED at the front of our convoy. I'd been right to order a halt of the trucks. The lead Humvee did a back flip and pancaked the vehicle directly behind it. Staff Sergeant Romlin hit the brakes and fishtailed us to a stop inches before we would have smashed into them both."

Everyone sat on the edge of their seat, silent and listening.

Maloney kept the same even tone of voice, never shouting or lowering it, never exhibiting the intense emotions that he must have felt while reliving such a violent ordeal. "All hell broke loose. AK's, M-16's, and M-60's barked all around. Tear gas canisters hissed by and exploded a few feet away from us. People shouted in English and Arabic. The wrecked Humvees in front of us billowed black smoke so thick that I couldn't have counted my cock and balls if I'd wanted to. Even though my ears were ringing I heard Sucier up top leaning on his fifty-cal, firing at any and everything breathing.

"I opened my door and bailed out with the rest of my team. We were taught to keep moving in a firefight, so that's what we did. Sitting in the Humvee was like painting a bulls eye on my head.

"So many camel-toes were running around that I didn't know who to aim at. I just started shooting. I plugged anybody coming my way who wasn't wearing camo—*anybody*.

"I looked around for cover, but the nearest building was fifty yards away, and I didn't want to leave my team. All was clear toward the back of the convoy, or as far as I could see. I was confident that no other IED's had been detonated at that point, but the whole damned city could've been booby trapped. Fucking terrorists will kill two-thousand of their own just to get one of us, you know what I mean? Luckily, other teams had boots on the ground running to help out, so I felt a little safer knowing that we weren't alone."

Maloney stopped talking. He stared down at the concrete floor, leaving us all in suspense. He cleared his throat. "I heard someone screaming for help inside the stacked Humvees. The vehicles were on fire and burning badly. I smelled smoldering flesh mixed with the stench of burnt oil and burning rubber. A combat medic from another team was over there trying to yank open one of the truck's doors. I froze at first, but I wouldn't have been able to live with myself if I sat there and watched them die. I kept thinking: *What if it was you in there? Wouldn't you want help? What if it was you?* Bullets whizzed past my head as I low-crawled toward the Humvees to help."

A telephone rang down the hall. In the office, Sarge picked up on the second ring. Two seconds later he was hollering Anderson's name. I spied her from the corner of my eye as she stood. My mouth watered at the sway of her hips as she walked down the hall.

Maloney went on. "I heard a faint whistle as I neared the burning Humvees. I saw the *Rocket Propelled Grenade* fly before my eyes like a football or a shooting star, but it was too late to react. I don't even remember the blast. I only saw a flash of bright light before passing out." He paused to sip his water.

Next, he turned his back to his audience and ran his finger up and down a long scar at the back of his head. "The RPG blew a chunk of shrapnel that's a little bigger than a two-twenty-three round through my helmet and skull. It was like being shot at point-blank-range. The doctors were surprised that I survived. They said the shard went so deep in that I should have been killed instantly."

Rynhold eyed him quizzically. "Did they take it out?"

"Nah. They were afraid I wouldn't survive the operation, so they left it in." Maloney knocked against his skull. "Right under this titanium plate."

Pender finished his sandwich. "Will it ever come out?"

Maloney shook his head. "Probably not. They'll try to take it out if it moves closer to my skull, but it's sunk a millimeter deeper into the center of my brain since I've been stateside. I'm really not pressed about it. I've only had one bad experience so far. I had the worse migraine of my life on the night that I received my Purple Heart. I was in my hotel room throwing up, and my nose wouldn't stop bleeding. It felt like someone was trying to cut my head in half with a dull hacksaw. I thought I was going to die that night, but I made it to the ceremony, and everything was fine after it. I have trouble with airport security sometimes. Other than that, I forget it's even in my head."

"That's gotta be dangerous, working in a prison," Jenkins added. "What if you fall while breaking up a fight or..."

Maloney brushed that off. "People get killed every day. It's not even safe to go to the movies or a marathon anymore. I'm not going to walk around with a foam helmet on my head. I'll go when it's my time to go. Besides, doctors aren't always right. They said that I shouldn't have lived in the first place, so what do they know?"

I tried to imagine a war-torn city street with stubby buildings powdered in layers of dust and soot. I tried to summon sounds of gunfire and the screams of people in distress, but the more that I tried to envision the violence and their suffering, the less I liked the idea of it.

"Danny!" Anderson wiggled the huge ring of keys in my face. "Come on," she whispered. "Grab a flatbed cart. We have to assemble an order for the gym." She peeked over her shoulder toward Maloney and his lame crew. A mask of mischief veiled her face when she turned back and jabbed me in the ribs. "Get your ass up before lunch is over. I'll be in the back."

Trying not to appear anxious, I stood slowly. None of the officers paid me any attention as I retrieved a cart from its parking spot against a wall.

She was waiting inside the twenty-nine cage, leaning against a shelf with her lips sparkling and chest heaving. I ran to her. I held her close as our lips crushed.

I don't know how long we kissed but when we finally broke away I was panting, hard as concrete, and ready for more.

Her hand snaked between my legs where she stroked me through my pants.

"Stop!" I whispered, wanting to push her away but not resisting when she open my fly and stuffed her hand inside.

While nibbling my lips, she said, "All I need is two minutes."

I leaned against a shelf, eyes rolling in their sockets from the sweet sensation of her hot, kneading hand. "Two minutes?" I managed to ask. "What can you do in two minutes?"

"Whatever you'll let me do."

She kissed me again. My eyes closed as our tongues went to work. I hated myself for being in prison—for not being able to give her the complete love that she deserved.

I pushed her away.

She held on, but I kept her at bay.

"We don't have time."

"We can make time, Danny." She weaseled her way back into my embrace, peppering kisses all over my face. "I've missed you so much. I hate the way things are now. Sometimes I'm afraid to look at you in front of him for the fear of what he'll think." She kissed me again. When we broke, she asked, "Don't you want me?"

"Of course I do. Why would you ask me something like that?"

"Do you lust for me when you're in your cell? Do you remember the way my body felt? Do you love me, Danny? Truly love me?"

My eyes bore into hers. "You're the only woman I will ever love."

We kissed again, but not for long. If we were caught we wouldn't be able to see each other ever again. I would rather admire her from a distance than risk the trouble of someone catching us in the act.

I handed her the letter I'd been toting around.

Crinkling her brows, she took it. "What's this? A poem?"

"A surprise," I said.

I began filling the order by stacking boxes on the cart I'd left in the hallway as she read. My back was to her when she squealed in delight.

"This is great news!" She ran over and wrapped her arms around my neck. "You could be out in less than a year! This is unbelievable!" I pushed her away, and this time she let me. "I was online searching for lawyers all night long. The cheapest fee that I found was twenty-five thousand, and that was just to get her to start working on your case. I had no idea it would be so expensive."

"You don't have to worry about that anymore." I said, stroking her cheek with my finger.Her eyes were aglow with joy. "It's real, isn't it? This letter...the possibility of you getting out?" When I nodded, she said, "Oh my god. I have so much to do. You'll need clothes and maybe a car. You'll need your birth certificate and social security card..."

"You would do all that for me?"

She punched a fist to her hip. "Who else do you have, Danny?"

I pulled her close for one last kiss. I held her long enough to make up for lost time and to cover the emptiness of our future yet to come. I kissed her in thanks for her heart and virtue. I kissed her for eternal love.

After, I finished loading the cart. We hurried back to the main foyer so the others wouldn't suspect our lengthy absence.

As we turned the corner, I saw that Maloney and his cronies had Critter surrounded.

"Leave me 'lone!" He shouted. His flaming red hair whipped this way and that as he tried to keep eyes on his tormentors like a fox boxed in by bobcats. "I came up here to see Danny!"

Laughing, Pender shoved him into Maloney who kicked him in the ass and sent him sailing toward Jenkins. Critter tried to run past him, but Jenkins wrapped him up in a tight choke hold. Maloney stormed over and twisted his fingers in the front of Critter's tee shirt.

I balled my fists and started their way.

Anderson blocked my path. "No, Danny!"

The fear in her eyes was real. "Someone has to stop him," I said.

"They'll lock you up!"

The implication was clear: if I intervened, I would be putting our relationship at risk. I thought about the letter and the future we could have if I got out of prison.

But something had to be done.

"I don't care," I told her. "What they're doing isn't right."

She nodded. "Well then...let me stop him. They can't do anything to me."

Holding Critter by his shirt, Maloney asked him, "Who gave you permission to come in here? Didn't you read the sign on the door stating: *Authorized Personnel Only?*"

Critter clawed at Maloney's hands. "I 'ont need no damned puh-mission'! I come up here when I git good and damn ready to! And I cain't git in no trouble long as ain't no truck comin' today!"

"Oh you're in trouble," Maloney told him with a smile. "I'm gonna..."

Critter bit down on Maloney's hand until blood dribbled out from the corner of his mouth.

Maloney let out a scream. He cocked back and pounded his fist into the side of critter's head.

Anderson ran over shouting, "Leave him alone!" Just as Maloney hit Critter once more, knocking him to the floor.

It was hard to stand there and watch. Adrenaline was a train running through my veins, yet I kept my distance, waiting for a chance to pull Critter out of harm's way.

Maloney sucked on one bitten hand and whipped out his baton with the other. He pointed to Critter with the tip of his weapon. "I'm going to kill you!"

Critter hopped up with his fists raised. "Not if I kill you first!"

Maloney advanced on him.

Anderson wedged herself between them. Shielding Critter behind her, she pointed at Maloney. "You won't lay another hand on him!"

Maloney tried to shuffle around her. "Move out of my way!"

"No!"

"I'll go through you if I have to."

She met his wild eyes defiantly. "What are you waiting for?"

They stared each other down. Maloney glared at Anderson as if he was seeing her for the first time—truly seeing her.

The other c/o's snickered like a man's life wasn't in danger. Glancing at them, I wondered what would have happened if Anderson had not been there to stop it.

"He bit me!" Maloney declared. "That's an A-charge, assault on an officer! He's going to do a year on lock-up for that!"

She shook her head. "He was defending himself against you."

Maloney lowered the baton to his side. "I'm the law in here. He can't defend himself against me."

Anderson asked him, "What do you call it?"

"I was doing my job. He entered an unauthorized area, and I was escorting him out when he bit me."

"That's a damn lie, Maloney." She gazed pitifully at the other officers. "Maybe the men here are too afraid of you to say something, but I'm not. You were wrong."

Critter broke free of her and pointed at Maloney. "I told yo' dumb ass that I's 'llowed up here! You backwood sum-bitch! You lucky she got a hold to me when she did, or I'da beat yo' cracka-ass cockeyed and knock-kneed!"

"Shut up, Critter!" She told him.

"Fuck him," he went on. "He ain't even good white folks! Actin' a damn fool front of his buddies! If we'd was alone..."

"Critter!" She pushed him into me.

Snatching him by the shoulders, I pulled him toward the exit.

I heard Maloney tell Anderson, "You'll regret this."

She replied, "No. I won't regret doing what's right."

He said, "You're playing for the wrong team."

"Maloney, this isn't a war, and it's not a game either. I took an oath to protect and serve, not to abuse."

"We're here to keep order at all costs," he said. "I signed on as a corrections officer, not a humanitarian."

Anderson sighed. "Do you need to be a humanitarian to know that we are all human?"

I hauled Critter to the front door and told him to never come back.

CHAPTER 16

Anderson and I dropped off the delivery to the gym. While heading back to work I kept my eyes open for Critter. Not one to let things go easily, I knew that he would still be fuming over his confrontation with Maloney. I hoped he wouldn't do something stupid.

Pulling the empty cart behind me, I fell in step beside Anderson. We needed to talk about what happened earlier, but we couldn't because other inmates were traveling the Six-tunnel with us. I kept quiet while they were in earshot.

The group of convicts followed us into *The* Center and around its circular path until she and I entered the Four-tunnel alone.

With the long corridor to ourselves, she slowed our walking pace and turned to me. "I hate working with him, Danny. He's too edgy—too unpredictable."

"You're an officer," I reminded her. "He can't do anything to you. Don't worry about it."

She stopped dead in her tracks. "It's not me that I'm worried about. He's started shit with you before…"

"That's why I've been avoiding him." I butted in.

"I know you have, but I hate thinking about what could happen on a day that I'm not working. You would have no way to reach me, and I wouldn't be able to protect you."

The concern in her eyes had me speechless.

"I don't want anything to happen to you, Danny."

I began to reply when two c/o's and a sergeant entered the Four-tunnel from the opposite end. We resumed our walk back to work in silence.

Once inside the warehouse, Anderson went into the office where Sarge and Maloney sat talking. I headed to the back.

It was dark outside on the loading dock—strangely dark for a summer afternoon. I sat on my bucket and propped my head against the brick wall, staring upward. Dense clouds blanketed the vast sky for as far as I could see. Cool winds raised hair on my forearms. Soon we would be overcome by a thunderstorm—a storm, or something much worse.

Lightning struck far off but never touched the ground. Instead, its fiery fingers cradled the charcoal underbelly of the clouds like an electrified hand holding them up.

Maloney stepped beside me as thunder rolled across the land.

I didn't look at him. I kept my eyes to the sky.

When he spoke, his tone was calm and disarming. "Looks like hurricane season is here early, huh?" Maloney rocked on his heels with his hands stuffed in his pockets. "We don't get hurricanes in Montana— too far inland. We get twisters though, and they can be just as bad." He looked down on me. "That's where I was raised. Montana."

I didn't know what he wanted with me, though I suspected the worst. I'd never heard of a predator stalking his prey with good intentions.

He told me, "Sarge said that I should apologize for what happened earlier with your friend. Anderson ratted me out right in front of my face. She wouldn't let it go until Sarge said that he would write me up if I didn't apologize. You just tell him that I did, if he asks."

I didn't respond. I recalled his fist twisted in the front of Critter's tee shirt. While cringing from that, I remembered that he had done something similar to me.

"Do you hear me talking to you?" He waved his hand in my face. When I continued to ignore him, he said, "I get it. You want me to think you're crazy so that I'll leave you alone, but I don't think you're crazy. I think you're scared."

Despite what he'd said, I felt that my calm bothered him. He wanted a reaction from me and the fact that I wouldn't give him one only fueled his anger.

His eyes searched the ground around me. After spotting Critter's bucket, he picked it up and looked to see if anything was inside.

Satisfied that I wasn't hiding any contraband, he set the bucket down. "How come you don't talk?" He asked. "The other blacks are loud and ignorant. They can't get a sentence out without yelling. Why do you think you're better than them?"

Still I didn't speak. It didn't matter what he said. I had more to think about than myself. I had Anderson. Her love was the solution to all my problems.

His foot struck out and kicked the bucket from beneath me. There was no time to save myself. I fell flat on the concrete, staring up at him through bulging eyes.

Lightning lit the dark sky behind him. "I bet you'll talk now, huh?" He inched closer, crouched with his fists raised. "Get up!" He snarled. "Nobody can save you this time. It's just you and me. Now get up and fight me!"

The wind picked up as sounds of pattering rain approached.

I stayed quiet, unmoving on the ground.

"Scared, huh?" He smiled a bit. "Just like I thought. You assholes strut around here like you're tough because you've killed someone, but you aren't tough. You're a bunch of bitches."

Fear driven adrenaline bum-rushed my veins.

I could beat him.

I had dominated bigger men, meaner, more hateful. I had beat two and three at a time. I could beat him so badly that he wouldn't have the life left to beg me to stop.

Yet I did not rise to face his anger with my own. I kept my place on the ground—beneath him—because that would keep the peace. I gave him victory at the expense of my own pride.

As the first drops of fat rain splattered the concrete around us, Anderson stepped out on the loading dock. "Danny? What happened? How did you end up on the..." She tossed an accusatory glare toward Maloney.

"I fell," I blurted, hopping to my feet. "I sat down too fast and lost my footing. It's no big deal."

She didn't believe me. Her eyes searched mine for the intention behind the lie, but I turned away from her, hoping that she would let it go.

After shrugging it off, she said, "We have another order to fill. So Danny, would you grab a cart and go with me to the nineteen-cage?"

As I walked away, Maloney and Anderson remained on the loading dock. She pointed at his chest and whispered a threat that I couldn't hear. Maloney laughed as she turned her back to him.

She and I headed toward the cages. I noticed Maloney following us. Anderson saw him too, and the hatred in her eyes turned my stomach.

She opened the nineteen-cage. I went in and began stocking the cart as quickly as I could. For a while the only sounds I heard were my own boots stomping the floor and the thud of boxes as I piled them on the cart.

Maloney leaned against the wall out in the hall, watching.

Anderson wasn't herself. She couldn't be still. She leaned to one side and crossed her arms, then uncrossed them. She gave the impression that she was supervising me, but her attention was on him the entire time.

She asked Maloney, "What the fuck is your problem?"

He shrugged. "I don't have a problem."

"Obviously you do. You're staring at me like I'm doing something wrong."

Maloney smiled. "Maybe you are—you and your boyfriend over there."

"Boy friend?" She asked. "What are you talking about?"

"You and Daniels."

A boulder settled in the hollow of my belly. My knees quivered beneath me. It took all that I had to keep moving—to keep working.

Maloney said, "I see the way you two look at each other. It makes me wonder how close you guys were before I showed up."

"You've got to be kidding me," she replied, but even I heard the fear in her denial. He'd taken the fight out of her with one accusation.

"No. I'm not kidding. I can only imagine how much time you two had alone together. Seems like it would be easy to carry on a sexual relationship between…"

"You're crazy!" She glanced at me. Her stare was like that of a deer catching the scent of a wolf, a bear, a mountain lion—some vicious carnivore on the prowl. "Me and Danny?" she turned back to him. "You can't prove that." Her chest heaved with each inhalation. "You can't possibly prove that."

He pushed off of the wall and stepped to the mouth of the cage. "I don't have to prove it. All I have to do is report it. Either he'll go to the hole for the duration of the investigation, or you'll be transferred to another unit. You two will be split up regardless. You'll probably never see each other again."

I wished that she wouldn't reply. He didn't know the truth. He was only fishing for a reaction from her, hoping that she would give him what he wanted: evidence. I hoped that she wouldn't let her emotions take control and feed into it by going on the defensive.

Please ignore him. Please.

"Why would you do that? You son-of-a-bitch." She said. "We haven't done anything to you."

Maloney began to reply, but he was interrupted by Sergeant Thompson who cleared his throat behind him. Sarge asked, "What in the world are you two talking about?" When no one replied, he said, "Quiet as two babes with teets 'tween their gums, huh? As soon as I leave you two will be at each other's throats again, right?" Sarge looked to me. "Danny, do you want to tell me what's going on back here?" I kept on stacking boxes. Sarge just shook his head. "Well, whatever y'all were fussing about can wait. We've got bigger fish to fry. There's a hurricane comin' to town, and the warden has ordered all first shift staff to remain on post past shift change."

Both Maloney and Anderson grumbled to hear the news. Sarge went on. "That don't mean we'll be staying the night—not yet anyhow. For now, I need one of you to go and help out in the operations building. They've got a list of contingencies to meet, and they're asking for extra hands."

"I'll go," Anderson said, tossing Maloney a sideways glance.

Sarge shook his head. "No. I need you here. You and Danny need to load up flashlights and batteries, then deliver them to the housing units. After that you'll stay up here on standby for emergencies. I need someone up here who knows the lay of the land so that I can get the supplies we may need as fast as possible."

Incredulous, Maloney complained, "You're going to leave her alone with him?"

Sarge wheeled on him. "Why the hell not? Ain't nobody had a problem with it until you showed up. Now, no one can rest easy. You pick on the inmates. You bully staff. You ain't been up here a hot two weeks and you're trying to tell me what to do." Maloney stared with his mouth wide open. Sarge continued, "I used to tell my young 'uns that you're born with two ears and one mouth, so you should listen twice as much as you speak. That lesson would serve you well, because you talk too damn much. Now come on with me. Captain Walker is waiting for you in the operations building."

Anderson suppressed a smile.

Sarge turned to walk away. After taking a few strides he turned back to see Maloney still standing in the same spot. Like an owner to his dog, Sarge clucked his tongue twice and commanded, "Git here, boy! Don't make me have to tell you again."

This time Maloney followed him.

Anderson and I locked eyes, snickering together. I felt safer thinking that Sarge was on our side. If Maloney did report his suspicions about us, maybe Sergeant Thompson's word would carry some weight in our favor.

After removing the boxes that I'd stacked on the cart before, I began loading up heavy boxes of C-batteries and flashlights. Anderson left me for a while to make a phone call in the office.

Ten minutes later, as I was reaching up high for a case of batteries, I felt her breasts against my back and her hands on my chest.

I sat the box on the floor and turned into her embrace. "They're gone," she whispered before kissing me deeply. "Sarge went to the warden's office, and Maloney is heading to the operations building. No one will be back for a few hours."

My erection was so hard that it hurt. Flashbacks of our love making crossed my mind. I remembered the feeling of being buried deep within her. I had new fantasies of ripping down her pants and bending her over…

"He's on to us," I panted into her open mouth.

"He's guessing," she said. "He can't prove it if he doesn't catch us."

"So we need to slow down," I said, still kissing her. "Maybe we should take a break."

"Mm-hm. A break."

Everything inside of me screamed *STOP! This is crazy!* But we didn't stop. I kissed her lips, her chin, and her throat. The slow seconds we spent suckling each other slipped by like snails sliding across a salty surface.

She didn't resist when I finally pulled away.

"We can't be careless. I don't want to be without you."

"I know, Danny. *I hate this*. It doesn't seem fair. Why is what we're doing so wrong?" She took my hands in hers. "Sometimes I want the whole world to know how much I love you, and I don't care what they think. Love isn't supposed to be bottled up and hidden. You make me feel beautiful inside when everything else in my life is ugly."

I wrapped her in my arms.

I closed my eyes with the gentle sway of our bodies.

My eyes didn't open again until Maloney shouted, "Get your hands off of her, now!"

The world stopped moving.

He stood outside the cage as brutal and menacing as I had ever seen him—a salivating beast staring down at his fresh kill.

Anderson stumbled to get away from me and tripped over the box of batteries that I'd placed on the floor. I knelt next to her as Maloney reached for his retractable baton.

"I said: Get your goddamn hands off her!"

I helped Anderson to her feet.

Maloney started toward me. "Put your hands behind your back!"

I froze. I couldn't move. His commands didn't register. All I saw was her. All I thought of was her. She was going to get walked-out because of me.

Maloney jerked his baton to its full extension. "I won't tell you again!"

"Don't hurt him!" Anderson stepped between us. "You don't have to act like this! We weren't doing anything!"

"I saw him kissing you!"

"Okay! So I'll quit! I'll transfer to another unit! I'll do whatever you want! Just don't hurt him! Please don't hurt him!"

She shook with sobs as she begged. Softly I placed my hand on her shoulder to move her out of the way. There was no pleading with him. It made more sense to surrender and accept the inevitable than to resist it.

Defiantly she shook me off. "Maloney it's not Danny's fault! I threw myself at him!"

With veins bulging in his neck, he told her, "Well when I finish with him, then I'll take of you too, whore!" He cupped his hand around Anderson's ear and shoved her to the floor.

She tumbled down in slow motion.

Her head hit the floor and bounced off the concrete.

My fists struck out before I could stop them. The first hit him with a short jab to the throat. He barely had time to gasp before the next tapped his chin. I'd hit him hard enough to knock out a bull, but my blows barely fazed him.

I swung again, and this time he dodged it easily—too easily for a brute his size.

I ran at him, trying to tackle him at the waist. The full force of my body hardly staggered him. I tried to lift him off of his feet, but he was too heavy. I punched his sides, striking out for his kidneys. My fists did no more than massage the solid muscle armoring his mid-section.

Maloney slammed his elbow into my spine. I dropped to one knee.

Anderson cried out behind me. She let out a wail of woe ending with a staccato of sniffling sobs.

I wondered what would happen if he beat me. Would he beat her next? I gained a renewed strength thinking that I had to stop him from hurting her, even if it meant losing my own life.

I punched him in the scrotum. That took the fight out of him. While he was still in shock, I wrapped my arms around his legs and lifted with all I had. We fell, tumbling to the concrete, and I struggled to climb on top of him.

He struck out to hit me. I laid my head on his chest to ward off the blows. Somehow he locked his legs around my waist in a martial arts wrestling hold that I couldn't escape. His thighs were like a python squeezing the air out of me. Desperate to gain an advantage I raised my fist to hit him, and he rolled us over so that he ended up on top of me.

He wrapped his hands around my throat and squeezed the life out of me. My frantic fists beat against his iron forearms. Maloney pressed all of his weight into the stranglehold, and I knew that it was over.

My head felt like a balloon rising into the air.

The light began to fade.

Through bulging eyes I saw Anderson rise behind him with a cardboard box held high above her. With a grunt she slammed the box down onto the back of Maloney's head.

Thick batteries scattered on the floor around me. Maloney slumped off. I scrambled to a far corner of the cage, gasping for air.

Anderson ran to me. After collapsing in my arms, she whined, "He was going to kill you, Danny!"

I kissed her forehead, thankful for her bravery.

I kissed her forehead, knowing that this moment would be our last together, until I became a free man.

CHAPTER 17

Fifteen minutes crept past and Maloney had not moved since Anderson hit him.

She trembled while huddling against me. When she spoke, her voice was small and shaky. "Why hasn't he come to?" Her nails dug into my forearm. "Is he okay?"

I wondered the same. "I don't know."

"He's been out way too long, Danny. I didn't hit him *that* hard— it was a tap, really. I wasn't trying to hurt him. I just wanted him to leave you alone."

"He'll be alright." I squeezed her tighter. "You probably knocked the wind out of him, that's all."

"It can't be so bad, Danny. There's no blood."

She was right. We stood fifteen feet away, and I didn't see a single drop of blood on the floor around him. Craning my neck, I stretched for a better view.

Maloney lay on his side with his back to us. He lay as still as road kill, but he didn't *look* dead. He looked asleep.

"Is he breathing?" She asked. "I don't think he is."

"Maybe…maybe I should go and check on him."

Gulping down her fear, she looked at me and nodded.

I let her go. Tingling nerves pulsated in my belly as I neared him. Something was horribly wrong. I felt it. After kneeling at his side, I examined the back of his head where Anderson must have hit him. His pale scalp was nearly bald, and I saw no bumps or redness marring his skin. It didn't look like he'd been hit at all.

Behind me she asked. "Is he breathing?"

I laid a hand on his shoulder and shook him. His limp body rolled toward me.

Anderson gasped. "Oh my god."

Now flat on his back, Maloney's eyes were wide open. He looked like a mannequin, a rubber doll, a cadaver—some lifeless representation of a man.

The pounding of my heart threatened to shatter my ribcage.

I leaned over him. With my face hovering a foot above his I tried to remain hopeful by ignoring the vacancy in his eyes. I pressed two fingers against one side of his neck.

He had no pulse.

Damn.

Hoping that I'd made some mistake, I felt around on the other side of his throat.

Still...no pulse.

Sweat beaded across my forehead. The cage grew sticky and hot—stifling. I struggled with each breath as if I was inhaling water. *This can't be happening.* Panic sunk spindly roots into my spine. *It can't be happening.* I knew that I needed to do something, but what to do eluded me. My mind drew a blank. I could only stare down into Maloney's cold green eyes as I kissed my future of freedom goodbye.

Try it again, I thought.

Try.

It.

Again.

My trembling fingers danced around his thick neck in search of a pulse—any sign of life. They went side to side, beneath his Adam's apple, even to the hollow where the base of his neck met his collar bone.

Nothing.

"Danny," She whined. "What's wrong?"

I heard her, but my brain was preoccupied with my own dreadful thoughts. *Please don't be dead. Don't let this rotten bastard be dead.*

My shaking fingers reached for his waist. I tried to keep them steady enough to check for a pulse there.

Anderson appeared at my side. "Why are you acting like this?" Why won't you tell me what's going on?"

"He's dead. I think he's dead."

"You *think* he's dead? Either he is or he isn't. Which is it?"

"He's dead," I said. My own words sounded more like an admission of guilt than a stated fact. "Maloney is dead. We killed him. He's dead."

Her once roseate cheeks turned cold and colorless before my eyes. Without saying another word she retreated to the rear of the cage where she paced back and forth.

I called her name. She ignored me. I walked to her. She continued pacing, eyes downcast, mumbling to herself.

I tried to stop her by grabbing her wrist.

She shook free. "Don't touch me! That's why we're in this mess in the first place, because I couldn't keep my hands off of you."

I opened my arms to embrace her. She fought me. She beat her fists against my chest and pushed me away.

"It's not my fault!" She screamed. "He was trying to kill you! What else was I supposed to do? Sit there and let him kill you? I love you, Danny! I would die without you! I love you too much to let anything happen to you!"

I succeeded in wrapping my arms around her. I held her until her screams died away and she was a sobbing heap against my chest.

I was about to get out of here.

After a year...maybe two.

I would have been a free man.

It was a grim situation, but I wasn't convinced that Maloney was dead. I gazed at him on the floor. She hadn't hit him that hard—not hard enough to kill him. Maybe I had done something wrong when checking for his pulse.

I held Anderson until she was calm enough to leave alone. Next I went back to Maloney and knelt at his side. I lowered my cheek over his mouth. He wasn't breathing. Anxiety welled inside of me, but I kept my calm. Further down I laid my ear against his ribcage. While listening for his heartbeat I saw Anderson crying and watching me from a distance.

No heartbeat.

I stood and stared down at him with my hands on my hips.

Anderson hurried to me. "Is he okay?" I shook my head. "What's wrong with him, Danny?"

"He's dead."

She glanced down at Maloney. "Why didn't you try CPR? Why didn't you check him earlier? Why didn't..."

"How was I supposed to know that he was dead? I thought the same as you, that maybe he was knocked out!" I paused because I realized that we were blaming each other, and we needed to stay calm and work together. I told her, "You need to decide what to do."

"Do about what?"

"He's not breathing, Anderson. His heart isn't beating."

"That doesn't mean that he's dead."

In her wide eyes I saw only a ghost of the woman I loved. I asked her, "What else could it mean?"

She took a deep breath and let it out. "How could he have died? There has to be some kind of mistake. I'm going to check him myself." She dropped to her knees beside him and fumbled through the same motions of checking his vital signs as I had earlier.

After working up a cold sweat she sat back on her haunches, sobbing in her hands. "I can't believe this is happening. What am I going to do?"

Her acceptance of Maloney's death solidified my own fears.

I was as good as free.

I was going to walk out of this place.

But not now.

Maybe not ever.

I knelt next to her. "You need to call *Master Control* and tell them what happened."

It was the right thing to do.

She wiped her tears and sniffled. She took a deep breath and stared down at the body. Slowly, she shook her head. "I'm not calling anyone."

I stared at her.

She wouldn't look at me.

"You have to call them, Anderson. What else can we do? Leave him here?"

Still staring at the corpse, she chewed the nails of her left hand. She stood on wobbly legs and backed away from me. "That's exactly what we're going to do." She paced the floor, hugging herself with one hand and pinching her throat with the other. "We're going to leave him laying right where he is like nothing happened at all."

I couldn't believe what I was hearing. I rose to my feet and faced her. "Somebody is going to find him. What will they think?"

Her lower lip quivered. "It doesn't matter what anyone thinks— all that matters is what they can prove. The only people who know what happened is you and me. No one else. We're the only witnesses."

I was beginning to get a headache. "Anderson...think about what you're saying. We're the only witnesses, sure, but we're the killers too!"

"They can't prove that."

"We work here! You've said yourself that no one comes up here, Anderson..."

"That's not true anymore," she cut me off. "Officers have been in and out of here since Maloney's been with us, and the whole prison knows it. Besides, the front door is never locked. Anybody that didn't like him could've snuck up here and killed him...*anybody*."

"I'll give you that—the front door is never locked, but the cages are. Who else would have the keys to the cages besides you..."

"Him!" She pointed down to Maloney. "I'll drop them next to him when we leave."

"Your fingerprints are on them."

"Danny, I'm here five days out of every week. My fingerprints are everywhere. So is my hair, spit, DNA—and yours too. That's nothing out of the ordinary."

I noticed that her tears of sorrow were now dried and gone. Her voice was smooth with the conviction that we could pull it off, but I thought she was taking it too lightly.

"I've been through a murder investigation, Anderson. You have no idea how thorough they are. Once they finish analyzing everything, they'll analyze it again and again."

"What difference does it make? There's going to be an investigation whether we admit that we killed him or not."

Her stubbornness was unnerving. "We'll be the prime suspects. Every trail will lead straight to us. There's no way to get around that."

She stepped close and made sure to meet my eyes. "Listen, Danny. You're a good man. You aren't anything like the men you live with. I know your heart is telling you to do what's right, but it's too late for that. What's done is done, and we can't take it back."

I didn't know what to say. We were in a bad situation, but how could I make her understand that it could become worse if we made the wrong choices?

"I don't want to go to prison, Danny." Her eyes bore into mine. "I know how bad we treat you guys, and I don't' want anyone to have that power over me. I would rather die than live the way you've had to for the last fifteen years."

"I don't want you to go to prison either, but we have to do something that won't dig us into a deeper hole."

It was strange to see this side of her. The Anderson I knew was compassionate; she had a warm heart and a wise intuition that helped me to see things from a different perspective.

The woman standing before me was a stranger.

I said, "I don't understand how you can be so selfish. We're in this together." "Selfish? Is that what you think—that I'm trying to weasel *myself* out of this? Are you out of your fucking mind? I'm trying to find a way to save us both!"

"Save us? Save us how? What you're talking about will…"

"Listen to me, Danny, and listen good. No rational thinking person will ever see our relationship as right. You're an inmate, and I'm an officer. We're wrong right off the bat. It won't matter that Maloney was a piece of shit or that he was trying to hurt you. If we tell anyone the truth, all they'll see is that you and I were fucking and Maloney is dead because he caught us in the act."

She went quiet and held my gaze.

I was speechless. It was hard to look her in the eye.

She said, "I hate to admit it, but they'll find a way to pin it all on you. Trust me. They'll say that you killed Maloney, not me. I'll scream the truth until my lungs give out, but they'll say that I'm only trying to cover for you. I don't like the way that our world works, but that is exactly what will happen if we let it. I'm not selfish. I was thinking of you first."

She was right. *Why hadn't I thought of that?* I was young and black. Already a convicted killer, I would be the focal point of any investigation. The media would paint me as a shifty opportunist who had sweet talked his way into a pretty white girl's panties. Maloney would be portrayed as the honorable war hero slain in the line of duty while upholding the law—doing what was right. Detectives would view Anderson as a pawn in some elaborate scheme that I had cooked up—a fallen angel; a damsel in distress; a hapless victim.

It was the only logical outcome.

Most likely I would be convicted of murder and sent to death row at Central Prison.

Yet with all of that hanging over my head I still didn't think that lying about what happened was a good idea. "It's not as easy as you think, Anderson. It will be worse on us if we try to hide it and we fail."

"How much worse could it possibly be? If we confess, it won't help us. They'll use our own words as evidence. No one gets a break for honesty. They will crucify us. The best thing that we can do is try to help ourselves while we have the chance."

She only thought about getting away with it, but murderers never get away with anything. The faces of those we have slain will always be with us—reminding us that life is a fragile flame flickering softer with each breath.

I glanced at Maloney on the floor...dead. "I was getting out."

She laid a hand on my cheek. "And you still can."

In that moment of decision making I realized why King David had put Uriah, Bathsheba's husband, on the front lines of a biblical war to die. I now knew how Paris and Helen had found it so easy to flee Macedonia and bring slaughter to Troy. I understood why Romeo and Juliet felt that they would rather die than live apart.

Love.

We do crazy things for love.

"They'll try to turn us against each other," I said. "They'll lie and tell you that I told them something when I didn't."

"I know." She nodded. Relief flooded her face. "I trust you, Danny. I know you wouldn't do anything to hurt me, and you should know that you can trust me too. We won't need to lie...we'll just leave some things out..."

"Well, we need to get our story straight right now."

"Okay, okay..." she said. "We just need to tell them that we left immediately after loading up the cart. It was only us two..."

I listened intently, knowing that we would go over our alibi another time to make sure we had it right

CHAPTER 18

It didn't take long to load batteries and flashlights onto the cart. Before leaving the cage, I stared down at Maloney lying dead on the floor. Looking him over once more, I saw no bruises—no lumps or abrasions suggesting foul play whatsoever. Anyone who happened upon his body *could* assume that he'd fallen or been the victim of some other innocent but deadly mishap.

Anderson dropped the ring of cage keys beside him on the way out.

The loading dock door was still open. Outside, black clouds rained down their fury upon the earth. The mist was so dense that I couldn't see three feet past the doorway. An echoing whine of a hurricane siren alarmed the townspeople of nearby Bonnieville that certain death was approaching.

I stared into the storm knowing that death had come and gone.

She said, "Should we close the door?"

Fierce rain blew in through the opening, drenching the concrete floor inside. If I closed the door I would leave footprints. I wasn't sure how that would impact the coming investigation. The best thing to do was leave as little evidence as possible.

"No," I said. "Leave it open."

We walked down the main corridor in silence.

Pausing at the exit leading out into the prison, Anderson took a deep breath and looked my way. Her eyes were still wet with tears, and I knew that more tears were yet to come.

She'll fall to pieces in the first moment that she has alone. She will look in the mirror and its reflection will be a stranger. Sleep will elude her for days, weeks maybe. His face will torture her forever. The memory of this day will allow her no peace. His death will haunt her no matter how much she'd hated him in life.

This is the way of regret.

Gazing upon her with sad eyes, I wished there was some way to spare her from the nearing future of pain, but it was much too late for that. Our decision had been made.

We stepped out into the Four-tunnel. I made a right.

"Why are you going toward *The Center?*" Anderson pointed to the left. "Why shouldn't we go the other way and start in Dorm Four?"

"Because we need to put as much distance between us and *him* as possible. We'll start in Dorm Three. Maybe the storm will hit before we make it back this way. If that happens…"

Her eyes went wide with understanding. "We'll have a good alibi if we're stuck somewhere besides the warehouse."

When we stopped at the closed slider door leading into *The Center*, I asked, "What time is it?"

She glanced at the pink digital on her wrist. "Two-twenty-seven."

"Okay. When they ask what time we left the warehouse, say two-thirty. Never change it."

She nodded.

Without looking directly at it, I gestured toward the surveillance camera mounted on the wall above us. "Those things are all over the place."

"So what? There aren't any in the warehouse. They're only in places where inmate traffic is heavy."

"It doesn't matter. Those cameras will be the only concrete evidence they'll have. That one there will show Maloney going into the warehouse…"

"But never coming out."

I nodded. "Exactly."

"That could be bad, right?"

"Could be." I made sure to stare deeply into her eyes. "That's why this will be so hard to pull off."

"What should we do? Go back? We can say we found him on the floor but we didn't know what happened to him."

Slowly the slider door hissed open.

"It's too late for that." I pulled the cart through the open doorway. "We'll say we left at two-thirty. We didn't know that Maloney was in the warehouse at all. Maybe he'd been in the office or out on the dock—wherever he was, we didn't see him. If we both stick to the same story they can't prove otherwise."

There wasn't a soul in *The Center*. No inmates were in transit. No C/O's were on post. The lack of people bothered me. If no one was in the tunnels, then who could have snuck into the warehouse to kill Maloney? Our chances of getting away with murder grew slimmer by the second.

It took fifteen minutes to drop off four new flashlights and batteries to the Sergeant in Dorm Three. I made it a point to strike up a brief conversation with the officer posted there, knowing it wouldn't hurt to be remembered by any and all.

We did the same thing in Dorm Two.

By the time we entered Dorm One, the routine of work and interaction with the staff had me calm and somewhat confident that we could pull it off. I felt as if we were building a foundation strong enough to hold up our word in court...if it came to that.

Dorm One was a mirror image of the other three housing units. It was a long corridor with four cellblocks housing one-hundred-twenty inmates each on one side of the hallway. Officer Rynhold sat at a steel desk adjacent to the blocks. As the officer on post, it was his duty to monitor cellblocks A, B, C, and D through floor-to-ceiling Plexiglas windows fronting them; instead, he was fast asleep with his feet propped on the desk's surface.

As we neared him, I heard voices coming from the Sergeant's office open door down the hall.

Anderson knocked on the desktop. Rynhold jolted awake.

In his startled eyes I saw none of the suave player who'd been trying to sweet talk his way into Anderson's pants. "Damn girl, you can't play like that!" He cast a nervous glance toward the Sergeant's office. "I almost peed myself."

She smiled down on him. "That's what you get for sleeping on the job."

"I wasn't sleeping," he told us. "I was resting my eyes. I've got a bad case of cataracts. The doctor told me keep them closed thirty minutes for every fifteen that they're open."

She giggled. "That doesn't make any sense. You're sleeping twice as long as you're awake."

He yawned and then licked his chops. "It makes perfect sense to me," he said. Rynhold glanced my way and then to the cart behind me. "Why are you all down here anyway? I heard there's going to be a lockdown soon."

Anderson replied, "We came to drop off flashlights and batteries. Do you guys need any?"

Rynhold pointed down the hall. "You might want to check with Sarge. He would know better than I would."

Anderson looked my way. "Danny, would you check for me? If they need any replaced, go ahead and handle it, will you? I need some time with Officer Rynhold."

As I pulled the cart away, I heard Anderson tell him, "I want to apologize for the way I acted toward you before."

I glanced back. Anderson sat down on the edge of the desk.

Rynhold gulped at the sight of her plump body. "Apologize for what?"

"Well..." she ran her finger up and down his forearm. "You went out of your way to ask me out, and I was rude. I was seeing someone at the time, but now I'm not. So..."

After witnessing that, I didn't want to see or hear anything else. I knew that she was trying to solidify an alibi, but knowing that did me no justice. She was the only woman I had ever loved. It broke my heart to see her flirting with another man, regardless of the circumstances.

I didn't dwell on it. I kept on walking.

A slim, dark-skinned Sergeant sat behind a big wooden desk in the office. I'd never seen him before. The velcro name-tag above his right breast pocket read *Browning*. Another black, male officer sat on a stepladder in the corner.

When I paused in the doorway, Sergeant Browning looked up with a frown. He asked me, "What the hell do you want?"

"I work in the warehouse. Sergeant Thompson sent me to..."

Suddenly all went black. Not only did the office lights go out, but every light in the unit. With the whole prison bathed in darkness, I heard someone stand up from their chair.

"Inmate? Inmate? Where're you at? Answer me! I swear if you..."

"I'm right here," I said. "I'm not going anywhere."

"Don't make a move! I want to know where you are at all times! If you do anything stupid I'll try my best to kill your black ass in here!"

Two flashlight beams came bouncing down the hall.

Out of breath, Ryhnold asked, "Y'all okay in here?"

Illuminated by the lamplight, Sergeant Browning told him, "We're fine." He pointed at me. "Someone put him in handcuffs."

"What? Why?" Anderson's voice was shrill with alarm. "What did he do?"

"He didn't do anything," Sergeant Browning replied. "I want him cuffed because I said so. I won't have an inmate on the loose in my housing unit during a hurricane and blackout. I don't know why he wasn't sent to his own cellblock hours ago, but since he's my problem, his hands will be secured. Somebody do it, now!" The officer who'd been in the office with Sergeant Browning stepped behind me hand handcuffed my wrists.

The five of us stood quietly in the darkness waiting for the lights to come up. After a few minutes had passed, one of the men said, "The generators must not be working. They should have kicked in by now."

A few of the others muttered their agreement. They seemed to share an anxiety of being in a dark prison that I didn't feel.

I wasn't worried about anything at all.

Anderson and I had just gotten away with murder.

I was sure that the power outage had killed the surveillance cameras too. On a playback there would be a long time lapse in the video footage—a time lapse long enough for someone to enter and exit the warehouse without being seen. Anyone could have went in after we left.

No one could pin Maloney's murder on us. Not now.

The lights finally came up after a thirty-minute blackout. Anderson's eyes met mine, and I knew she'd been thinking exactly what I had.

With a cackle, all of the officer's walkie-talkies came to life. A woman's monotone voice filled the small office. *"Attention in the institution! Code seven! Code seven! Institutional lockdown! All inmates are to be secured in their cells immediately!"*

We all listened as the command was repeated. Afterward, Sergeant Browning asked me, "Where do you sleep?"

"Dorm Four," I replied.

He hoisted the walkie-talkie to his lips. "Eleven to Master Control. Eleven to Master Control."

The radio hissed back, *"Go ahead for Master Control."*

"This is Sergeant Browning. I've got a seventeen en route to forty-one from eleven, over."

"Negative, Sergeant. Your seventeen must remain at your twenty until the code seven is lifted. Over."

Sergeant Browning frowned my way. Into the radio he muttered, "Ten-four." He told his two unit officers, "We need to secure the inmates in their cells. We'll do it together, starting with A-block."

Rynhold and the other officer nodded.

Anderson asked, "Do you need my help?"

Sergeant Browning gestured toward me. "Since he's your helper, you babysit him." As the three men headed toward A-block, Sergeant Browning looked over his shoulder and said, "Don't take the handcuffs off until I get back."

Anderson turned to me once we were alone. "It's working, Danny! The storm, the blackout...everything is happening exactly like you said it would."

Things were going good, but it was too early to celebrate. "It's not over yet," I told her. "Keep your fingers crossed and hope nothing bad happens to change our luck."

Just then, we heard voices out in the hall. Anderson and I peeked out of the open doorway and spotted two officers wrestling Critter through the slider door.

"Turn me loose!" Like me, he was handcuffed behind his back. Each c/o escorting him had a tight grip on one arm as they dragged his thrashing frame. "I ain't done nothin'! Why y'all doin' me like this? They got illegal Mexicans pickin' turnips er'where you turn—hell, I'm an American—go git one them and leave me 'lone!"

I nudged Anderson with my shoulder.

She caught the hint and walked into the hall asking, "Hey! Hey! What's going on out here? Why do you have him handcuffed?"

Critter settled down once he spotted her through a ragged part in his clumped hair. His mouth was coated with fresh blood.

One of the c/o's told Anderson, "He was wandering the tunnels by himself. Captain Walker called from *Master Control* and told us to get him."

After surveying Critter's face, she asked, "Did Captain Walker tell you to beat him up too?"

The officer shrugged. "The whole prison is under lockdown. Policy says that an inmate's hands are to be secured during a Code Seven. I'm not going to lose my job for an inmate. We caught up with him down by the warehouse and he wouldn't submit to the cuffs, so we had to use force. We didn't do anything wrong."

Critter spat a glob of blood on the floor. "You kicked me in the mouth you country mother-fucker!"

Cautiously I stepped out into the hall behind Anderson. Critter stood up straight once he saw me. His eyes were glazed over and heavy-lidded. His lower lip sagged sloppily. His head rolled around on his neck as if no spine held it in place.

I shook my head, knowing that he was high.

"Danny? I's lookin' for you, Danny! You gotsta tell'em that I ain't don' nothing'! They gotsta cut me loose! Y'all told my dumb ass not to show up on truck days, but I ain't listen! I swear I won't go up there no more, Danny, just tell 'em that I ain't done nothin'!"

Anderson glanced my way with confusion in her eyes. I returned her stare with a shrug. I had no idea what he was talking about.

To make matters worse, he rambled on and on. The more that he spoke, the antsier the officers holding him became.

All of the staff at Broutal knew that Critter was a little off. I hoped that they were only planning to lock him in his cell until the lockdown cleared.

Before I could tell him to calm down an ear-piercing whine of feedback screamed from their walkie-talkies. The shriek lasted a few seconds. Once it died down, we all heard the voice of my boss Sergeant Thompson panting into his own radio. "*All available medical staff report to the central warehouse! Code Red! Code Red! Officer down! I repeat: Code Red! Officer down! Oh god hurry! Someone please get here fast!*"

And so it began.

Time stood still as I watched the officers that held Critter perk up to Sarge's distress call. They were attentive, but not alerted by it. I glanced at Anderson and reminded myself that she and I were the only two who knew that Maloney was dead.

Keeping her composure, she asked the officers, "So what are you going to do with him?" She nodded toward Critter. "Are you going to lock him up?"

The two c/o's glanced down at their charge. "I guess so," one of them said. But then, after a moment of deliberation, he said, "Well nobody told us to take him to segregation. Maybe we could just lock him in his cell until the storm blows over. Captain Walker can deal with him later if he wants."

Anderson nodded. "I could go for that." She pointed down the hall. "He sleeps in B-block."

As they led him away, Critter pleaded with me, "You gotsta tell 'em, Danny! I ain't don' nothin' but walked up on 'im! Xplain it to 'em!"

The officers tightened their grip and pulled him harder. He struggled to get away from them.

Still handcuffed myself, I told him, "Just go with them. You'll be fine."

"I ain't gon' be fine!" He shouted. "They gon' lock me up, and they ain't gon' let me out again! Why won't you help me? You s'posed to be my friend!"

They dragged him into the cellblock.

Once they were gone, Anderson asked me, "What was that all that about?"

I couldn't get Critter's face out of my mind. He'd looked more afraid than I'd ever seen him. "I don't know."

Sergeant Browning and his two officers walked out of C-block. On their way into D-block he stopped to ask Anderson, "Who was that inmate out here in the hall?"

"James James," she admitted. "Captain Walker said to lock him in his cell. They said he'd been wondering the tunnels."

"During a lockdown?" The Sergeant thought about it for a moment and then shook his head in disgust. He headed into D-block shouting, "Lockdown! You know what it is! Get in your goddamn cells right now! Anybody who doesn't comply gets their head cracked tonight!"

Anderson and I were left alone again, but neither of us was in a hurry to say anything. Too much was happening at once. We barely had time to focus on one incident before another tumbled to the forefront.

They'd found him.

I stared at her. Heavy bags puffed beneath her chocolate eyes. She'd aged ten years in the hour since the tragedy. Hard lines of worry furrowed her brow. The corners of her lips downturned in a perpetual frown, freezing her face in a doleful mask of uncertainty.

There was nothing I could do or say to comfort her.

A person's own shame is far worse than any guilt that another can impose. It is the same for forgiveness. The true debt of dirty deeds done can only be paid from the inside out...if that debt can be paid at all.

I wanted to give her space to deal with what she was feeling, but time wasn't on our side.

"Anderson. You need to go to the warehouse and find out what's going on."

She turned to me with tears in her eyes. "I know." The woman of composure that she'd been in the presence of her peers was gone. Her hand trembled to wipe hair from her face. "I can't think, Danny. I'm trying to hold myself together. I don't know if I'm ready to go up there. I don't know if I can handle their questions."

"Don't do that," I said.

"Do what?"

"Fall to pieces. This was your idea." Maloney's death was eating me alive too, but the bite of the handcuffs around my wrists was a constant reminder of what was at stake. "If you try to backtrack and tell the truth now it'll be worse for us."

"I know," she whined, "and I'm going to stick it out. It's just…it's hard…I keep seeing him. I keep *seeing* him."

Fingers of doubt wrapped around my throat. *We shouldn't have done this*. If she was acting this way now, what would she say to the detectives once they had her alone?

We were silent when Sergeant Browning and his officers returned. He asked Anderson, "What's going on in the warehouse?"

She glanced at me before replying, "I don't know."

Their walkie-talkies hissed to life. An officer radioed to *Master Control* requesting an ambulance.

My heart beat triple-time.

Maybe Maloney was alive.

Why else would they call for an ambulance, not a hearse?

Then again, if he was alive he would be able to tell everyone what he'd seen Anderson and I doing…and what we'd done to him.

The two officers who'd escorted Critter to Dorm One came out of B-block. Sergeant Browning told all four of the males to report to the warehouse to help out. "If everything is under control," Sergeant Browning told them, "Rynhold, you and Johns come back. We're still under a lockdown and I need as many hands as I can keep."

Quickly I glanced to Anderson, raising my eyebrows.

She picked up on it. "I'll go, Sarge." She said. "After all, I do work up there."

"No," he replied while gesturing toward me. "You brought him down here, so you'll stay with him."

She didn't challenge his authority. She stuffed her hands into her pockets and watched silently as the four officers headed toward *The Center*.

CHAPTER 19

An hour had passed since the officers left for the warehouse, and not one had returned. Anderson and I flanked Sergeant Browning on opposing ends of the officer's desk. She slumped in a chair to his right. I squatted to his left with my hands still cuffed behind my back.

We sat in silence for the most part.

Awhile back Sergeant Browning had received a phone call, and although he seemed content with the brief chat, he didn't tell us who he'd been speaking to or what the conversation was about. He sat quietly in his chair, staring into the vast cages before us.

His walkie-talkie stood upright in the center of the desk. A continuous stream of radio traffic gave us clues about the progress they were making in the warehouse.

An officer at the front gate of the institution radioed *Master Control* to inform the *Officer In Charge* that an ambulance had arrived. Later, there was radio communication when a sheriff's deputy showed up. An agent with the *State Bureau of Investigation* had been admitted shortly after.

My eyes were drawn to the little black radio each time it hissed to life. I felt like a kid in the fifties, listening to a radio show, closing my eyes to images of the spoken words that I heard.

As time passed the vocal tone of the airwave traffic gradually lost its edge of lifesaving urgency and was replaced with somber voices devoid of hope.

They knew that he was dead.

The situation was panning out exactly as I thought it would, but still, I felt a pang of dread deep within my core. The discovery of

Maloney's death wouldn't be cut and dry. Discovery was only the beginning.

If the coroner determined that Maloney's death had been murder, the hunt for his killer would begin.

We will pay.

All of us.

There will be lockdowns, midnight searches, and violent interrogations. They will kill for information, gossip—anything leading to whodunit and why.

Their revenge will be merciless.

We will pay for it in blood.

My only hope was that they never found out it was me.

I'd been squatting for so long that I couldn't feel my feet. My hands tingled while cuffed behind my back. My bladder was full. "Sarge, I need to use the bathroom."

He shook his head. "There's no inmate bathroom down here."

Glancing toward the end of the hall, I spotted a closed door with a sign reading: RESTROOM—*No Inmates Allowed*. I saw myself as a little black boy in a southern town, staring up at the words: *WHITE'S ONLY*, and I wondered why the world hadn't left that era.

I stood up. "I really need to go."

"You're gonna have to hold it."

"Why should he hold it?" Anderson shouted, pointing down the hall. "The fucking bathroom is right there!" I saw the stress of the day as fire in her eyes. "What's wrong with you people? How would you like it if someone told you that you couldn't pee after you'd been holding it for an hour? How the fuck would you feel?"

Sergeant Browning grit his teeth. It sounded like he was chewing rocks as his jaws worked. I expected him to let her have it, but he didn't. He reached behind him for the phone bolted to the wall. He dialed a number and when someone on the other end picked up, he asked them, "Is the lockdown cleared? Captain Walker called thirty-minutes ago and said the storm was over...so why are we still on alert?" He was quiet, and then, "*Are you serious?* So what...will there be inmate movement after?" He glanced at me. "I have an inmate down here that's housed in Dorm Four, and I need to get him there. What? I'll ask him." Sergeant Browning lowered the receiver to ask me. "What's your name?"

I said, "Woodrow Daniels Jr."

He repeated my name into the phone and then listened as he was instructed on what to do. After hanging up, he stood and led me down to the employee restroom at the end of the hall.

As he was removing the handcuffs, he asked me, "What did you do in the warehouse?"

While rubbing the ache out of my freed wrists I faced him. He was deadly serious. "I didn't do anything."

He said, "You did something."

I began to reply when his radio crackled: *"Sargent Thompson to Officer Anderson."*

Sergeant Browning and I stared down the hall as she answered the call. Sergeant Thompson told her to report to the warehouse. She explained that she had me to look after. Over the radio, he said, *"Leave him there."*

Sergeant Browning didn't look surprised as we watched her leave. Before I turned to enter the employee restroom, he told me, "It won't be long before someone comes to get you too."

Two other officers showed up an hour later. Sergeant Browning instructed me to go with them. Silently we walked through the empty tunnels of Broutal to the big steel door leading into the warehouse.

A dozen somber-faced correctional officers lined the main corridor. Men and women alike met my eyes as I was led past them. Their hollow stares weren't accusatory—not yet.

As we neared the office, Anderson burst through its door with tears rolling down her cheeks. Two female C/O's ran to her, offering their support. She buried her face in her hands and mumbled, "I can't believe this is happening."

I was stopped in the hall. Anderson met my eyes when an officer told me to stand still while he went inside to ask if they were ready to see me.

I noticed that no one moved to put Anderson in handcuffs.

"We're not in trouble," she was careful to tell me. "They just want to ask you a few questions. They'll take you to your cell once they've...once they've..." She began to cry again, and her co-workers led her away.

Someone from inside the office shouted, "Bring him in!"

I went into the office and was told to sit in a chair resting against a wall. All of the correctional officers left after I was seated.

I faced two strange men. A white sheriff's deputy in full uniform sat stiffly in Anderson's chair. His gun holster was empty. The other was a white man in a navy blue business suit. He sat at Sarge's desk with a pen and pad in his lap.

The deputy's eyes never left me.

The suited man acted as if I wasn't in the room for the first few minutes. He kept his eyes on a yellow legal pad resting on his lap, reading notes he'd taken earlier. Without looking up, he said, "Mr. Daniels, my name is Special Agent Davis, and I'm with the *State Bureau of Investigation*." He pointed to the deputy with his ink pen. "This is Deputy Harold. He'll be sitting in as an impartial witness while you and I go over a few things." He looked up then. His gaze was warm and friendly. "I'm going to ask you some questions and you'll be free to go after you answer them."

"Questions?" I asked. Sweat puddled beneath my pits. "Questions about what?"

Special Agent Davis glanced toward the deputy, who shrugged, and then he turned back to me. "Didn't anyone tell you? There's been a death."

"*A death?*" I asked. "Who?"

Agent Davis flipped a few pages of his notes, searching for the victim's name as if he hadn't said it enough in the last two hours to know it by heart.

He looked back up. Watching me closely, he said, "Michael Maloney. Sergeant Thompson found Officer Michael Maloney dead."

"Maloney?" I let a long pause still the air between us. "What does that have to do with me?"

"That's what I'm here to find out, Danny. It is, *Danny?* "

I nodded, realizing that he knew much more about me that I had assumed. Before my arrival he'd probably been through the prison's database studying my life behind bars. Everything there was to know about me was at his disposal, and I was sure that he'd taken advantage of it.

I sat still as he flipped to a blank page in his yellow notepad.

He said, "The first thing we're going to do is create a timeline of what you did today."

I nodded.

"What time did you wake up this morning?"

And so it went, routine questions, all the way up to the present.

I remained calm and kept my voice even. I held eye contact, never looking left or right when asked a question. I told the truth for the most part—only omitting our encounter with Maloney.

Once my day had been recounted, he handed me a blank sheet of paper and a pen. "We're going to go over it again," he said. "But this time I want you to write everything down."

I didn't have a choice. To refuse would be an admittance of guilt.

Surprisingly, he didn't ask what I had done that morning. He asked about the ten minutes prior to entering the office for the interview with him. After I had written that down, he then asked many of the same questions as before, but in no sequential order.

I gave the exact answers that I'd given the first time. When it was done, I felt confident that neither Anderson nor I was a suspect.

"Good, Danny," Agent Davis told me. "We're almost done here." He thumbed through the timeline I'd given him. "Hmph," he said, sounding puzzled. "Now, Danny, you seem like a very intelligent man. I'm willing to wager that you're one of smartest men in this prison, and I mean officers and inmates. But for the life of me I can't figure out this one missing detail."

"*Detail?* What do you mean?"

"Well," he began, "you stated that you didn't leave work for your lunch break, right?" He stared with one eyebrow raised in expectation.

I nodded.

He went on. "You gave a detailed list of the officers who were present at that time, but you never mentioned another inmate being there. Why is that?"

Critter! I'd forgotten about Critter!

"He's nobody important. He's a friend of mine. He comes up here all the time," I explained. "I guess it slipped my mind."

"Slipped your mind?" His eyes never left mine. "What about the argument this friend had with Officer Maloney? Did that slip your mind too?"

I'd forgotten all about it. I had been so caught up in trying to appear innocent that I hadn't mentioned it at all. Maybe I'd blown it off because Critter and Maloney's spat was insignificant to the death. Then again—*I knew what really happened.* Special Agent Davis did not.

Again I said, "I guess it slipped my mind. I've known Critter for so long, and he's always arguing with someone." I gave my best attempt at a disarming smile. "It's not unusual."

Agent Davis nodded along. "If it was so usual, why don't you explain everything that happened?" He sat back in the chair and crossed his arms. "Tell me what you saw."

192

I didn't understand why he was pressing me about it. I glanced over at the sheriff's deputy. He sat stone-faced and silent.

I told them how the officers had surrounded Critter and harassed him.

Agent Davis listened, and when I was finished, he said, "You're still not being straight with me, Danny. How do you expect me to trust you when you aren't telling the whole truth?"

"What are you talking about?"

"You left something out, Danny. Your friend, *Critter*, bit officer Maloney. Didn't he?"

"I don't remember."

"What about the threat?" He said.

"What threat?"

Agent Davis flipped through his notepad.

As he did this, I said, "This is pointless. Why do you keep on asking about...?"

He waved his notepad in the air between us. "I will tell you in just a second."   While scanning the pages, he said, "These are written statements from the officers who were present during your lunch break. They all describe the violent confrontation between inmate James J. James and Officer Maloney." He paused on a sheet of paper to read: "'Inmate *James James told Maloney that he was gonna kill his cracker ass*.' " He flipped a few more pages. Reading from another, he said: "*Critter yelled, 'I'm gonna kill your cracker ass!'* " Davis lowered the stack of papers and met my eyes. "Every witness in that room said the exact same thing—everyone except you."

My fists clenched.

Critter didn't have anything to do with Maloney's death. I wondered how Agent Davis was tying it all in. *Did he know about me and Anderson? Had we been suspected of having a relationship all along?* Was he using Critter as a sledgehammer to break me down in hopes that I would reveal the truth?

I shrugged. "He said a lot of things, but I didn't hear him say that. Besides, *they* started it with him. Everybody wants to put the blame on Critter, but he wasn't the aggressor. They were picking on him. What would you expect a man to do, stand there and take it?"

I wanted to explain that Critter was a mentally-challenged fool who had no real control over what he said, but Agent Davis wouldn't care. He'd had a preconceived notion of what or who Critter was before I had even stepped into the room. Nothing I said would change that. The fact that I'd spun such a web of lies and deceit to cover my own ass made it look like I'd been covering for Critter all along. My misleading statements only solidified the twisted truth he'd had in his mind the whole time.

"Do you admit that he bit Officer Maloney?"

My teeth grinded. "He wasn't trying to hurt him. He just wanted to be left alone."

"It's a simple question, Danny. Did he bite Officer Maloney?"

My heart was a piston punching a hole through my chest. "Critter isn't like that. He's not the way you're thinking."

"But did he bite Officer Maloney?"

"They were kicking him around!"

"Did he bite Maloney?"

"He isn't...he didn't...you don't understand! You've got it all wrong!"

"Answer the question, Danny! Did he bite...?"

"Yes! Yes! *Yes!* He bit the rotten son-of-a-bitch! He should have bitten his whole damned hand off for the way they treated him! But that's what you don't understand! Critter doesn't start fights! He isn't mean! He just reacts to what people do to him! He isn't mean! He isn't violent! He's just misunderstood!"

"Misunderstood?" Agent Davis took a moment to stare at me, tapping his pen against his notepad. "Your friend—James J. James—was convicted of First Degree Sexual Assault Of A Minor. He was convicted of that, Kidnapping, Attempted Murder, and Assault With A Deadly Weapon. He shot a twelve-year-old girl four times in an attempt to kill her and cover up the fact that he'd been holding her hostage and raping her repeatedly for six days. Thinking that she was dead, he buried her alive in a landfill. Lucky for her she still had the strength to climb out and crawl six miles for help."

I noticed that he'd said that without looking at his notes.

"Isn't that violent, Danny? Isn't that mean? Did that little girl *misunderstand* him? Did she push him around? Did she kick him? What did she possibly do to make him *react* in such a way that you say is out of his character?"

I never knew that about Critter. I had never wanted to know. In the fifteen years that we'd been friends I'd never asked him about his crime, and he'd never asked me about mine.

"I'm not his judge or jury," I said. "I've got my own past to deal with. It doesn't matter what he did to end up here—not to me it doesn't. Maybe it's hard for free people to believe that a man can come to prison one way but learn to live another—maybe it's hard for you to believe that he's not the same…"

Special Agent Davis shook his head. "He's been punished for fighting over sixty times in the seventeen years that he's been in prison. That may not sound like a lot to you, but it is to me. He's been caught with knives, drugs, homemade alcohol. He's assaulted officers and inmates. He's been written up for masturbating while looking at a fully-clothed officer. If that is a display of him as a changed man, then he should never get out of prison. Yet you want me to believe that although he threatened the life of a man who is now dead, he had no violent intentions against Officer Maloney. That's not logical."

I hated the way that he twisted questions into insinuations, making them seem like two-headed snakes—each as poisonous as the other.

I was at a loss for words, but I sensed that I was expected to say something. "They started it with him. Critter was only reacting to what they did."

"Don't get me wrong, Danny, I'm not disputing that. I've been around long enough to know how the system works. I'm sure there is some level of intimidation by officers, whether minimal or extreme. I don't agree with it, but I'm not investigating a human rights issue. I'm investigating a murder."

There it was, out in the open.

"A murder?" I asked. "Somebody *murdered* Maloney?"

Davis smirked, giving me the inclination that he thought I already knew and was playing him for a fool. "Your friend, Critter, came in here and killed him."

My heart stopped beating. "That's impossible," I managed to get out. "He wasn't here. He'd left hours before the last time I saw Maloney alive. He couldn't have been here."

"How would you know?" His eyes scrutinized my reaction. "What are you holding back, Danny?"

"Nothing…"

Special Agent Davis read from his notepad before telling me, "Officer Anderson stated that you and she left the warehouse around two-thirty. You told me the exact same thing. So as far as you two knew, Critter left the warehouse and had not returned."

"That's right," I said. "He'd been gone at least two hours."

Agent Davis didn't say anything else. He flipped open a laptop computer resting on the desk beside him and began tapping keys. I wondered how he had come to the conclusion that Critter was the killer. There was no evidence pointing to him. Why did Agent Davis think that Critter had done it?

While watching him at his computer, I thought about telling him the truth. There was a time when I was sure that Anderson and I were going to get off scot-free, and we still could, but at what expense? It wasn't Critter's fault that any of this had happened. I didn't think that he should be blamed for something he didn't do.

Had I been alone in my guilt, I would have told Special Agent Davis the truth. But I wasn't alone. I was in love. Whatever guilt that I placed on myself would affect Anderson as well.

There was no need to damn us both. If I told the truth, Anderson would go to prison, and I didn't want that to happen. The absolute truth wasn't an option, yet I needed to convince Agent Davis that Critter was innocent.

Davis turned his laptop toward me. He said, "This is footage from the prison's surveillance cameras." He tapped a button. On the screen, Anderson exited the warehouse and held the door open for me to pull my cart through. "You and Anderson left at two-twenty-seven."

How can I take the blame and spare them both? I could say that Anderson had been alone in the office the entire time. I had lured Maloney to the nineteen-cage. *But was it the nineteen-cage?* I couldn't remember. So much was running through my mind...*THINK!*

Agent Davis tapped another button and fast-forwarded the video footage to three-twenty pm. At that time, the Four-tunnel was empty.

It was the nineteen-cage! That's where we stored the flashlights.

I could say that Maloney and I had a confrontation as I was collecting the flashlights. I could say that I'd hit him over the head with one—they were clunky enough to do damage. When I realized that he was dead, I left to go meet Anderson in the office. I could say that we left without her knowing what had happened.

It would work.

It had to.

I could make him believe it.

Davis' eyes were locked on the surveillance footage.

I said, "I'm going to be straight with you. I need to tell you something."

He raised a finger to stop me. "Hold on. You need to see this. Here he comes."

"No, you've got it all wrong?" I tried again. "I want to tell you what really happened."

Shushing me once more, he pointed to the computer screen.

At three-thirty-two, Critter came stumbling down the Four-tunnel. He took stutter steps, weaving like he was drunk or high.

He went into the warehouse.

I couldn't believe it. I leaned in as close to the screen as I could to make sure my eyes weren't deceiving me. Whatever I had intended to say was now frozen in my throat.

The computer screen went fuzzy and black.

Davis said, "That's when the blackout hit."

When the screen jumped back to life, the time stamp read four o'clock. Critter bolted out of the warehouse six minutes later, running at full speed, nervously looking behind him as if he'd seen a ghost—a ghost, or a dead body.

My jaw dropped wide open.

Special agent Davis turned to me. " Now what was it that you wanted to tell me? What was it you wanted to explain?"

I didn't say anything at all.

What could I say?

CHAPTER 20

Following the interrogation I was taken to my cell.

The lockdown lasted twenty-three days.

It came as no surprise. Institutional lockdowns are a regular occurrence at violent facilities. Locking us in our cells is the prison's best response to a natural disaster, riot, gang violence, or anything else threatening the security of the institution.

Once that cell door closed, there was no coming out.

We weren't allowed freshly cooked meals from the kitchen. We were fed *Nutri-loaf:* a clump comprised of hominy grits, oatmeal, pinto beans, tomato paste, sweet peas, and cornstarch molded together in a football-shaped brick and baked to an unsavory crisp. We were fed the Nutri-loaf twice daily with a carton of warm milk to wash it down.

I quickly learned that a few big bites was enough to satisfy my hunger. Even then, I didn't chew. I pushed the food to the back of my throat and swallowed it in chunks.

During the first night, inmates shouted to one another through the steel doors, everyone wondering why we were on lockdown. As far as they knew, we had been locked in our cells because of the storm. This belief held up until the morning after the tempest when a brilliant July sun rose high in a clear blue sky.

They cut off the water a day later.

They shut down the air conditioner the day after that.

The first week of their retaliation was hell. We were trapped in sweat boxes with no water to drink. Everyone complained about the stench of stagnant waste rotting in our toilets. Some female c/o's refused to enter the cell blocks because inmates were lying naked on the concrete floor of their cells—lying naked on the floor to stay cool.

No explanation was given for the lockdown. Most inquisitions were met with tight-lipped silence. "Why y'all doin' us like this?" Was shouted at them. "How long we gon' be locked in here?" And… "Can you at least turn the water on? I ain't washed my ass in two weeks!"

Even the friendliest guards remained quiet when making rounds.

Only I knew that we were being punished for Maloney's death.

Only I knew that this was the beginning.

Only I knew that the worst was yet to come.

We received no mail, made no telephone calls and had no connection to the outside world. Our only form of news came from listening to public broadcasts on our AM/FM radios. Never once did I hear any mention of Maloney's death, nor any news of Critter's arrest for murder.

Things got easier after the first week. To beat the heat I stayed awake at night, when it was cool, and I slept during the hot days. I covered my toilet with a pile of clothes to dampen the smell. I moved around as little as possible. I did whatever I had to do in order to gain some semblance of comfort, but there was no comfort for the way I felt inside.

Why did you go back Critter? Why didn't you stay away?

I never made a conscious effort to write. I just needed a release—something to expel what I could not rationalize. The manqué expressions that came out of me were directionless and difficult to decipher, but I knew that the solutions to the inner ills I faced were tangled within those beautifully ugly webs of words.

love letters
A bonfire burns for those who yearned
Needing pleasures as treasures like ashes need urns
Desperate to reap lessons from all we have learned
Respecting the storm and how quickly winds turn
Easing our needs for realities affirmed
Asking for mercy not easily discerned

Pages of nonsense. Melancholic distiches of heartache drenched in dregs of misery. Flowing elegies of exotic words that were only the rambling rigmarole of a deranged mendicant.

Inoculated cryptic code of conduct
Lost in riddles my morbid mind constructs
Overwhelmed by life and bullshit run amok
Veering toward the brink where fools self-destruct

Enshrouding black hands cradle luminous fears
Yanking down rain as dimorphic tears
Opening our love was an irascible sear
Untrussed a lust that will linger all years
love letters

I twisted sacrosanct words in devious ways. I perverted their chaste definitions in order to paste them inside wicked phrases, not as a show of supreme intelligence, but in protest of the sacrilegious way that some men were misunderstood by other men; and to show that deeper meanings lie beneath shallow surfaces if you choose to search for them...

the black rose
will we love in the future as we loved in the ancient?
through a forbidden affair man's law has tainted?
HIS gift, forsaken, makes Santa into Satan.
father giving love, but that love birthing hatred
with poison in the soil where the black rose grows
where the silence of misfortune saturates all those
lovers entwined by a passionate prose.
hoping forgiveness shines through feathers of dark crows.
the black rose

I confronted my anger through rambling versification. I realized that I had always hated myself for killing my father and ruining my own life at the same time.

I blamed myself for the mess Critter was in. It was my fault, because I had fallen in love—because the sickest part of me would rather see my friend suffer for something he didn't do than see my lover punished and taken from me.

I hadn't even tried to save him.

I didn't think that I could save him.

I am the scarlet minion crouching atop a smoldering peak in the hottest hell. With the teeth of my pitchfork I skewered an innocent and shoved him over a cliff's edge into the blazing lake of fire.

I am Judas.

I am Lucifer.

i am
to the world i am faceless, to you i am known. to them; motives
baseless, only you have i shown. footprints in sand, once walked
hand in hand. now listless and bland, bleak barren land. scattered
with the molds of brittle loveless bones. battered by cold—waves
of heartless soul.

to the world i am no one, to you i was love. to them; a pseudonym,
an identity of none. volcano of treasures, once pleasured beyond
measures. now beaten and weathered, no climbers will endeavor.
deadened by hatred, packed with clotted crust. cooled by
impatience—the ailment of lust.

to the world i am distant, to you i am near. to them; i am mystic,
only to you am i clear. stars in skies, once traveled in your eyes.
now blackened and blind, from whence nothing will fly. nebulous
cage, space of weightless stones. battered by cold—remnants of
a bartered soul.

i am

Without the distraction of everyday life, I couldn't keep my mind from the tragedy of love—how a person must sacrifice the greatest part of themselves in order to receive love's potential. I thought of Critter and the sacrifice he was making for me. I thought of Anderson, and I wondered why my experience of a first love had to turn out so horribly.

When I thought of her I couldn't think of anything else.

The love consumed me. It overshadowed everything. I never knew how much in love I was until the thought of losing it made me sick.

I wrote until my hand cramped and the cell floor was blanketed in paper. I wrote until tears slid from my eyes and the ink smeared beneath their salty droplets.

selfish

i would give my last breath to see you again. i'd give my arms, my
legs, the flesh beneath my chin. if only i could love you until the
very end. lost in your gaze, waiting to descend.

i don't care if heaven crumbles or which angels fall. i don't care
about apocalypse or if judgement is stalled, all i want is you, just
you, and that's all.

selfish

I was trapped in a realm where love and self-hatred were strange bedfellows. I couldn't see a way where one could exist without the other. How could I truly love another without hating myself? How could I put her on a pedestal if I couldn't find my rightful place kneeling at her feet?

I wrote until I could no longer hold the pen. I wrote until I was delirious. I wrote until every attempt to shape a letter was finalized with a long streak—a streak like the slash of a tiger's claw across a goat's hide.

Crying, I curled into a ball on the floor. The concrete's chill seeped deeper than marrow in my bones—deeper than the hollow hole left by the beating heart ripped from my body.

The misery was no stranger. It had always been a part of me in the same way that I would always be a part of the prison. Love's embrace had been warm, while it lasted, yet I remained every bit as cold as the heartless stone caging me.

Beast. Captive. Slave. Broken.

With my cheek lying flat against papers I'd defiled, my horizontal view glimpsed words here and there: *Love. Her. Hate. Me. Apart. Us. Forever.*

Those meaningful reflections were more revealing of myself than a picturesque image in a perfect mirror.

I was truly introduced to my inner-self for the first time in that lonely cage, and I didn't like the man I met.

CHAPTER 21

They let us out of our cages at seven a.m. on a dreary Monday. There was no forewarning. The airlocks hissed as they were released, and the doors slid open in a banging succession like dominoes crashing in a row.

After hopping out of bed, I crept to the doorway for a peek outside. I didn't go all the way out, I only poked my head past the threshold. The air beyond my cage door was fresh and cool and inviting. I inhaled deeply, suddenly aware of the sour squalor I'd been wallowing in for the past three weeks. My gaze swiveled from left to right meeting the eyes of other astonished convicts whose curious expressions also wondered if the lockdown had been lifted, or if our supposed freedom was a mistake.

The open doors weren't enough of a clue.

We were too housebroken to think on our own—too well trained.

We needed authority to permit us to exit our cages.

Over the intercom a man's voice said, *"Lockdown cleared! All inmates will report to their assigned work detail following breakfast!"*

Cheers erupted all around me. Moments later the sound of flushing commodes filled the cellblock. Some cons hurried to the showers while others gathered in small groups to discuss the joy of being freed from such a long ordeal. They smiled and laughed and recounted instances when they thought we wouldn't make it out alive. Although we had spent weeks in solitude, we'd survived our misery together. For those first few minutes of freedom I saw not enemies, rival gang members, or racial adversaries—among me were brothers bound by the bondage of a shared hardship. But I didn't join in their elation. The comradery on display alienated me.

I was the only con who wasn't happy.

For them it was a new day. Their troubles were behind them.

My troubles were about to catch up with me.

After showering and shaving my head I went to Dorm One to check on Critter. An inmate named Schoolboy explained that a group of officers had removed Critter from his cell during the first night of the lockdown. Everyone figured that he'd been moved to the hole because no one had seen him since.

In the tunnels everyone was talking about the lockdown, but they were still unaware of the motivation behind it. Ignorance didn't stop the rumor mill from spinning out of control. Inmates speculated about the harsh conditions that had us on lockdown for so long. They said that the hurricane had picked up and carried off a quarter of the prison; Warden Shelly had been arrested for statutory rape; the town of Bonnieville had been so storm ravaged that some of its citizens had been forced to camp inside the prison until federal aid was provided. They lied and guessed about everything except the truth.

On a usual day I would have rushed off to work in a hurry to see Anderson. Instead, I sat alone at a steel table in the chow hall staring at food I couldn't stomach, dreading what awaited me in the warehouse.

I was sure that the investigation was over. Special Agent Davis had pegged Critter as the culprit from the very start. No one had reason to investigate any other truth. The video of Critter entering and exiting the warehouse was good enough evidence to charge him with murder. The chance of freeing him from the trouble he was in was slim to none.

Slowly I stood from the table and headed to work.

The Four-tunnel was quiet. I was the only inmate around. No officer stood as centurion near the warehouse, nor was there any yellow tape blocking its entrance.

Pausing before going in, I hung my head in remembrance. I imagined seeing Critter slumped on his bucket while sleeping with his wild hair hanging over his forehead.

He didn't deserve what was coming to him.

We'd been friends with no expectations besides keeping each other company and passing endless days with long talks about nothing. He'd been the best friend he was able to be. That was more than I could say for the kind of friend I'd been to him.

I went into work knowing that what I had to do wouldn't be easy, and hoping that Anderson would understand.

Sergeant Thompson was working at his computer in the office, squinting at the monitor. Upon noticing me in the doorway he stopped typing.

His lips were a flat line of concern. "You okay, Danny?"

I thought about the eternity I'd spent in prison. I thought about free people my age who lived successfully happy lives—the people who would never know the musty bowels of a correctional institution. I thought about the cool mountaintops that I would never see in person, soothing sounds I would never hear, and the sweet freedom that I would never taste. I thought about Critter and the fact that I was taking his chance of living a good life—the second chance he'd been waiting for these last seventeen years.

Finally, I thought of Anderson and the truth about what we'd done—the truth I needed to tell.

"No Sarge," I answered. "I'm not okay."

He offered no reply. He stared at me as if he knew exactly what I was feeling.

The telephone rang.

He cursed and held up a finger as if to say: *gimmie a sec*, before answering.

I walked away.

The loading dock door was closed. Even as I freed the latches in preparation to raise it up, I feared the memories awaiting me on the other side.

It was an overcast day. The blacktop beyond was still slick from a downpour the night before. The air was heavy and thick. A warm breeze swept across my face as I gazed into gunmetal grey clouds that threatened to rain again.

A guard hunched over the outer railing of his gun tower. He wore dark sunglasses, and a rifle was strapped to his shoulder. Yards below the guard a gathering of sparrows flitted in and out of razor wire coiled atop the perimeter fence. Oblivious to the tangle of knife-life blades, they dove through the murderous mesh in play, chasing each other, perching right on the razor's edge. They seemed not to care that one wrong twist could sever a wing or end life as they knew it.

The more dangerous, the more exciting.

And such was the way of love.

Except Anderson and I weren't mindless fowl. We were intelligent beast who knew what we were getting into.

I had to retrieve my bucket from where Maloney had kicked it almost a month before. I carried it back to its rightful resting place. Exhaling, I sat down and leaned my head against the brick wall behind me.

Her scent wafted my way when I closed my eyes. I smelled purple petunias and passion fruit. I tasted berries on her lips and mint on her tongue. I felt her breasts against my chest and her bottom in my hands.

Soft-soled shoes squeaked to a stop beside me. Without opening my eyes, I asked, "She's gone...isn't she?"

Sarge cleared his throat. I imagined him with his hands stuffed deep into his pockets, gaze downcast and locked on the pavement.

"Yeah," he said. "She's gone."

Tears caught fire in my throat. I closed my eyes tighter, telling myself that tears don't cleanse the soul, they remind you of how filthy you truly are; but still they spilt, bathing me in sorrow.

"How long ago?"

Critter's bucket scraped the concrete as he sat down. He told me, "She gave two weeks' notice. She thought that she would have a chance to tell you goodbye, but none of us expected the lockdown to last as long as it did."

"How long ago, Sarge?"

A moment stretched between us. "This past Friday."

Damn. I'd missed her by a weekend. I felt like the jilted lover running beside a departing train, chasing a woman's fading face behind a shrinking window. *Damn.*

A long time passed as Sarge gave me time to recover. I tried to clear my mind in the silence—to think of nothing at all—yet her face remained, beaming like a beacon in my darkness.

"She didn't leave because of you, Danny."

Somehow I already knew that.

"She made me promise to tell you that. She was scared, Danny."

I was scared too, but I couldn't quit my job or run away. I had to stay and deal with it. I couldn't hide.

But I wasn't angry. I understood why she left, and if I'd had the opportunity I would have left too.

I thought back to Sarge's words and the careful way they'd been delivered.

He knew that Anderson and I had been in love. It was in his voice. He had always known.

"She has a daughter, Danny. Did you know that?"

Another tear dropped from my closed eyes. "No."

"Prettiest lil' girl you ever wanted to see. Anderson brought her over to the house back 'round April or so. I'm guessin' she was five or six years old. Judging from talk 'round town, Anderson ain't seen the father since he found out that she was pregnant. Son-of-a-bitch skipped town soon as she told him. It's a damn shame too. It oughta be illegal to abandon a good woman and a child like that. He oughta be locked up in here with you."

Sarge paused, deep in thought, and then he smiled. "My wife Lulu taught her little girl how to shuck corn and square dance too." He laughed a little. "Ain't no greater joy than watching a child learn something new. I wish you could've been there, Danny. We had a time unlike any other."

I wished that I had been there too.

My eyes opened toward the dark sky. Silent tears held at low tide, licking against their shores, harboring the swell of sadness within me. I felt Sarge staring my way, but I couldn't face him. Not yet.

He went on. "She figured you'd be upset because she hadn't told you, but she did want you to know. She hoped you would understand that she had a family to think about."

Gazing above I saw Anderson and her daughter hovering in the clouds like two hazy angels smiling down on me. In my imagination Anderson knelt curbside on a little country road with a little country house in the distance behind her. She embraced a little girl—a chubby-cheeked sweetling with her mama's big brown eyes and pouty lips. I envisioned Anderson helping the girl onto a school bus, and then wiping tears as the bus grew smaller and smaller against the horizon.

Why didn't she tell me? Why did she feel that she couldn't tell me? What didn't she trust about me?

Then again, *why did it matter?* She'd loved me when I needed it most.

Closing my eyes once more, I said, "Maybe it's best that she kept some things for herself. She gave all that she wanted me to have and it was more than enough."

"I guess you're right," he said, "as long as you know now."

A quiet peace overcame us. His easy breathing told me that he was relieved to get that burden off his chest, but we weren't done talking.

I sat still, knowing that we'd only climbed a molehill and had a mountain left to scale.

Sarge's radio came alive. An officer called in a code for a gang fight down in the gym. A crow pranced in the gutters above my head. An airplane zoomed by. A gentle breeze rustled my eyelashes.

I tried to ignore it all.

I focused my mind on Anderson and her little girl. I saw them playing and laughing and living, and I didn't want to let go of that vision. I clung to it like a climber clinging to loose branches on the edge of a slippery slope. I wished that I was a part of her family too.

"What's her name, Sarge?"

"Stephanie."

"Not Anderson's the little girl's."

"Oh." Softly he said, "Deanna. Deanna Destiny."

"*Deanna...*" I repeated it quietly, over and over, until the echo of its syllables was a familiar friend that I would always know.

I thought about my own estranged mother, and I remembered what it was like to grow up without one—the emptiness that I would always feel. I thought about that and the fact that I didn't want Anderson's daughter to grow up without her mother. No child should be so imbalanced. At the same time that I cursed the little girl's father, I wished that Deanna was my child, because I would never have left her or her mother.

"Sarge," I said, opening my eyes. "I need to tell you something."

"You do?"

"I killed Maloney, Sarge." I waited for him to reply, but he didn't. I could still see Anderson's daughter in my mind, and I hoped that I could make sure her mother would always be there. "Anderson answered a phone call in the office. I waited until she was on the phone, then I snuck back to the cages and hit him in the head when he wasn't looking."

Sarge sat motionless on his bucket, blinking at me. "No you didn't."

I met his eyes. "I'm going to tell them that I..."

Sarge spat on the concrete between us. "The hell you are! You didn't kill that boy no more than Critter did."

My body stiffened. "Did she tell you that? Anderson?" A part of me wanted him to know everything. I was reminded of the last time he and I had sat out on the loading dock. Back then he had given me words of wisdom, and although I had made the wrong decision, I needed his sagely advice again. If Anderson had told him and he hadn't said anything to anyone, then he could be trusted. "Did she tell you all of it?"

He shrugged and spat again. "She told me some. I don't really know the rest. It doesn't matter much to me. I know your heart and hers too. If y'all had something to do with it, it couldn't have been on purpose."

I got the feeling that he was holding something back. He needed to tell me something but was reluctant to do so.

"Why didn't you try to stop us, Sarge? Didn't you know something was going to go wrong?"

He cocked his head at an angle. "Did you want to be stopped?"

I remembered the good way her body felt in my arms, the sweet taste of her tongue, the intensity of her touch, and the way her eyes lit up when she read one of my poems.

Then I remembered how it felt to know that she was gone.

"No, I didn't," I admitted, "but I knew that I couldn't stop myself."

Sarge said, "Trying to stop two folks from falling for each other is like trying to stop the sun from shining. It's going to happen no matter what anyone does against it."

Fresh tears fell from my eyes. "I just hate that it ended so badly."

Shaking his head, he declared, "I ain't ever known something *bad* to come out of love. What y'all had was good for the both of you. Everything on the outside was bad. If you had found each other on the street you'd be inviting me to a wedding."

I held his gaze, amazed at the conviction in his voice.

He told me, "I didn't stop you because I didn't want to. You've been in prison for a long time, and strangely, the only man Anderson ever talked about was you."

"She told you about us? From the beginning?"

"Not in the way you're thinking. She just talked about you a lot. *'Danny works so hard. Danny's always on time. Danny's so strong...'* Danny this, Danny that! I suspect that she liked you from the first time y'all met. It was funny to me. She'd sneak and look your way when you weren't paying attention, and you would do the same to her. I knew it would happen sooner or later."

"And you were okay with that?"

"It ain't like I hooked y'all up! I just turned my head left when y'all went right. I know my job says I'm not supposed to do that, but who am I to stop the natural course of things? Falling in love changed my life for the better. I didn't know what it meant to be a man until I had a woman to love."

I stared at him. Despite the outcome of our relationship, I wanted to thank Sarge for giving Anderson and I the space to find love, but I didn't think that he'd been looking for gratitude. He'd done what he had because he felt that it was right.

"My wife Lulu been dragging my ass to church every Sunday for twenty-seven years, and you know what I've learned?"

I shook my head.

"I learned that God is everywhere. He's in the good and the bad. Just because you're in prison doesn't mean that you aren't human. Everybody has desires, Danny, and no one on this earth can tell their heart when to fall in love. None of us knew something bad would happen. There was no way to tell. If Maloney had never been assigned up here...well, there's no telling how long things could have gone on. I didn't see anything wrong, so stopping y'all never crossed my mind. I just moved out of the way."

Sarge had been respecting our privacy all along. He'd never come to the cages when Anderson and I were back there alone. He'd never let on about his suspicions or said anything about it.

I would have smiled if I hadn't felt so horrible.

Knowing how he'd helped us made me feel worse about what I had to do to set things right.

"I have to tell the SBI that I killed Maloney."

"But you didn't," he said.

"It doesn't matter. If I don't, they'll charge Critter with murder, and I can't let that happen. The only reason I didn't say anything before was because I didn't want to involve Anderson. This is the only way to make things right."

Sarge shook his head while standing up. He paced around on the loading dock, visibly upset. I knew he didn't like it, but I had to free Critter. I had to.

I expected him to tell me that I was thinking foolishly and that I should be patient and let things proceed as they would, but instead, he said, "In the beginning we all thought something foul had happened to Maloney. That's why they moved Critter to the segregation unit—to isolate him because we assumed they were going to charge him with murder. All the evidence pointed his way. But when the autopsy report came back, it read that Maloney had a chunk of metal lodged in his brain. It had been there for a long time. It was well documented in all of his

210

medical files with the State's Employee's Association. To be honest, he shouldn't have been working in a prison at all."

"What are you saying, Sarge?"

"I'm saying that the autopsy report determined that Maloney wasn't killed. He died because that piece of metal moved too deep into his brain. The SBI and coroner ruled that he died of natural causes...but it was already too late."

"Too late? What do you mean, *too late?* "I hopped to my feet. Suddenly I remembered a time when Maloney had been telling a war story to his buddies about a day when he tried to be a hero in Iraq but ended up a victim instead. "Why didn't you tell me sooner? Anderson didn't have to quit! They have to let Critter go! They have to..."

Sarge held up a hand to stop me. His skin was pasty white. His eyes were as hollow as a skeleton's. "Critter is dead, Danny. Some of the officers jumped the gun, thinking he'd killed Maloney. They went in to rough him up, but...they went too far. The autopsy report came back a week later. By then he was already dead. They'd beaten him to death."

CHAPTER 22

Sarge called my name as I hurried out of the warehouse, but I ignored him. I had to get out of there. I knew that he was following me, but I kept on going until I was out in the Four-tunnel heading toward *The Center*.

Critter dead?

I didn't want to believe it.

It wasn't possible.

I thought back to my conversation with Sarge. Only moments before, I had asked him, "*Why didn't you stop them?*"

He'd replied, "*How, Danny? There was an external investigation going on. There wasn't a damned thing I could have done for him. I wear a uniform in here, but in the real world I'm just as powerless as you are.*"

"*You could've done something, Sarge. You could have protected him.*"

"*How? He was locked up in segregation. He may as well been on a deserted island. I didn't even know it had happened until it was done and over with. One day I went home, and he was dead when I clocked in the very next morning. I don't know what else to tell you.*"

That's when I'd left him. We had nothing else to talk about.

The slider leading into *The Center* opened. I thought of Anderson as I walked through. She hadn't quit her job because of her daughter. She'd quit because she knew that Critter's death was our fault. He would still be alive if we had only told the truth. Maybe she'd blamed herself. Maybe she couldn't bear to face me after it...

The Center was packed with inmates. I'd never seen so many congregated in one place. It was as if the entire population was moving in the same direction.

I fell in behind a crowd with no destination in mind. I was just walking, thinking about Critter, and wishing I had told the truth when I'd had the chance.

I noticed other convicts staring at me. Quite a few casted sidelong glances my way. While pointing, they shielded their mouths and whispered to one another. Some wore masks of pity; others, disdain; most, anger.

They knew.

Somehow they knew.

The kid Kelly fell in step beside me. His beard had grown thicker. Heavy bags hung under his eyes. He'd lost weight, and I wondered if I looked as malnourished as him after being on lockdown for so long.

I said, "What are you doing out of the hole? I heard you busted New York's head open with a lock."

"I did," he said, "but he refused to write a statement so they had to let us out." Frustration was in Kelly's eyes. "He tried to kiss me, man. I don't even remember everything that happened, I just know that I lost it. He didn't even try to fight back. I hit him a couple of times and he ran away."

I didn't reply. There was no need to. He'd acted accordingly. I was glad to see him walking and talking and free.

He said, "I saw Critter in the hole."

"You did?" He nodded. "Were you there when they…"

"No," he said, "and I'm glad that I wasn't. I heard about it though."

"What is everyone saying?"

Kelly regarded me with sadness in his eyes. "They're saying that the police killed him for nothing. They thought he murdered some c/o that had been picking on him, but it turned out that the cop really died from a heart attack or something like that."

I nodded somberly.

No one knew the absolute truth, but they knew enough.

"What about the officers that beat him? What happened to them?"

Kelly shrugged. "Nobody's talking about that. They probably got away with it. You know how it is."

Yes, I did know. But the real injustice was that Kelly knew. He hadn't been in prison for half of a year, yet he had already learned to accept the struggles of hardship.

Other inmates kept their eyes on me. We all seemed to be heading in the same direction. Even Kelly and I were following the crowd.

I asked him, "Where is everybody going?"

"Don't you know? Everyone is down at the gym waiting for you. I thought that's where you were headed all along."

"Waiting for me?"

Sure enough the crowd turned and went through the Six-tunnel slider and headed toward the gym. Inmates lined the corridor on both sides. All conversations ceased when they spotted me. A thousand eyes stalked my every move. Those men who blocked my path parted before me as if I was Moses on a mission from god.

Strangely, I felt no fear.

Somehow I knew that no one was there to hurt me.

A man patted me on the back. He said, "Sorry about your little homeboy. Don't worry, we gon' make it right," but I didn't see who the man had been. His hand was replaced by another and another. Before I knew what was happening, I was bombarded with robust condolences and endearing words of encouragement.

I turned to look for Kelly, but he was lost in the crowd. The men thrust me into the gym where a larger mass of cons was gathered.

A Muslim stepped to me. He said, "Brother Nasir is waiting for you on the yard."

So that is where I went.

The dark clouds had grown even darker. Thunder rumbled, pulsing like a heartbeat for the soul of a violent storm.

Nasir stood alone in the center of the vast rec yard. He didn't look at me when I approached. He kept his eyes upward into the sky. Today he wore no kufi. His unkempt beard was ragged and streaked with grey. His disheveled appearance let me know that the lockdown had been hard on us all.

"It's time," he said.

"Time for what?"

"Retribution." His gaze never left the cloudy sky. He blinked as sparse rain drops began to fall. "They've been killing us for too long. What they did to your friend wasn't right, so we're going to do something about it."

"Who is we, Nasir? The Muslims?"

214

He turned toward me, but his eyes rolled somewhere beyond mine. "*We* is everybody, Danny. All of us. Look behind you."

I turned around. Hundreds of men were spilling out of the gym and onto the rec yard. None of them spoke. Their presence was voice enough.

Rival gang members were now unified and standing shoulder to shoulder with their sworn enemies. Pedophiles stood with thieves, Jews with Catholics, and skinheads with Muslims. In the forefront of the crowd stood the clique of Mexicans that Critter and I had fought only a short time ago.

They stood tall, together, and ready for war, but I knew that Critter's death wasn't their only reason for being there. In that crowd were men who had once despised Critter. They'd hated him for being different. They'd called him retard, redneck, and a slew of other insulting names. Some had exploited his mental inadequacies, pressuring him into stealing, arguing with officers, getting him into any kind of trouble so they could laugh at him.

I wondered why a man who had been the butt of so many jokes was now a martyr.

"They never gave a damn about him." I told Nasir.

"No," he admitted, "they didn't. They're here because they don't want the same thing to happen to them."

I looked over the silent crowd. I met as many eyes as I could, hoping to see beyond the cold stares for a glimpse of their true motivation. All I saw was rage.

He said, "They ruled your friend's death an accident. Did you know that?" His eyes searched mine. "That's the real reason we were on lockdown. They were looking for a way to cover up their mess. The official report reads that he fell down a flight of steel steps in the segregation unit. His death was never investigated as anything else. Whoever killed him got away scot free." He turned his gaze back toward the sky. "How does that make you feel, Danny? Does knowing how your friend was treated give you a reason to fight?"

Critter's killers weren't the only guilty people who'd gotten away with murder.

Anderson and I had too. We killed Maloney, and Critter was dead because of it. How many more would die because of Critter's death, and when would the chain-reaction of violence stop?

"We can't change the past, Nasir, and revenge won't make a bad situation better."

He shook his head. "You're missing the point. Some men want to make a stand because the phone rates are too high. Someone is upset because we aren't allowed conjugal visits. Maybe a man wants to fight because he wasn't allowed to go to his mother's funeral. A hundred men will find a hundred different reasons to fight for a single cause, but at least they fought for the one thing that they believed in. We cannot continue to let them treat us however they want. This system is evil in all its ways. It is a virus that sickens us. So don't think we're trying to change the past. We're going to pave the way for a better future."

I faced him. I forced him to look into my eyes. "Nothing gets better by fighting violence with violence. The only outcome is death, and dead people can't change anything. What happened to your soapbox sermons about a non-violent petition? What happened to organizing a workers' strike?"

"A strike isn't enough," he said. "They showed us that by locking down the prison for three weeks. We have no power there. If we refuse to work they'll just lock us down again. We need to do something to really get their attention—something extreme." There was bloodlust in his eyes.

"What kind of leader are you? What Shepard leads his sheep to slaughter? The last time that I checked *Islam* meant peace. Where is the war in that?"

"So you're my teacher now?"

I shook my head. "No. I'm your voice of reason. You need to break this up. These men have no reason to be here."

"They do, he said." "And so do you, your friend died."

"He didn't die for this."

"It takes a single spark to ignite a forest, Danny."

"Yes, but the fire won't die unless there is nothing left to burn up."

He gave me a half-smile. "You misunderstand me. I don't want violence either, but there is no other way. What reason do they have to respect us now? Isn't it bad enough that they've taken our freedom? Why make things worse by taking privileges and our lives too? When will the oppression stop? A wound will feaster if not sterilized and bandaged—it will only grow worse if left to rot. Don't you see that?"

I understood why they wanted to riot. Many of us were serving life without parole. A lot of those with numbers as sentences had decades left to serve behind bars without any hope of an early release. Prison was no longer a place of reform, it was a warehouse. A cage. A cage for men.

With every passing year or new gubernatorial administration life in prison got worse. We weren't considered good people who had done something bad. We were treated as bad people who didn't deserve anything good...not even a second chance.

I felt the same anger as them. I'd been living with that disparity my entire life. But the difference between me and them was that I knew violence would only make things worse.

I said, "I want more out of life than a shallow grave and a tombstone etched with my name."

"It's not about you, Danny. It's not about your friend either. It's about the arrogant way they look down on us. It's about them stomping on our children's pictures during a shakedown or the inflated price of medical or the long prison sentences with no parole. It has nothing to do with you. It's about the way things are and how they should be. It's about us! It's about *US* against *THEM*."

Nasir's lips were curled into a sneer like a madman.

I spoke softly in attempt to calm him. "There is no *THEM*, Nasir. There is only *US*. Why view us as separate? We are all the same. You're judging them in the same way that you say they unfairly judge us. There is no difference between an African and a Mexican. The distinction lies within our own eyes and how we choose to see each other." He turned away from me. "Please listen, Nasir. You can stop this. No one has to..."

There was a commotion in the crowd. I stopped to look. The inmates parted as Sergeant Thompson pushed his way through. He headed straight for me and Nasir.

I was amazed to see him. "What are you doing out here, Sarge?"

He said, "I came to keep you out of trouble, Danny." He glanced toward the gathering of convicts, then back to me. "I don't know what's going on out here, but y'all need to break this up. There have been seven fights since they let y'all out of your cells, and Warden Shelly is about to order another lockdown. He's already called in the PERT team to make sure y'all comply. I came down here to warn you so that you don't get hurt."

The *Prison Emergency Response Team* (PERT) was known for its brutality. Made up of selected officers from numerous prisons, the PERT team only mobilized for institutional shakedowns, prisoner escapes, and a slew of other emergencies. They are the state's highly trained elite. Heads would roll if they met any problem from inmates at Broutal.

Sarge pleaded with me. "Danny, I know you're upset about Critter. Hell, I am too—but there isn't anything we can do now."

Nasir faced us both. "He can stand up for himself. He can make sure no other convicts die at your hands."

"Stay out of this!" I told Nasir. To Sarge I said, "You shouldn't have come out here."

Men from the crowd moved toward us with their eyes locked on Sergeant Thompson. I noticed that some of them brandished padlocks, homemade shanks, or broken broom sticks.

"Stop!" I shouted at them.

But they didn't stop.

"It has begun," said Nasir. "It has begun."

A hollow sphere of fear twisted my belly—the same as I had known the instant I'd discovered that Maloney was dead, or when Anderson tried to kiss me that first time, or when I'd gazed upon the sticky knife I had used to stab my father as it lay in a pool of his spreading blood. It was the helpless feeling of being caught up in an avalanche— swept away, knowing that the course of my life was out of my control.

Sarge felt it too. He fumbled to retrieve the walkie-talkie from his utility belt. Lightning struck above, startling him, and he dropped the radio at his feet before he could call for help.

The men advanced on him.

In that instance I imagined Critter alone in a cell, handcuffed and helpless. A blur of blue uniforms stormed his small space and beat the hell out of him for something I had done. I heard him cry out for help with his dying breath...but no help came.

And so I threw the first blow of the riot; not fighting for my rights as a prisoner, but to somehow undo my wrongs as a friend.

CHAPTER 23

We're going to die.

There are too many of them.

I'd broken Nasir's jaw with the blow that set it off. He didn't fall. He reared back with a grunt, eyes wide, chin slumping slack against his throat at an unnatural angle. If it was a fair fight I would have advanced on him. I would have kept up the pressure until he was begging me to stop...

But it wasn't a fair fight.

Nasir's Muslim brothers were the first to converge. They attacked quickly. I didn't have time to count how many. A blur of brown fists swarmed my face like wasps. Some stung their mark, most punches fell short as I ducked or blocked them with my upraised forearms.

By hitting Nasir I'd hoped to stall the rioters long enough for help to arrive. The diversion worked momentarily. Many of the men stopped and stared, confused about who was supposed to be fighting who.

Somehow I kept Sarge safely behind me. I heard him radio for help as I smashed the nose of a would-be attacker. The man retreated, but I didn't have time to enjoy the victory.

The next two were smarter. One side stepped to my right, the other went to my left. Both crouched in fighting stances and inched toward me in concert.

"Why are you protectin' him?" One of them shouted.

"You s'posed to be with us!" The other declared.

I charged one as he spoke, punching him in the throat and then the eye as he back-pedaled. His friend hit me from the rear. I wheeled around, swinging wildly until my knuckles met flesh and bone. I felt his front teeth buckle when my fist caught him in the mouth. I sent another blow racing behind the first to cram the rest of his teeth down his throat.

He wouldn't fall. He fought back, and I saw a flash as his fist connected with my own lips. Along with the blood, I tasted rage coming to a boil on the tip of my tongue.

His friend got to me from my blind side.

They attacked at the same time, their fists were jackhammers drilling into my face.

There was no way that I could handle them both.

From the corner of my eye I caught a glimpse of the rest of them—vultures surrounding us, waiting for me to fall. It was only a matter of time before they overwhelmed us.

Suddenly a heavy hand clamped my shoulder and pushed me down. I tried to resist, but the fingers were a vise and the palm an anvil. Peering up as I sank, I saw that it was Sergeant Thompson towering over me and pushing me down.

He had no fighting stance, no discernable game plan or strategy of attack. He lumbered toward one of the inmates like an ogre with his hands outstretched. Sarge grabbed the guy by his neck, lifted him a foot from the ground, and slung his flailing frame headlong into another man.

The clouds above opened up and unleashed a heavy downpour.

Through the mist I spotted another con attack Sarge. The prisoner knuckled-up with his fists raised, ready for a fair fight. Sergeant Thompson pulled out his retractable baton and slapped the man in his face with the knobby end, sending the guy stumbling to the wet ground.

Three others ran at him. One dove at his legs, another leaped onto his back, and a third snatched the baton out of Sarge's hand.

By the time hopped to my feet in an attempt to help, one man was flying past me. Sarge kicked another four feet into the air. The last he lifted high above his head and launched him into the mass of inmates watching from the sidelines with bloodthirsty eyes.

I hurried to Sarge's side. "There are too many of them! We can't fight them all! Let me hold them off while you run back into the building for help!"

"And leave you out here to die?" He asked. "Fuck that!" He said. "If you stay, then I stay, and we'll die together!"

There was no more time for talk.

A group of guys started toward us cautiously. Sarge reached for his pepper spray and sent two poisonous bursts into the eyes of a pair in front of us. They yelped in unison, falling to the soggy ground while clutching their eyes with closed fists.

Others in the crowd stood hunched in preparation to attack. Sarge swiveled his canister in open threat of anyone else who wanted to try something stupid.

Mace wouldn't hold them off for long. The rain limited its range and he would only be able to spray a few men before it went dry.

A fight broke out on the left flank of the crowd. Two cons stabbed each other with homemade shanks. To the right, four or five inmates swung at each other with tightly clenched fists. Frays among the rioters jumped off everywhere. I imagined that the riot was a good time to settle scores, whether individual or gangs alike.

I didn't care if they killed each other.

I only wanted them to leave us alone.

As the riot entered the point of no return, black clouds replaced the grey, giving way to a morning with sinister intentions. Lightning struck, illuminating a million eyes of our foes. The rioters cried out, and I realized that it wasn't lightning, it was a concussion grenade.

Another went off to the right, then the left. Men in fatigues and full riot gear poured out of the gym like ants, hollering at the top of their lungs. Instead of instructing the rioters to get down, they came out swinging long black sticks.

A handful of inmates stood as a single unit apart from the mêlée raging behind them. Sarge shouted to the men, "It's over! The PERT team is here! Go to your cells! I don't want to see you get hurt!"

"Fuck you!" Was shouted back.

And so we faced them, a squadron against two.

Searing spots sizzled my skin where someone's knuckles had been. I asked myself, *when will it stop?* I'd been fighting since the day I entered prison. Most times I thought that I was fighting for survival, but now I wasn't so sure that I wanted to survive in a place where some men hated other men simply for the act of hating. I once thought that I fought to prove my manhood, so why did I leave those fights feeling lesser of a man than I'd been before I fought them?

There's no such thing as fighting for a noble cause.

There is no honor in violence.

In the crowd stood a stocky, white convict with a swastika tattooed on his cheek. He inched toward me. When lightning struck, I saw that he had a metal pipe in his hand. I thought, *where did he get a pipe?*

He charged with the pipe wagging beside him. I tried to step out of the way, but he was too fast for me. Lightning crashed again as the pipe struck the bridge of my nose.

The next thing I knew, I was on the ground, staring up into the black clouds above. Rain poured over me in tidal waves, filling my nose and mouth. Some thick liquid clouded my eyes—whether blood or mud, I couldn't tell. I only knew that a man sat on me, stabbing me in the chest.

I was weightless, drifting in space, reaching out, trying to grasp something—some purpose of life, some reason to live.

The sounds that I heard were hollow thuds as his fist pounded my chest and scrapes as the point of his shank raked against my ribcage.

I felt no pain.

I tried to open my eyes, but I couldn't see my attacker, *i saw Anderson smiling at me. she raised the hem of her yellow sundress as she tiptoed, barefoot, across a shallow creek. our blue sky was cloudless and beautiful. her smile, flawless. laughing at the sight, I held her squirming little girl in my lap.*

I wondered if I was dying. I wondered if this was the last vision I would ever see. I'd heard of a man's life flashing before his eyes in the moments before he died, but I didn't want to see mine—not as I knew it...not as I had lived it.

Quickly my attacker was lifted off of me. I felt a momentary relief. I tried to inhale, but no air would enter my body. Panic set in. It was as if my lungs were filled with cement. I tried to cry out for help as the rain-slick sole of a boot stomped me in the face.

Thoughts of breathing disappeared.

and there was the girl with her mama's big, brown eyes. she rose from my lap and grasped her mother's hands. they square danced in the shallow creek, giggling and kicking up water into the air.

If there was ever a reason to live, then I wanted to live to see that. But she was gone, and I was left holding the bittersweet remnants of our love like shards of broken glass slicing my palms.

But I wasn't sad...*i was still floating on a couch in the gulf stream. remembrance so fair, but only tangible as dreams. like smoke on the water rising in wispy steam. a mystery of sorts, unreal as i once deemed.*

The boots stomped me over and over again.

When is help going to arrive?

Someone kicked me in the belly, and my lungs filled with air. I coughed and blood spewed from my mouth. It was hard to breath, but my vision began to clear. Many men stood in a circle around me. They took turns stomping me—all of them.

Yet I felt no pain.

No physical pain.

miserable love, the ghost of affection. companion of pain from its very inception. like the beauty of birth, or the hurt of its conception. makes me wonder if the gift was worth the hard lessons.

Convicts screamed for mercy all around me. Superiors shouted commands. I thought I'd been time warped into some alternate reality— a past life where I'd once been a fallen soldier on a bloody battlefield.

Sergeant Thompson pushed the men away from me. "My god, Danny, what did they do to you?" He knelt by my side and cradled my lolling head as a father would his child.

A man ran over and tried to kick me again. Sarge caught the boot and pushed it away. "Leave him be!" He shouted. "He ain't done nothin' wrong!"

Someone replied, "He's just a fucking inmate."

"No," Sarge said, looking down on me. "He's my friend."

The PERT team officers who had been stomping me turned and left me to find another victim. I wondered how I had come to be hated by so many, but by then it didn't matter...

eulogy

when i die, they'll burn me in a box for one. they'll engrave my urn with: loved by none. they'll forget my name and good deeds i'd done. they'll recount my shame while scattering my crumbs.

eulogy

Tears streamed from Sarge's eyes. "Hold on, Danny!" He wiped rain-plastered hair from his forehead. Holding me close, he called out for help. "Somebody bring a stretcher!" His horrified eyes roamed over my body. Finally, he shook his head and said, "Father God, I come to you in my hour of need. There are men on this earth who deserve to die...but not this man here. Danny has made mistakes, but we all have. I beg you, father god, to let him live a little while longer..."

I began to slip away. Sarge slapped my face. "Hold on, Danny!"

Hold on for what?

If I lived, the deaths I caused would haunt me all my days. Life was grief. Happiness was not meant for me. Even the love I'd found had ended in tragedy. Why should I want to live?

I tried to smile for him. I tried to show that it wasn't so bad. Dying.

Whether I succeeded in comforting him or not...I would never know.

Darkness consumed me.

cage

if you should read this and happen to shed tears, know that i cried first while exploring my fears. i cried in my cage while wishing she was near. i cried in my soul where no one else could hear.

loosing love is worse than dying a death. love can be a sanctuary when you have nothing left. love is your heartbeat—the purpose of your breath. without it you are plain, as bland as the rest.

so when tears melt down your cheeks, like picasso's clocks. when you watch ships set sail while alone on your dock. when your heart needs togetherness, but loneliness will not stop. then you're me, in my cage, when bathed in tear drops.

cage

When I opened my eyes—and they did open—on the other side, I lay on a beach of black sand with water crashing at my feet. It was pitch black, yet I could see. I sat up, looking all around me. I was stranded on some deserted island—some lonely limbo. The same dark clouds that I'd known before blanketed this sky as well, but there was a break in them. Way out, over the open ocean was a circle of white. From that halo within the cloud cover spewed an inviting rainbow of bright light. Beaming rays shined down to create a spotlight on the surface of the water a mile or so out from the beach.

I climbed to my feet. Immobile on the black shore, I watched black waters ripple as I stared out into infinity and beyond.

I didn't feel dead.

death

reality or legend? fairytale for kids, or a place in the heavens? are you a point of no return, or the start of a journey? are you the finish of one race, or triumph of the tourney?

death

I looked over my shoulder.

Behind me lay a wasteland. Beyond the black beach, the mainland was bordered by a wall of twisted trees that held no promise of peace. Through brittle and leafless limbs I saw the glowing eyes of beasts awaiting my return.

Hidden within those darkened branches was the image of my mother—frozen in photos with an eternal smile that had never smiled for me. I saw my father in his study, hunched over an open book with a kitchen knife protruding from his back. I saw Maloney laying lifeless on the concrete floor of the nineteen-cage. And there was Critter, strumming his guitar with busted fingers, singing through a broken jaw.

I saw myself on the elevator at the Morganton High Rise for Boys, fighting off three kids who had tried to take my newly purchased deodorant and toothpaste. I remembered the gang fight at Polk Youth Center when fifteen guys jumped one man whose only defense was a rusty horseshoe. I thought of my year at Marion Correctional where there was only one black guard in the entire institution, and the white staff made it a regular habit to address the black convicts as boy, nigger, and darkie. I was transported to Scotland Correctional in the early two-thousands when there was so much money and drugs changing hands that an inmate could have acquired a kilo of cocaine if he'd had the money to buy it.

This was the life that I knew.

I stared deep into those twisted trees knowing that if I climbed through I would only be going back to a life of misery. Even if I was to get out of prison, how could I forget? How could I turn my back and ignore those days as if they didn't exist? How could I get over it? I would never be free. I would always be boxed in by what I had done and seen. There is no greater cage than a confined mind that has no key, no door, no way out—no escape.

So I turned and walked toward the water with my eyes locked on that halo in the cloudy sky. I waded in and fought the waves as they tried to push me back.

Within that circle of light, I saw Ms. Anderson and her smile. I saw the only happiness I had ever known...

into the abyss i sought for bliss. braving black seas, succumbing to their kiss. hoping for the pain to go, go adrift. while clinging to the memories of her soft, soft lips.

I treaded water until the waves crept over my head and the distant circle of light was a dab of shimmering white beneath the water's surface. All else was black, yet still I saw her face, and I swam to it, hoping to get wherever I was going so that I could sit and wait for her to arrive.

That's when it all made sense.

the darkness is life.
love is the light.
this is why we search.
why we cry.
why we cannot let go.

the darkness is life.
love is the light.

CHAPTER 24

It was dark when I awoke. The door leading into the hall was half-open, and a sliver of light lit a slender strip on the floor just inside the room. Soft sounds of ringing telephones and friendly voices wafted to my ears from the outer lobby. I moved around a bit, but my back was stiff and sore from laying in the hospital bed for so long. A digital clock on the wall read five-forty a.m. As my eyes adjusted to the darkness, I made out the shape of an armed correctional officer dozing in a far corner of the hospital room.

I lay still and silent, trying to forget the fact that I had to pee and I couldn't get up without waking the C/O because my left wrist was handcuffed to the bed.

Shift change was at six, so I decided against waking him so soon. The dark quiet of the room was comforting. I figured that I could lay in peace for a little while longer.

Although I didn't like being battered and broken up, I was enjoying my hospital stay. Bonnieville General Hospital's food was better than the prison's, the nurses were nice, and it was always quiet.

I'd been recovering there for two weeks.

During the riot I'd been stabbed eleven times. The most serious of the stab wounds had punctured my lung. It took one surgery to repair the damage, and after it was done, I began the fast track to getting better. Besides the punctured lung, I also suffered from a bruised rib and fractured jaw. A day before, the doctors told me that I was healing quickly, and soon I would be well enough to be moved to the prison's infirmary.

The sleeping guard shifted in his chair. My bladder began to burn. I thought about waking him, but then I looked at the clock. Ten minutes had passed, and I knew that I could wait ten more.

I rarely spoke to the officers who sat in my room. Most of them watched TV for the entire shift or talked on their cell phones. A few mentioned the riot, explaining that the prison was back on lockdown and probably would be for a long time. I learned that four inmates and one officer had been killed during the violence. None of the officers mentioned Anderson or Sergeant Thompson to me, and I didn't ask about them.

I asked for a pen and writing paper a few days after the surgery. To be honest, I didn't feel like composing anything—poetry left a bad taste in my mouth—but a pen and paper had been my constant companions for so long that I felt normal with them near. A nurse bought me a composition book from the hospital's gift shop, and one of my doctors donated an ink pen from his own pocket.

The items sat idle for the first week. I couldn't write about just anything. I had to be spiritually connected to something in order for my words to make sense. When I did finally decide to write, I didn't like what came out.

is there any reprieve for the brokenhearted?
estranged, lost vows of the dearly departed
like jumping the broom over a cliff's edge
falling with a smile mere moments before death

What I wrote was a reflection of the turmoil within. I'd lost my vision. I couldn't write beautiful things anymore—I didn't think of anything as beautiful. The vivid landscapes of love and passion that I'd described before had become blackened wastelands of depression that I could not escape.

After a few attempts I left writing poems alone.

Though I couldn't write, I still felt connected to the pen and paper. Each time I sat up to eat my eyes wandered over to the little nightstand beside my bed, and I thought about it. Poetic lines flowed through my mind, but I ignored them. I had to let go of the past. I convinced myself that writing would only keep my thoughts on Anderson, and I had to get over her.

Our time together was a chapter read and forgotten. Maybe she'd left because she realized the one truth that I wanted to ignore: we should never have gotten together in the first place.

It was a test of my will not to write—to not even try, because I loved her so. Yet I thought of her constantly.

And one night, I dreamt of her. It was the most vivid dream I'd ever had. I was still an inmate, and she was a uniformed guard, but instead of being in Broutal's warehouse, I quietly sat behind a sewing machine, and she sat across from me on the other side. We laughed and spoke and she read some of my poems. In her hands she held jagged scraps of pink and red material, which she handed to me one at a time and gave me directions on how to sew. Once I had stitched in the last scrap of material, we stood together and held up a quilt of two mended hearts sewn together. Soon after, we lay naked beneath that quilt while making love.

When I woke from the dream, I was hot, sweaty, and miserable. I squinted through the dark room toward the open door. I thought that I was still dreaming because there was no light in the hallway, yet I swore that I saw Anderson smiling at me in the darkness.

I whispered her name with tears burning down my cheeks, but she didn't answer. I blinked once, and her ghost turned and walked away.

The officer who'd been in the room with me was asleep. I lay there, silently crying, wishing that I could find a way to let her go.

I asked myself: 'Why doesn't someone close that door?'

Before I knew it, I had the pen and paper on my lap...

the open door

an open door lays before sun rays cutting shade
feeling betrayed, i reiterate promises she made.
whether open doors or windows, both lead to someplace else
our love is an open chest, that rests, stagnant on a shelf.
its hinges are rust, its walls layered in dust
to substitute what was within will cause it to combust.
i love you
and i continue chasing your dream
with my fingers slipping through you, as if a banshee.
people spend too much time trying to close old holes
clinging to the next, so their beds won't grow cold.
failing to fill the void of broken promises spoken
unwilling to shut a door that will always remain open.
knights fight for a princess, princesses kiss their toads
but is all that kissing and fighting, only, so we won't be alone?
hazy flashbacks of hindsight cloud my twisted path
so i can't foresee my future for dwelling in our past.

no promise is much better than a broken promise
could've saved ourselves some pain if we'd only been honest.
you honest with me; but me, more with myself
i knew it wouldn't work, i whipped myself theses welts.
yet i find myself asking: "is it better to close
those open doors that may retract exactly what fate stole?
can we still have a future if our past remains alive?
does an open door mean that our love will never die? "
the open door

I wrote until my hand cramped and I fell asleep with the pen still in my clutches.

I couldn't write anymore when I awoke the next morning. I reread the poem, sometimes glancing over at the open door leading into the hallway. I had to admit that I didn't want closure. I wanted to continue dreaming of her—seeing her face as if she would always be mine. I decided to leave that door open so that she could walk back into my life if she wanted to.

The C/O woke up at six and took off the handcuffs so that I could pee. Officer Rynhold was standing in the doorway when I came out of the bathroom.

I asked, "What are you doing here?"

He didn't answer. He flashed me one of those pearly white smiles as the other officer led me back to the bed and handcuffed my wrist to the rail. Rynhold relieved the night shift guard, and once we were alone, he scooted a chair close to my bedside.

"How are you, Danny?"

He was still smiling, and oddly, I felt that he was truly happy to see me. I said, "I've been better …but why are you here? Don't you work in Dorm One?"

He shrugged. "Operations is short-staffed, so I volunteered to come down here and help out. Today was my day off."

I raised an eyebrow. "You came here on your day off? Why did you do that?"

"I figured you needed somebody to talk to," he said. "Besides, you saved Sergeant Thompson's life. He's a good friend of mine, and I wanted to say thanks. If you hadn't fought for him, there is a good chance that he'd be dead."

I shook my head. The awe in Rynhold's eyes had me uneasy. "He wouldn't have come to the yard at all if I hadn't been out there."

"It doesn't matter," he told me. "What happened-happened, and you did what no other inmate would have done."

"No. I did what any human being should have done. But don't think Sarge was some damsel in distress. He got in his fair share of licks too. He probably helped me more than I helped him."

Rynhold laughed a little. "Yeah, we've all seen the video footage. It's safe to say that each of you had the others' back. That's a rare thing to see in a prison. We're so used to hating each other. You and Sarge showed a lot of people that we don't have to be enemies. We don't have to be friends, but we don't have to make things any more difficult than they already are."

Rynhold opened up about the lessons he'd learned from my actions in the riot. While listening, I was reminded that I had hated him once. Of course he'd hit on Anderson, but there was something more. I had disliked him just because he was an officer. I never looked at him as a man with a job to do. I had been as prejudiced against them as they had been against me.

I wondered if things between us would have been different if we had looked beyond our positions in life from the beginning—if the labels didn't exist, or if the barriers were somehow erased. That was a clear example of Anderson's inner beauty. She had found a way to love me despite what I'd done my in past and where I was in my present.

Would the riot have happened if the opposing sides had shared a basic respect for each other instead of a blind distant hatred?

Probably not.

He said, "Sarge carried you to the front gate of the prison. He wouldn't let any wounded officers be treated by the paramedics until you were in an ambulance of your own."

We were both quiet for a long time afterward.

Finally, I asked, "How is he? Sarge?"

"He's doing good. He had some bumps and bruises," Rynhold's eyes traveled over my body, "but nothing like what happened to you. As a matter-of-fact, he threw a retirement party last night. I never knew that he had so many friends and family. We ate ribs and barbecued corn on the cob. He got drunk and square danced with his wife Lulu. We had fun all night long."

I smiled, thinking of it. Rynhold told me about the liquor and music, and I closed my eyes and saw it almost as if I'd been there myself. Just the thought of being around so many joyful people made me happy.

Until he said, "Anderson was there too."

The still way that he held my gaze let me know that he knew about us—he knew about us, and he was okay with it.

I asked him, "How is she?"

He sighed before answering. "She's miserable, Danny."

In my mind, I saw her again. I stared into her brown eyes, losing myself a thousand times. I felt her squirming in my arms as I rained down kisses upon her lips. I tasted honey on the tip of her tongue as she slid it against mine. It was a bittersweet vision that broke my heart, because I knew that it would never happen again.

"Is that why you came here?" I asked him. "Did she give you a message for me?"

"No," she said, standing in the open doorway. "He worked on his day off so that I could come and see you."

The breath caught in my throat at the sight of her. She stood immobile, staring straight at me. She wore a thin white blouse and blue jeans. Her brown hair rippled down over her shoulders. Her face was freshly made and angelic. I was afraid to blink for the fear that she would disappear.

Rynhold stood and walked toward the door. Anderson gave him a little hug and asked, "How long do we have?"

He glanced at his watch. "I'm here for twelve hours. If you try to stay any longer than that, you're on your own. Besides, that little nurse behind the counter has been checking me out since the minute I walked in. I'm gonna go and say hello. Hopefully I'll be a long while myself."

She giggled and hugged him again, then said thanks as he strutted out into the hall.

She closed the door behind her. She took tentative steps toward me and sat down in the chair at my bedside. She reached into her pocket for a handcuff key, and as she removed my restraints, she said, "I hate seeing people in these things."

I didn't reply. I just watched her.

She gave me an uneasy smile. "You didn't really think that I was done with you, did you?"

"I didn't know what to think. You just left. What was I supposed to think?"

A slow tear trickled down her cheek. "I didn't know what to do, Danny. So much

had happened. I mean, I knew that quitting wasn't fair to you, but I just couldn't..."

I reached over and took her hands in mine. "I love you," I said, "and you're here now, so don't worry about it."

She wrapped her arms around my neck and kissed me—she kissed me like the sun and moon rose and set by the beat of my heart and her world would end without it.

She smiled as she sat back in her chair. "I love you too."

While staring into her eyes and living by the good feelings I felt, I was suddenly overwhelmed by grief. Critter would never know what it was like to look into the eyes of a loved one.

It had been her idea to try and cover up Maloney's murder, but I couldn't blame her for something the both of us had done. We loved each other. Despite the beauty of love, the dark lurking shadow of our past would always be there. I would always feel guilty for Critter's death, even though we hadn't killed him with our own hands.

She said, "We've got a lot to talk about."

I couldn't explain how good it felt to be with her. My stomach tingled and my hands trembled. I didn't want to do anything but smile.

"What do we have to talk about?" I asked.

"You getting out of prison."

"Let me guess, you've been talking to my lawyer."

She nodded. "I have. He says things are looking good, but it will take longer than he once thought. It will be five years before you go in front of a judge. The only thing that he is able to do now is file for an Appeal Bond so that I can bail you out until your re-sentencing. If that happens, maybe you won't ever have go to back."

I thought about the shit-stained cinderblock walls that had been my home for as long as I could remember. I had never thought that a day would come when I could live beyond them. Listening to the confidence in Anderson's voice gave me hope that it would actually happen.

Hope.

Hope was a strange sounding word that I was beginning to get used to.

"We've got a back-up plan though," she said, smiling.

"You don't say."

"Sarge and some other officers are going to have a meeting with the governor."

"The governor? What are they going to talk to him about?"

"*You!* He has a yearly meet and greet with SEANC: the State Employee's Association of North Carolina. They're going to take the video footage of you and Sarge trying to stop the riot. They plan to press him to give you a commutation. It's something like a pardon."

I took a deep breath, not believing my ears. "Whose idea was that? Yours?"

She shook her head. "It was Warden Shelly's. He was impressed that you had the heart to stand up for what was right."

Right...

Who can say what was right or wrong? Those men didn't riot for nothing. Oppression had been the catalyst driving the violence. When I fought, it wasn't to stop the riot or to purposely go against the grain. I too saw a need for us to rise up so that we could be treated fairly, but I didn't think people should die to get it done.

"I can't go back to Broutal." Her blank face told me that she knew it was true. I probably had a price on my head.

She said, "You're not going back there. You've already been assigned to another prison."

I nodded, not wanting to talk about it. I'd betrayed my clan. Sooner or later I would run into convicts who knew what I had done, and I would have to suffer the consequences. There was no way around it.

"I can visit you when you get to the other prison. I'll come every week if it isn't too far away. We'll be in constant contact. You've got to give me input and make some important decisions concerning your book."

"My *what?*"

She laughed. "Your *book*. It's really a collection of poems, but it's good. I've been typing it and painting scenes to go along with every poem, so actually it's *our* book. I sent a few samples to a publisher, and they loved it! They want to see more. Who knows, maybe one day you'll be a big time writer."

A book? It sounded too good to be true.

"What's it called?"

She pulled my hand to her lips and kissed it. "It's called: *floating on a couch in the gulf stream.*"

We laughed, and she held my hand when the pain of my bruised rib made me double over in agony. Once the ache subsided, she said, "I've already painted the cover art. You and I are drifting across the ocean on a dull red sofa. I'm lying on top of you with our legs all tangled up. My head is resting on your bare chest, listening to your heartbeat. Our hands are in the water, cutting trails through the waves. An orange sun sets in the distance, and into its brilliance is where it seems we are floating."

I saw it—I saw it as clear as I had seen it when I'd written the words on paper. Our connection was so deep that she saw the world through my eyes, and I saw it through hers. It's like we had been together since the tallest mountain was but a pebble in the sand, or when the longest raging river was a trickling stream slinking along.

"Danny, everything will be perfect for us when you get out. I don't want to worry about money or the past, or anything at all. We've made mistakes, but we can get past them. We have to. Things are bad now, but they won't be forever."

...And I'd been laying up thinking that she'd left me alone. Not only did she want what I did, she was already making them happen.

I was so happy that I really didn't know what to say. "Sounds like you've been busy."

She grinned. "Oh, there's more."

"There is?"

"Yup."

"What is it?"

She whispered, "You're going to be a daddy."

*****

ABOUT THE AUTHOR

vance phillips is a new author on the writing scene who loves to mix a dose of reality with a little romance. Look for more titles from this author in the near future.

www.ingramcontent.com/pod-product-compliance
Lightning Source LLC
Chambersburg PA
CBHW070604130626
46556CB00001B/268